To Vicky, ♡ ♡

FOREVER LOST

By Laura Morgan

True Love never
was easy...

Laura
Morgan x

Forever Lost

Limitless Publishing, LLC
Kailua, HI 96734
www.limitlesspublishing.com

Formatting: Limitless Publishing

ISBN-13: 978-1-68058-004-4
ISBN-10: 1-68058-004-3

Dedications

For Ethan and Elizabeth, the loves of my life and the centre of my world. You both bring me such joy and happiness; I am both proud and honoured to have you and to know you.

For Brian, my lover, my friend and most importantly, my rock. We've never been perfect, but together we're an imperfect match and I'll cherish what we have until the end of time.

I'll love you all forever.

Chapter 1

"Come on, it's your first night off in ages," Hanna teased, fluttering her eyelashes at Cassie in a blatant attempt to sway her decision to stay in on her night off from the busy Soho restaurant where she worked as a waitress.

"I have big plans already. There's a bottle of chardonnay in the fridge with my name on it," Cassie replied, shaking her head.

"Suit yourself, but one of these days you're coming out with me whether you like it or not," Hanna retorted with a cheeky smile.

Although Cassie wanted to go and spend time with her roommate, she didn't dare tag along to the parties and places where her friend usually ended up. The dark world of escorts, dancers, and prostitutes Hanna was a part of was not what Cassie needed in her life right now.

"Maybe." Cassie grinned.

"I do love you, sweetie. But sometimes I worry about how much time you spend here alone with your old friend, Mr. White." She pointed at the tall glass of cool wine in Cassie's hand.

"I know, Hanna, but I'm not ready to get out there yet. I'm already better than I was when we first met, remember? Who would've thought a year ago when this shy girl came looking for a roomie things would have worked out so well?" Cassie replied, planting a kiss on her best friend's cheek.

"Absolutely, and I would thank that douchebag of an ex-husband of yours for bringing you into my life if he hadn't put you through so much."

"Me too, sweetie, me too."

Hanna finished getting herself ready and was later picked up by her boyfriend, Jamie. They all used the term 'boyfriend' in the loosest sense of the word. Hanna was a hooker. She had worked for a call-girl agency called Cyrene's for over six years. She had started out on a strictly escort basis, but had then progressed to the inevitable 'option for more' contract later in her career. She made fantastic money and was well protected when it came to her alone time with the clients, but it still scared Cassie more than she would ever admit. She worried for her constantly, but she admired Hanna for her independence and free spirit.

She seemed really happy in her work and had been honest about it before Cassie had moved in. She informed her that she didn't bring her work back home with her, and clients would never collect her from the apartment, so she wouldn't have to worry about her own safety or privacy.

Jamie had been the recent exception to that rule. He wasn't rich enough to buy her affections exclusively, nor was he in a position to offer her a life away from the escort business, but Jamie reserved his beautiful companion on as many nights as he could. He worked hard to keep her for himself, having fallen head over heels for her after Hanna had been invited along to an intimate party held by Jamie's boss, gangster and all-round scary guy, Leonardo Solomon.

After Hanna and Jamie left, Cassie sat back and drank her wine, thinking of some of the terrible stories Hanna had told her about the companion business. Tales of women being victimized, raped, and sometimes even tortured by their clients—usually resulting in a large payoff and some time off—but the women almost always returned. They loved the life; otherwise, they never would have gotten into it in the first place. Seemingly gone were the days of girls being forced into the sex industry, at least on the New York prostitution scene. Nowadays, women who openly enjoyed sex would gladly get paid to do it. They enjoyed having the power over the men they frequented rather than feeling ashamed.

***

When Hanna and Jamie came stumbling in a few hours later, Cassie was still up. She had been watching a movie while relaxing on the sofa, and paused it while the pair of them regaled her with stories of the party they'd attended at a nightclub owned by Mr. Solomon called Odyssey.

"It was amazing. There was free champagne, and we were in the VIP area. Leo was there, but he kept himself separated the whole time. I've never spoken to the guy, but the others seemed quite taken with him. I think he's been on his best behavior with the girls lately, and can turn on the charm when he wants to. He's hot, and apparently he's British. I had no idea!" Hanna said, joining Cassie on the sofa while Jamie grabbed them some drinks.

"I'm glad you didn't speak to him. Sounds like a right piece of work, if you ask me," Cassie replied, thanking Jamie for the fresh glass of wine.

"Definitely. He's just interested in business and fucking, and not necessarily in that order. Rumors are he had a girlfriend back in England who broke his heart, and when he came over here he was done with relationships for good, surrounding himself with sluts, and then prostitutes. Never been married, no kids, just a hard ass with a temper you never wanna get on the wrong side of, trust me," Jamie said, sliding in beside Hanna and wrapping her in his arms.

Cassie could tell Hanna loved him back, as best as she could, anyway. Neither of them made a big deal out of it, but Jamie was now at the apartment most nights, a fact Cassie was pretty sure Hanna had not told her madam about since he wasn't paying for her time.

"I'll get the gossip tomorrow, I suppose, but in the meantime, I need to speak with you in the bedroom, Mr. Drug-dealer. I've been a bad girl," Hanna teased.

Jamie immediately jumped up and pulled her off toward her room, waving goodbye to Cassie on their way. She rolled her eyes and settled back down on the sofa to watch the last hour of her paused movie. Cassie was glad their rooms were soundproofed, knowing full well she would've been kept up all night by their lovemaking otherwise. But she didn't care. If anything, she was jealous of what they had. She missed being happily married. Cassie had not been with a man since her husband, and because of how he treated her, she still didn't feel ready to let anyone close enough to try. Jonah's all-consuming addiction to cocaine had been their undoing. In the last few weeks before she had finally left him, he had put her through so much. Cassie knew he was the reason she had gone looking for a life so very far from what she'd had with him.

Jonah had gotten through his addiction eventually, but by then the two of them could not reconcile and had decided to split. Jonah was a precious commodity in the theatrical world, a star on both stage and screen.

As the images of the happily ever after for the movie's main character played out before her, the landscape reminded Cassie of home. She missed London, the person she had been there, and the life she had led. Memories flooded back to her, unbidden and yet not unwelcome. She and Jonah had met eight years ago while Cassie was painting and building theatrical sets in the West End during her spare time around college. She sang in the chorus on occasion to fill empty slots if the actresses were sick, and had loved the life she had there. She'd met Jonah when he was just starting out in his career. He was talented, beautiful, and so sweet to her that Cassie was quickly putty in his hands. They were married less than a year after having gotten together.

Now, at the age of twenty-five, Cassie hated the fact she was already a divorcee. Her ex-husband was over ten years her senior, so she knew it wasn't an issue when he had to tell people he was divorced. But for her, she felt like it was seen as a failure. Relocating to New York City had brought with it many challenges for the couple, but they had loved the Broadway experience. The first few years had been truly blissful and they were extremely happy, but over time Jonah's stresses and strains soon made their way home with him, and their happy bubble deflated.

Snapping back to reality, Cassie took stock of the new life she had made for herself. Hanna had saved her in a way therapy couldn't. She had happened upon her through a mutual friend at the family-run Italian restaurant where Cassie now worked. Hanna was looking for a new roommate, and Cassie needed a place to live following the divorce. As if by fate, they had clicked instantly.

The two had become closer friends than Cassie would've thought likely during this past year. She'd confided everything to Hanna about her failed marriage, including the abuse she suffered at the end of it, without judgement or pity. She readily gave Hanna that same understanding and acceptance of her choices in return.

One day she would get back out there and start dating again. For now though, Cassie would settle for nights spent with a bottle of cheap wine while living vicariously through her professionally promiscuous best friend.

Chapter 2

When Cassie's next night off came around, Hanna dragged her almost kicking and screaming out to a party. Cassie promised a long time ago to give it a try, and they had gone over all the rules beforehand, so she knew where she stood and what might be expected of her. Despite Cassie not wanting to have a contract with Cyrene's, she couldn't help but be intrigued by Hanna's world. She was even turned on by a lot of her stories, so she decided to give it a try.

"The madam, Delilah, is paying you for tonight as a trial. Just think about those cute designer shoes you were eyeing up the other day. A few of these parties, and you can go straight out and get them. You don't even need to get naked to earn money in this town, sweetie. You're beautiful, skinny, great tits, and you're British, for Christ's sake. They're all gonna follow you around like little puppy-dogs. You'll feel sexy, like a goddess to them. And all the while knowing nothing is expected of you, so you can just come home at the end of it a thousand dollars richer and your ego a little bit fatter." Hanna grinned cheekily, and Cassie had to smile back. This really was a good deal, and she could definitely do with both the money and self-esteem boost.

"Okay, I'm ready," Cassie said, checking herself in the mirror one more time. She looked amazing and felt it too, dressed in a skimpy gold dress and high heeled shoes, lots of makeup, and her hair coiffed to stylish perfection by her roommate. It was as though she was no longer looking at the same person she usually saw in the mirror.

Cassie almost felt like she were playing a role now, a demure, sexy, and alluring woman who would soon be lapping up the attention of the men at the party. She would toy with their affections before sending them off in the direction of willing partners, who would then take the rest of the client's night in a much more desired direction. It was the perfect scenario, and she was more excited than she would ever admit.

***

Later that night, Hanna pulled Cassie over to a closed doorway where a burly bouncer guarded the entrance to the bar.

"Cyrene, times two," she said, lifting two fingers up playfully as she greeted him. He asked their names and then checked them off a list before letting them pass, not needing to question them further.

Cassie found herself both delighted and scared.

She wondered if this was how they all started. She worried that in a few short years she'd make the same progression—not caring who she was sent to by her madam as long as the money was headed her way. Cassie vowed to herself she would never become that person, never trade her body in that way, and she meant every word of her silent personal pledge.

Within seconds they were inside the bar, full to the brim with businessmen and women who were surrounded by scantily clad escorts who were all ready to flirt and tantalize their clients in whatever way they required. Hanna led the way around the edge of the crowd, and soon they were ushered into a small cloakroom. Their jackets were quickly checked in, and the madam, Delilah, arrived to give them their wristbands.

"Welcome to Cyrene's, Cassie," she said, smiling warmly. "I hope you're happy with everything so far?"

"Absolutely, thank you," Cassie replied, staring into the beautiful woman's eyes as she mentally prepared herself for the night ahead.

"That's wonderful to hear. Hanna will be a great mentor, but obviously the two of you are at different levels, so you might have to split up here and there. Please take your bands and head into the party. Drinks are free, but not too many, of course," she said, and both girls nodded, understanding they were never to get drunk while on the job. "Have fun, and Cassie, your money has already been wired to your account. I hope you'll enjoy tonight and continue to work with me. If you need me, here's my number," Delilah finished, extending her card, which Cassie tucked into her purse. She then watched as the stunning woman wandered off toward the party.

"Whoa, I have a pimp," she whispered, making Hanna laugh.

"Yeah, yeah. Get your red band on, shy girl, before someone tries to fuck you," Hanna teased, indicating the boxes to the side. Cassie immediately took a thin red bracelet from one of them and slipped it on.

"So, red means completely off limits?" she asked and Hanna nodded.

"Yep, look but don't touch. They may touch your arms, back, and face while talking. Or they might take your arm or hand when walking, if you are comfortable with it, but nothing else. If you ever do decide to do anything with anyone, go to see Delilah first. She will make the necessary arrangements," she reminded her, and Cassie nodded.

"Not that I would, but yes, I know. Safety first, don't ever go off with anyone without going through Delilah," she replied, going over the rules with Hanna one more time. Her friend seemed happy she had it all clearly engrained in her mind.

Cassie watched as Hanna slipped on a green bracelet, the signal to the clients that she was unbound for the evening and ready to procure for their pleasure. All they had to do was approach her to chat, and if they were interested, she would make the arrangements. She'd then be free to go with the client to a nearby hotel with a guard, where they would carry out the agreed transaction.

There were also boxes of yellow bands, which meant the girl wearing it was a more complicated case. Women who had been procured by a client for part of the evening wore these bands, or those who were open to propositions by clients of their choosing. It also meant they might be picky and had reserved the right to choose for themselves. These women, while more in control of their careers, were usually far too complicated for the men at these types of parties to bother with. Most of the men there were just looking for a bit of attention and would enjoy the company of the red band wearers, or they were there for a full night of frolicking and would only look twice at those with green bands. The yellow wearers needed to be something special for the clients to deal with the hassle involved in procuring them, so most of the women went for either the red or green.

"Better to decide yes or no right from the beginning of the night, and then everybody knows where they stand," Hanna had told her earlier. "I know you don't want any touching or trying to get in your pants, so make it clear, and don't tease—unless it's in the right way, of course."

The party was great fun. Cassie tried to stick with Hanna as much as possible but was separated from her when Jamie arrived and immediately bought her for the rest of the evening. She didn't so much as grumble as he whisked her away with him for a night of passion, and Cassie was left chatting with some of the men she had been introduced to earlier in the evening. These guys were all clearly married, looking for a kind smile and an affectionate woman who hung on their every word, and Cassie played the part well. She was naturally warm and gentle with others anyway, and she remained so in their company. She chatted with them as much as she thought necessary, laughed at their jokes, and sent each of them home with a happy smile and the weight of the world a little less on their shoulders.

"You're gonna be good for business, Cassie, I can tell," Delilah told her at the end of the night, before sending her home in a waiting car with some of the other girls. One of the bouncers accompanied them, dropping each off at her home, as was the protocol to ensure they all arrived there safely. "Lots of good comments on you tonight. You certainly made an impression," the dominant madam added before waving her goodbye.

Cassie smiled sheepishly. It was very flattering to have the men say nice things about her. She tried her best to give them what she thought they needed and knew now that Hanna had been right. It really was an ego boost to have rich and powerful men lapping up her affection and enjoying her company so openly. There was no pretense of anything more. They all knew where they stood, and before she even got into bed, Cassie made up her mind. She had to admit, she was impressed by the whole setup and felt safe the entire time.

She was already sure she wanted to get booked in for more parties with Cyrene's.

Chapter 3

"Mrs. Smith, how wonderful to see you again," said the kind doorman whose name she could never remember. Cassie smiled and returned the compliment, omitting the name as she didn't want to be rude. He opened the door for her, ushering her inside the timeworn, yet still elegant theater with a graceful bow. She didn't bother explaining she had now gone back to her maiden name, opting to leave the conversation for another time, if ever. The old theater seemed so grand, so regal, and she couldn't help but reminisce over the person she used to be while walking these halls and living in this world.

"Hey, honey, he's just gone for a coffee run," her old friend, and now up and coming Broadway star, Liam Casterly, said as he caught Cassie making her way toward Jonah's dressing room.

"Oh, okay. I'll wait," Cassie replied, hugging him tightly. It had been far too long. "And don't call me honey."

"Well, usually I call everyone a slut, but I know you aren't one of those." His camp demeanor seemed to have doubled along with his stage presence, and she grinned. "You look different. Happy and confident or something. Did you get your groove back?" He looked her up and down with an approving gaze.

Cassie's smile broadened. She had indeed, 'got her groove back,' thanks to her inflated confidence after having her company sought after at many a party over the past few weeks. She had gone along to them all, red band firmly in place, and had enjoyed every moment. The array of men she had met was astonishing. She always thought the city seemed so small before, but soon realized that was just her little slice of it, where she had worked the same restaurant almost every day for over a year and knew the regulars like old friends.

The real New York City was a bustling throb of millions of people, most of whom you would never happen upon again even if you went to the same places over and over. Cassie played a different role at each party, relishing in the adoring gazes from the men who were drawn to her warm smile and gentle nature. Her self-esteem was now definitely on the mend.

"I think I have, Liam. I think I have," she replied, grinning up at the tall, skinny man with an affectionate gaze.

He hugged her tightly again and then dropped the façade. "I've missed you, we all have. This place just isn't the same without you, and he isn't the same either. We all know why you left, we know he pushed you away, but sometimes I wish it was you who'd stayed and he who went," he whispered, stroking her cheek gently before kissing it.

Cassie knew Liam had never loved a woman, and he had no idea where to even begin figuring them out. Something about them was different, though, and always had been. Liam had told her once she was the only woman who had even gotten close.

She remembered how he used to tell her stories of his childhood. Liam had known he was gay since he was ten years old, supposedly having begun fantasizing about boys alongside the little girls who swooned over their boyfriends and practiced their anticipated married name in signature. Cassie always knew he didn't love her that way, but he truly was a close friend, and she missed having him in her life.

"That's mean, but thanks," she replied, shrugging. "I miss you too, you slut."

"Cassie? What are you doing here?" came a voice from behind them. She turned to find her ex-husband staring at her wide-eyed from the doorway, two trays full of paper coffee cups and a bag full of muffins in his hands.

"Can I have a word?" she asked, releasing her grip on Liam. Jonah nodded, setting down the trays and leading her into his dressing room. He went to close the door behind them, but caught the flash of fear in her eyes and seemed to think better of it.

"It's good to see you. You look amazing," he said, taking a seat in the corner while Cassie stood, feeling uneasy being alone with him for the first time in over a year.

"I'm not here for pleasantries, Jonah. I need you out of my life for good. I know the agreement included alimony, but I don't need it anymore. I have a much better job alongside my restaurant work now, and I'm earning more than enough to get by. Please, would you stop the payments? I don't want your money." Her entire demeanor was cool, but it was either that or get upset, and Cassie wouldn't let him see her falter.

"If that's what you want, honey. I just wanted you to have it so you'll always be safe, always have a roof over your head," Jonah replied with a hurt look in his eye.

"Don't call me honey," she insisted, her expression now turning icy.

"Sorry. I'm sorry for everything, Cassie. I'll do as you ask, and you'll be free of me for good now," Jonah said, looking down at his hands with a defeated sigh.

"I'll never be completely free, Jonah. You were the biggest part of my life for such a long time, and then it didn't just fizzle out like most people's relationships do." Cassie began pacing the small room. She hated how rattled he made her. The memories of the monster he had inside of him blocked her from seeing the genuine sadness that deep-down she knew was not a mask. "Our marriage was obliterated in one awful moment after another. I need to live my life now and be me again, whoever that person is. I wish you all the best," she said, heading out before he could say another word and before the tears that were pricking at her eyes dared to fall.

***

The next morning Cassie had both a night off from the restaurant and as a Cyrene. She intended to grab a DVD and a cheap bottle of wine, change into her pajamas, and become one with her sofa. Hanna had plans with Jamie again, this time at his boss's house for a small gathering for his many worker bees, but this time Jamie did not seem worried about taking Hanna into the fray.

"He's been crazy busy lately. I think things have gone sour on a recent deal. He's just after a distraction tonight, so he's already ordered in a bunch of green girls to keep him occupied," he informed them, waiting patiently for his lover to get ready. "I've told the other guys I've paid up front for Hanna for the whole night, and I ain't sharing. They know the drill," he added, smirking.

"If only they knew how many freebies I give you, baby." Hanna leaned down to give her boyfriend a kiss before turning to Cassie. "You should come. Jamie's friends are good guys."

"Nah, babe, they'll expect more from her. Leo doesn't have red girls at his parties. No offense, Cassie," Jamie said.

She shrugged. "None taken. I am intrigued about his house, though. A few of the girls have said it's beautiful. Maybe next time," she replied, grabbing her wine and taking a long sip as she nestled herself in the nook of the sofa. Hanna had told Cassie all about the villainous, self-made billionaire boss, and he sounded like the sort of person she never wanted to know. Still, she was intrigued and astounded by the stories Jamie and Hanna had to tell about him. Leo took no prisoners and was a merciless drug-lord, something Cassie hadn't actually thought still existed off the television screens. Jamie had warned Hanna right from the start not to get too close to his boss during any of his parties, and she had opted to follow his advice.

Cassie took comfort in knowing his professional lover always stayed by his side, while the boss-man broke many of their rules and heartlessly worked his way through many of the girls. Hanna had told her Leo was often required to pay some of them off for their silence, thanks to his aggressive sexual preferences.

"Why don't you say you've bought her for the evening, too? We'll be your girls for the night. Just say you were feeling flush and paid for a threesome with us. We can go along with a little lesbian role-play, can't we, Cassie?" Hanna offered, one penciled on eyebrow raised. "There might not be a next time. Leo never has parties at his place, does he, Jamie?"

"She's right, and yeah, if we told people I have already paid for you both, they wouldn't be allowed to proposition you. You'd have to play it up, though. And, FYI, I'm not against watching the two of you fondle and kiss a little for the maximum effect," he teased. "It'll be fun, and if you can't trust your hooker best friend and her drug-dealer boyfriend-slash-client, who can you trust?" He laughed when Hanna slapped his shoulder in retaliation for the 'hooker' comment.

"You'd stay with me the whole time? And no

one would try anything?" Cassie asked thoughtfully, genuinely interested.

"Absolutely, we won't leave each other's side," Hanna promised with an enthusiastic smile. "We'll play it like Jamie's hired us both for a threesome after the party. We'll stay with him the entire time and have a bit of fun."

"Sure, why the hell not?" Cassie sprang from her seat and followed her beaming best friend into the bedroom to start getting ready.

Less than half an hour later, Cassie had changed out of her pajamas and discarded her wine, ready to go and see the big, bad mob-boss's house. They made their way out of the city and into what seemed like a very normal, suburban area. However, it soon opened out into country roads lined with gated driveways that no doubt led up to mansions with vast grounds and their wealthy owners nestled comfortably inside.

Leo Solomon was no exception to his neighbors in terms of his wealth, and neither was his home. The girls both gasped and watched in awe as Jamie drove them inside the electric gates. Within a few minutes they were led inside, each holding one of Jamie's arms, and they had to contain their gasps at the lavishly furnished and stunningly decorated home that belonged on a movie set. Cassie took it all in, smiling at the other men and women she made eye contact with, but she kept her body language and affections focused on her supposed client for the evening.

The girls had wanted to go along for the sheer intrigue of the party, but poor Jamie's funds were running low. Cassie agreed not to take any money from him tonight, seeing the evening as nothing more than three friends going out together to have some fun. They already warned the gentle-natured man they were going to tease him senseless, using their feminine wiles to seduce Jamie and play with his libido before eventually heading off home— Cassie would then retreat to her room and let the pair of them enjoy unwinding their frenzied emotions alone.

"I really think I'm falling for him," Hanna said back at the apartment when they had a moment alone. "It's his birthday, and I want to give him tonight as a kind of present. You don't mind, do you?"

"Not at all. I really like Jamie. He's always been kind with me, and I already feel like you two are a real couple. I have for ages. He's my friend, and I know I'm safe with him," Cassie replied, being honest about the man who was frequently part of her life now. She'd honestly never felt scared or intimidated by him, and was glad Hanna seemed to finally be coming to her senses about Jamie before potentially breaking his heart.

"Good, thanks. I hope you don't mind, but I told him about you and Jonah. He knows you don't have sex, but I thought I better let him know the full story so he understands why you're so careful. Please don't be mad." Hanna's brows furrowed, reflecting her concern.

"I'm not mad, sweetie. It's better that he knows. He'll keep me safe, I know it," she told her, smiling to reassure her friend.

"Absolutely. I've already warned him to grab us and take us home if he feels like we might be in trouble. He can make out as if he wants to get his money's worth or something. I don't mind. As long as we can go and see this guy's mansion for a little while, I'll be one happy girl."

***

"Champagne?" Jamie led the two ladies over to a small table where a variety of drinks and drugs were on offer to Leo's guests. Cassie and Hanna each took a glass, but nothing more. Cassie was glad her friend hadn't had issues with substance abuse. If she did, it would've been a deal-breaker right from the offset for them, as she could not be around an addict ever again.

The two of them then went for a lap of the house's open areas on Jamie's arm, smiling as they were introduced to his colleagues, but the boss-man himself was nowhere to be seen. Jamie's co-workers were friendly to the girls, having met Hanna plenty of times, but their attention didn't linger on them long. These men were not interested in an affectionate ear or a flattering of their egos. They were only interested in sex, so fulfilling their physical needs was the top priority. Cassie stayed quiet, sensing the difference between them and the men she usually entertained at parties.

"Why don't you two take a seat and amuse yourselves for a few minutes while I talk business with my boys?" Jamie asked them, clearly needing to talk shop out of earshot. Hanna nodded, taking

Cassie's hand and leading her toward a chaise lounge in clear view of the room, but secluded enough for them to be away from most of the partygoers' gazes.

Looking around at the visually gratifying group of people, Cassie could tell every guy in the room was a drug-dealer or was associated with that business in some way. They may have varied in areas of expertise or the military style rank structure within their boss's rule, but she knew they were all in the same line of work.

The women, of whom there were at least two to every one man, were all prostitutes. None wore bands or obvious signs of their place in the sex trade, but they were clearly all procured for the enjoyment of the party. They were courtesies, just like the alcohol and drugs, purely for Leo Solomon's guests to enjoy at their leisure.

"You okay?" Hanna whispered, leaning closer to Cassie so they could talk while maintaining their cool amongst the other partygoers. They had been there over an hour already but were still sipping on their first drinks, careful not to let their hair down while on the job. Cassie was reeling with excitement at being here, trying her best to hide her eagerness.

"I'm fine. This place is amazing," Cassie whispered back, stroking her hand down her friend's arm as though they were being flirtatious with one another. They enjoyed playing their roles as Jamie's upcoming threesome partners and did so with ease because their mutual affection for one another negated the need for any exaggerated deception. Neither one of them was gay, but they were both happy to tease Hanna's lover and endeavored to give him his tantalizing treats periodically throughout the evening.

"Good to hear." Hanna tucked a stray lock of hair behind Cassie's ear.

"Also, I don't see anyone undressing or doing anything publicly, which is good. They all seem to be taking their partners off to the guest rooms to play," Cassie added, and Hanna nodded in agreement.

"Yeah, I noticed that too. As long as we stay away from the bedrooms, I think we'll be okay," Hanna concurred, brushing her fingertip over Cassie's top lip and leaning in for a deep, passionate kiss.

Cassie was surprised by her friend's forwardness at first but went along with it, trusting Hanna not to push her.

She was more than likely only doing it to get Jamie's attention, so she kissed back just as enthusiastically. Cassie let her tongue delve into Hanna's mouth, their lips caressing one another's while their hands stroked each other's cheeks. When they finally pulled away, they felt eyes on them. They exchanged a grin before turning to look up at the group of men who had silenced their mini-meeting and stopped to watch, evidently enthralled by the action going on before them.

"Boys, if you'll excuse me," Jamie said, breaking the quiet that had descended, and the others all headed off in search of a woman or two to enjoy. Jamie slipped down on the chaise between them and placed one hand on each of their cheeks, looking from one to the other with a wicked grin. "Fucking hell, Hanna. Talk about playing on my threesome fantasy," he joked, making them both smile wider. "Do it again," he asked, his breath catching with excitement.

Cassie and Hanna obliged, leaning over his lap to kiss again while he watched from just inches away, shuffling in his seat as though his hard-on might already be pressing against his pants uncomfortably.

Chapter 4

"Do you wanna go upstairs?" Jamie whispered, stopping Hanna and Cassie in their tracks. They pulled back from their kiss and eyed him carefully. Cassie could tell Hanna was interested in taking things further. She was flushed and panting after kissing her friend so intimately, and peered longingly at Cassie's lips, seemingly desperate to taste them again. Cassie knew she was the only thing holding Jamie back from grabbing the two women and leading them upstairs to have his way with them, and she thought it over for a second, the panging in her core driving her toward their shared thrill.

"It's up to you, sweetie," Hanna said, stroking her cheek lightly. "We'll do as much as you feel ready to. You set the boundaries."

"I won't try to fuck you, I promise," Jamie added in a hushed voice, a cheeky grin on his face.

"I should hope not," Cassie teased, her British accent heavy and seeming far too classy in comparison to the situation at hand. She laughed quietly, but eyed Jamie. She couldn't deny she wanted more, too. "Okay, but I'm out of bounds downstairs," she whispered, making it clear, and both Hanna and Jamie nodded.

"That goes without saying, sweetie." Hanna's voice was hardly more than a whisper, but they were so close Cassie heard her perfectly.

"Everywhere else is okay, though. I'll lick, suck, and kiss whatever you want me to. And my hands will go wherever you tell me to put them," she added, biting her bottom lip.

Without hesitation, Jamie jumped up and wrapped his arms around them, his hands gripping their hips, pulling Hanna and Cassie toward the staircase.

They soon found an empty room. Cassie noticed the open doorway instantly, but they were to be expected. It was one of the biggest rules in the kinds of gatherings where sex was anticipated, and downright encouraged. If you decided to enjoy a sexual encounter there rather than wait for the privacy of your own home or hotel room, you were expected to allow others to watch. If your observer then wished to join in, they had to ask first and respect your decision. Either way, the three of them knew they might find themselves being watched, but they were also too hot for each other to care.

Cassie was ready, her core already tense and excited for her first night of passion since Jonah. It didn't matter in the slightest that she was not actually going to be having sex; the rest would be more than enough for her to get off.

She and Hanna stood side by side before their

master for the evening, his power over them unspoken. Their submission was part of his present. They were at his command, ready to do as he demanded, and Jamie openly enjoyed it, his eyes alight and excited.

"Happy Birthday, baby," Hanna whispered, smiling seductively.

"How did you know?" he asked, cocking his eyebrow, but she wasn't telling. He just shrugged. "Who cares? Best present ever."

"So, what would you like us to do?" Hanna asked, her smile never faltering. "Anything goes."

"I want to watch Cassie make you come," Jamie replied, looking over at Cassie with heat in his eyes. "Take your clothes off and get on the bed, Hanna. Slowly."

"If you insist." She turned so Cassie could help her unzip the short dress she was wearing, and placed it over the back of an armchair to the side of the bed. Cassie came back over and the two girls kissed, their hands entwined and roving over one another's bodies.

Cassie slipped her finger under the cup of Hanna's bra and lifted the soft flesh upward while pushing down on the lace. Her nipple sprang loose, and her supple breast overflowed from the now half-sized bra cup. She did the same with the other nipple, and then kissed them, one at a time, before running her hands down to Hanna's panties and slipping the tips of her fingers under the hem. Cassie hesitated just long enough to let Jamie know she was waiting for his command, and he didn't delay in giving it.

"Take them off," he muttered, watching in stunned silence as the two women took the next step for him. Cassie was still dressed when she adhered to his command and slid down his lover's lace panties, tossing them over the armchair. She then kneeled before her waxed nether lips while running her hands up and down Hanna's thighs.

"I never kissed a girl here before." She stared up into Hanna's eyes with a playful grin, and her friend laughed. They were close in so many ways, yet this was the first time Cassie had ever seen her fully naked.

The awkwardness which might've then settled around them could have been a normal couple's undoing, but not them. Hanna was a skilled and experienced lover of both men and women, and Cassie was so excited at the prospect of having her first threesome and lesbian encounter, neither of them cared. Jamie watched them in enthralled silence, his hands balled into fists at his sides and his panting breath giving away his excitement.

Hanna reached her hands back and unclipped her bra, sending it flying toward the chair, while Cassie ran her hands up her thighs to her ready opening. Hanna trembled and panted in anticipation.

"Please." The word left Hanna's lips in a rush.

"I'm the one on my knees, and you're still begging. How much do you want this?" Cassie's fingertips skimmed her mound, and Hanna groaned loudly.

"Do it," Jamie whispered, stepping around Cassie and unzipping her dress at the back. She leaned closer and laid a gentle kiss on Hanna's moist lips while he continued to watch. Both girls groaned as she flicked her tongue over Hanna's swollen nub, the tender nerve endings ready and eager for her touch, and she teased it gently for a few minutes while holding onto Hanna's hips. She continued until she sensed her friend's readiness for her release, but Cassie wouldn't let her have it too soon. She too wanted to enjoy herself and prolong Hanna's pleasure in the process.

Cassie leaned back and stood, planting a soft kiss on Hanna's mouth before pulling her own long hair out of its tie and shuffling out of her open dress. Her still trembling friend moved over and lay down on the huge bed, watching as Jamie began circling his new present, his eyes taking in every inch of Cassie's body.

Jamie unclipped Cassie's bra and slid off the satin cups before lifting her firm, full breasts with each hand. He kissed them, sucking on her hard nipples in turn while she groaned in appreciation of his touch. She had already given Jamie permission to go anywhere except 'downstairs,' and he was taking full advantage of the night's twists and turns. She hoped he was enjoying his birthday treat as much as she was. Cassie moaned loudly, a deep rumble coming from somewhere primal inside of her.

"Yeah, that's it. Let it go, Cassie. Let yourself go," he breathed against her breast, and she shuddered at the warm breeze. She moaned again as he latched on and sucked hard.

Cassie had never found herself attracted to Jamie sexually before, but in this place she was utterly captivated by him. When his mouth eventually found hers, she did not shy away from his lips, or the tongue that snaked its way inside to command her own. His hands still caressed her ample breasts, and Jamie pressed his hard-on into her thigh.

After a few minutes, Hanna's panting breath caught her attention again and she pulled back from Jamie's kiss. Cassie wandered over to the bed, giving him a wink as she went.

"Down, boy. I haven't finished with her yet," she whispered, grateful he had left her panties on. She climbed over the still so wet woman and opened Hanna's legs. Cassie was mindful of her posture and wanted to seduce Jamie using more than just the sight of her mouth on Hanna's cleft. She purposely lifted her hips as high as she could, arching her back seductively as she leaned down and enveloped Hanna's clit with her mouth. Two fingers slid inside her ready opening, and Cassie proceeded to pleasure her friend with her sights set on delivering nothing but pure ecstasy. It wasn't long until Hanna cried out as her orgasm burst through her.

"Yes!" she cried, bucking and writhing on the bed until the throbs finally ceased and Cassie pulled away gently.

"Come here," Jamie said from beside her, and Cassie looked up, noticing his fly had been undone, and his hard cock was now set free from its restraints. He was huge, intimidatingly so, but Cassie didn't hesitate. She climbed over and sucked the tip, rubbing her hands up and down his shaft while rolling her tongue over the end of his impressive length. When she felt him nearing his climax, Cassie pulled her mouth away, rubbing him and directing the flow of his release down onto her breasts, watching as he came undone for her.

Chapter 5

Cassie grinned up at Jamie, and they laughed loudly once he came down from his sexually gratified high and she'd wiped herself clean with some tissues from the bedside box. They switched back to their friendly personas ever so slightly following their intense moments in that bedroom, glad no one had decided to watch them after all. Hanna soon joined in, and the three of them fell about laughing on the bed. In that moment they were nothing but a group of friends, laughing together in a genuine display of affection with their fun natures shining brightly in the aftermath of their shared satisfaction.

"I wanted to come in your mouth," Jamie said, discarding the last of his clothes and then joining Cassie and Hanna on the bed, a roguish grin on his handsome face. Both girls peered up at him, and within seconds the air changed back to the sexually charged atmosphere that had temporarily dissipated. Their laughter subsided, and Jamie began running his hands over the lengths of their bodies, and their sexual needs began taking precedence over their friendship again.

"I know, but no one gets to do that. Not even birthday boys," Cassie joked, running her hands over her breasts to remind him of her moment of brazenness when she had covered herself with his offering. Hanna watched their interaction from between them on the bed, a satisfied smile on her face. She reached up and captured Cassie's mouth with hers.

"Hmmm, I can taste him on you," Hanna groaned, delving her tongue deeper and lapping at Cassie's.

"Are you ready for him?"

"Yes."

"Not yet," Cassie teased. She climbed over Hanna on the bed while Jamie kneeled at their feet and watched. Hanna wrapped her legs around her friend's waist, and the pair gyrated together, their bodies so sensitive and their tensions so high that Cassie soon felt a climax building in her belly. She pressed hard, rubbing her clit against Hanna's mound, and then she came, her cries of pleasure drowned out by the lips that still possessed her mouth. She continued to push against Hanna even once her throbs subsided, the pair of them completely lost in their moment.

Jamie was ready again after watching their show, and slid his hand between their entwined thighs. He didn't touch Cassie but groaned his affirmations as she continued to move against the back of his hand, his fingers rubbing Hanna's swollen nub until a second orgasm claimed them. After she came down from her high, Cassie shuffled backward with a delighted smile, her cheeks burning hot from her climaxes and her body trembling. She lay next to Hanna on the bed, running her fingertips over her friend's still pulsating, naked body while Jamie took Cassie's place between her thighs. When he slipped inside, she kissed Hanna's lips again, enjoying being part of their wonderful lovemaking and still not ever having been touched in a way she found uncomfortable.

She and Hanna kissed while Cassie's fingers twirled each nipple in turn before sliding down to rub her clit, and Jamie continued to thrust inside of her. He kissed Cassie's lips and groaned with appreciation when her fingers pinched his nipples as he moved inside his lover, his own hands taking advantage of her exposed breasts.

"You two are so fucking beautiful," he muttered, leaning down over the pair of women and sucking on one of Cassie's nipples. The three of them remained entwined until both lovers came again and they lay back on the bed, resting and reveling in the afterglow of their entangled ecstasy.

When they were dressed again, they made their way back to the party, giggling like teenagers and openly fawning over each other. Following their incredible time in the bedroom together, the girls were glowing, and Cassie felt more relaxed than she had in ages. Jamie led the girls toward the pool and deposited them on a lounger close to where most of the other women were congregating. Some of them were in their underwear in the pool, lapping up the attentions as the men watched their half-naked bodies glide effortlessly in the water. Hanna and Cassie stayed to the side, enjoying one another's company and not needing anything else. Jamie kissed them both deeply, still clearly enjoying their role-play, and then wandered off in search of his friends, probably eager to tell them the story of his birthday threesome and enjoy their jealous stares.

"Did you enjoy that?" Hanna asked Cassie quietly when they were alone, their bodies still buzzing.

She nodded. "I did, I really did," Cassie admitted. "I got what I wanted even though I never took off my knickers. You were both amazing and never once forgot what I needed from the experience. You gained my trust in that bedroom, Han, you and Jamie."

"I'm glad you felt that way. I wanted to be sure you enjoyed it. After all, you didn't even get yours properly. You could've fingered yourself if you wanted. Neither of us would've minded," she replied, her hand stroking her friend's thigh.

"I didn't need to. Giving you guys what you needed was an amazing feeling. I was so turned on, I still am," Cassie told her. "You weren't angry that Jamie and I were doing stuff, were you?"

"Not at all. He has to share me, comes with the territory, and even though he and I are more than just a business relationship, I still loved having you join in. Watching the two of you make out was so fucking hot. I almost touched myself but didn't want to ruin my climax by going too soon. I wanted you to make me come, and when you finally did, I think it was honestly the best orgasm of my life,"

Hanna replied, blushing slightly. "Seeing him come on your tits nearly sent me over the edge again. You have no idea how sexy you are, Cassie."

"It was hot, wasn't it?" She giggled, scanning the pool area and watching the supposed lesbian pairings fawning over one another in the depths. They were great actresses, but Cassie was sure they had nothing on what had just taken place in that upstairs room.

"I've never admitted this to anyone, but I'm bisexual. I guess it's 'cause I've never needed to look for female lovers, thanks to my wonderful job." She gave Cassie a wink. "I thought every one of my fantasies had been fulfilled, until now. Thank you, sweetie."

"You're right, Jamie, these two really do make the perfect company for a hot threesome," came a deep, sultry voice from over their shoulders, and the two girls looked back to see who had spoken. A tall, broad, ruggedly handsome man stood beside Hanna's lover, staring down at them with an intimidating smile. Even Jamie seemed uncomfortable in his presence. Cassie knew right away this must be his boss, Leo. The girls stood and walked over to them, reaching out to shake his hand and introduce themselves in turn before sidling over to their date in the hopes of losing his ominous attention.

"We were just heading back. Thank you for your hospitality, Mr. Solomon," Jamie said, gripping both girls' waists tightly and turning toward the doorway.

"Surely you aren't ready for round two just yet? I

insist, you've yet to see my new billiards room and my collection of vintage sports cars, Jay. The girls can join us if they like," Leo insisted, his powerful gaze making both girls squirm uncomfortably. He had given them no other choice than to stay, they all knew it, so they each accepted a fresh glass of champagne and followed the powerful man's lead.

Leo chatted away about his art and collectables on their way to his underground garage. They hung on his every word, but only Jamie replied, the conversation seeming forced and unnatural. There was something about Leo that Cassie found herself drawn to, though. Underneath his unfeeling, uncaring exterior she sensed something pure in him, and before long was glad he had insisted they stay a while longer. He was sexy and driven, ambitious and fierce. She didn't know if it was simply because she hadn't had a proper sexual release up in that bedroom, but Cassie felt herself buzzing for him, her core tensing with every elegant syllable he spoke. His still strong British accent reminded her so much of home, and even that sent her body reeling for him.

The girls sat silently as the two men played pool, their postures poised to look the perfect arm candy, and their faces in permanent half-smiles as they watched Leo beat Jamie in just a few moves.

"Do you play?" Leo asked, breaking Cassie's reverie. She looked up to find his dark brown gaze boring into hers from across the room, a wide smile on his lips as he took in her surprise at having been spoken to.

"I used to, but I haven't played for a very long

time. I'm afraid I'm not very good," she answered, remaining modest, although she had played many a game in her college years back home in London. She was actually quite skilled at the game, but would never show this powerful man. She had the feeling Leo liked to win.

"Come here, I'll help you," he said, beckoning her over to him. She did as he commanded, knowing better than to bother looking over at Jamie for his approval. Even he would have to acquiesce to his boss's wishes. Cassie was now in full escort mode. She had a feeling if Leo asked them for anything, they better be ready to say yes. The very idea scared her stiff, but it also made her heart beat faster in her chest, her body forgetting all about its past trauma. Cassie mentally chastised herself for being so ready to be dominated should this forceful man say the word.

When she reached him, Leo turned Cassie around so he pressed himself into her back, her thighs pushing against the pool table in front of them. She felt his thickly muscled thighs pressing against her backside, and her breath caught in her throat, giving away her reaction. Leo lifted the cue and placed it in her hands, pushing Cassie's lower back gently so she leaned forward over the table, and her hips instantly tilted up to meet his. He slid the wood between her fingertips while he helped her get the correct posture for a good shot, his hands gripping her tightly and shuffling her back into him. Cassie waited for his next instruction, and looked over her shoulder where she caught the wry smile curling at his lips. Leo leaned down over Cassie, and his lips found her ear, sending shudders down her spine as he spoke.

"I didn't realize you're British," he said, his voice quiet and full of desire. His interest both excited and frightened her, but she couldn't resist him, so she played along, enjoying their back and forth more than she would have ever thought.

"I was warned your parties are the kind where the women are seen and not heard, Mr. Solomon," she breathed, cursing herself for being so foolishly brave when deep down she knew she should not be flirting with him. Cassie sent the white ball hurtling perfectly toward her chosen color ball, potting it expertly. She grinned and sidestepped so she could escape his body's vice-like grip on hers. As she wandered down the length of the table to take her next shot, she caught the eyes of her friends, each of them appearing scared she might be attracting the wrong man's attention, but she didn't know what else to do. He was the one talking to her and making every move. Cassie had no control, and something told her it was exactly how Leo Solomon liked it. She took her next shot while under the constant scrutiny of her clearly intrigued opponent, purposely missing her intended ball, and she shrugged as though unperturbed by her miss.

"Leave," Leo said coolly, his eyes on Cassie, but his tone making it clear he was talking to Hanna and Jamie. The two of them stood and walked to the door, Hanna turning to quickly look at Cassie and mouthing 'sorry.' Cassie couldn't react but hoped her friend wouldn't be too worried or feel too guilty about leaving her there. Cassie was a big girl, and she was aware what he might want from her, but also that she had many ways in which to gain his affection rather than his lust, and so she worked on ideas to steer the powerful man in that direction now that they were alone.

Chapter 6

"So, what brings you to the States?" Leo asked once Jamie and Hanna had gone, taking his first shot while Cassie watched him intently.

"The theater," she replied. The smirk on his face made it obvious he assumed she was a failed actress. Cassie quickly corrected him. "My ex-husband is the actor. I was working the sets as a designer until last year, and I was pretty damn good at it too. I left when he and I split up. My choice," she told him in a more determined tone, opening up more than she possibly should have. He seemed to draw out her honesty without even trying.

"And now you're a whore," Leo said coldly, standing just a couple of feet away, his body language tense and unreadable.

"If you say so," she replied, not taking her eyes from his.

"Well, you see, this is where I am confused. Jamie said so. He told the other guys up there all about the antics you three apparently enjoyed in my guest bedroom this evening, but he failed to mention the fact that you did not even remove your knickers the entire time, nor did you let either of your friends touch or fuck you. I find it strange that a whore would be so conservative during a threesome that had been set up and paid for in advance," he said, wondering aloud what had gone on, but also giving away the fact he had somehow been watching them. Cassie flushed but held her ground, knowing he was calling her out, having caught them at the lie. And there she was thinking they'd played out their deception so perfectly. "Are you even a real whore, Cassie, or are you just playing one for the night so you can have some fun with your friends?" Leo asked, stepping closer.

"I am a Cyrene, my madam is called Delilah. I can give you her number if you wish to check my credentials," Cassie replied, trembling slightly under his intense scrutiny.

"But," he insisted.

"But, no. I am not a whore. I am a red girl," she admitted, readying herself for whatever he might do to punish her for lying. Most powerful men in his position, and, according to Hanna, even Leo himself in the past, would deliver a lying whore a slap or drag her off to his bedroom to be taught a lesson for her dishonesty. But tonight he merely smiled and shrugged. Leo seemed genuinely pleased to have figured her out at last and stepped closer.

"Your turn, and this time play properly. I saw you miss on purpose last time."

After a few games of pool, all of which Leo won, though Cassie managed to give him a good run for his money, they left the billiards room. She followed him down another corridor toward the underground garage. This house was truly spectacular and so sprawling Cassie couldn't be sure where they were anymore. The thought scared her a little, but so far Leo was being the perfect gentleman, so she remained calm. It surprised her that he seemed to enjoy her this way rather than the brazen, sex-kitten persona many of the other girls adopted around him.

"Do you have cameras in every room of your house?" she asked as they walked, following his lead through to the vast, cold room where over twenty stunning cars were parked. Cassie gasped as she took in the fantastic array, all of which had been restored to perfection. They were no doubt worth millions of dollars.

"Yes, I like to watch people," he replied, observing her every move as she trailed her hands delicately over the bonnets of his impressive collection and peeked inside the windows at the intricately upholstered interiors.

"Even when they're having sex?" Cassie asked, unable to help herself.

"Especially when they're having sex." Leo came around in front of Cassie and pinned her against one of the stunning vintage cars that had bright red paintwork and a black roof. "But, you didn't have sex, did you? Why?" Leo pressed her, demanding to know her motives.

"Because I don't have sex at all, ever." Cassie placed her hands on his chest and pushed him back. Leo stared down into her eyes, waiting for more, and she knew he would not stop until she gave it. "My marriage ended badly, and I haven't been with anyone since."

"I'm gonna need to know more than that," Leo replied, his expression dark and his strong jaw tense. Cassie sucked in a deep breath, not wanting to carry on with her story, but she could tell by the look on his face that Leo was not going to let her off.

"My husband went on a cocaine bender that eventually sent him spiraling into a complete mental breakdown. He was somehow convinced I was going to leave him, and he tied me up and held me hostage for over a week until we were found. Ever since then I have had trust issues, to put it bluntly," she said, talking as fast as she could to get the words out, needing them gone from her mind so she could escape the powerful man's intense gaze. She felt hot and bothered, her body reacting to Leo in a way it hadn't in well over a year, and she was angry with herself for letting him affect her this way.

"Did he rape you?" Leo asked. His expression hadn't changed, his brown eyes still peering into hers, and Cassie hated him for asking.

"Yes, repeatedly, thanks to his snapped mind. He doesn't even remember doing it," she replied, looking down at Leo's perfect and expensive shirt, focusing on his shimmering buttons in the dim light rather than on the tears that were now pricking at her eyes.

"Did you press charges?"

"No, just rehab and a quick divorce," Cassie replied, becoming upset.

"Hmm, I figured you were damaged goods, but I never took you for a victim." He grinned, clearly enjoying the stern look she shot him.

She felt full of defiance, and her emotional turmoil shifted to anger.

"I'm not a victim. Maybe I was back then, but not anymore. You have no idea what I've been through, so I'd appreciate it if you'd keep your assumptions to yourself." When her outburst was met with a smile, Cassie knew he was toying with her. She reacted in exactly the way he wanted her to, but she hadn't been able to hold her tongue.

"I apologize, Cassie. Well, I was gonna ask you to fuck me, but seeing as you don't do that…" He tailed off, as if hoping she might offer him something else. Cassie stayed quiet, gazing up at the powerful man in the darkness, a smile curling at her lips uncontrollably. "How about one of those amazing blowjobs, like the one you gave Jamie? I wanna come all over your tits like he did."

"Well, that depends," Cassie retorted, enjoying their closeness now. She actually did want to see more of him, to feel more of this connection they obviously shared, but she didn't dare risk a liaison with this violently renowned man. She tried to turn his attention away, reminding him of the details of her contract. "I'm officially off the clock, as you've so cunningly discovered. So I would need for you to call my madam and arrange it. Once our business is over with, I'll go home and you'll never see me again, because I'll never be anything more than another whore to you."

"What if I pay you ten million dollars right now to spend the night with me? Off the books, you'll keep every cent." Leo's counter offer was mind-boggling, but Cassie shook her head.

"That's incredibly generous of you, Mr. Solomon, but the answer is still no. Goodnight." Cassie stepped away from his grip and his gaze. She made her way over to the doorway and began walking back the way they came without another word, hoping he would let her leave. She got as far as the billiards room when powerful arms gripped her from behind, and Leo's strong body pressed her into the wall. She remained calm, determined not to end up like all those other girls who had supposedly taken his money to stay quiet after he'd had his way with them.

"What will it take for you to be mine, Cassie?" Leo whispered in her ear. His voice was rough, his breath ragged, and he sounded desperate for her to change her mind. She peered back over her shoulder, her breath quickening and her stomach twisted like a pretzel.

"Time, patience, and trust. All the things I fear you do not possess, Mr. Solomon. I can never be yours, just as you can never be mine," she replied. She cried out with shock when he turned her around an instant later and kissed her lips so delicately it was as though he were an utterly different person. She had expected a harsh, deep kiss, but this was something soft and passionate. Her hands found his stubbly cheeks and grabbed them as she kissed him back, their mouths locked on one another's before he eventually pulled back. Leo peered into her face intently as though really taking her in, creating a lasting memory of her in his mind.

"I'll see you again soon, Cassie." He stepped back to let her leave, and she walked away quickly, heading toward the sounds of the party above.

"I don't think so. Goodbye, Mr. Solomon." Cassie replied, her voice quiet and full of tension.

"We'll see. You can call me Leo, by the way," he shouted after her.

"No. Not unless I'm ready to be yours," Cassie stopped at the bottom step and looked back into the face of the man she feared more than anyone she had ever known, yet was so drawn to that she couldn't stop herself from enjoying one last look.

She ran up the rest of the stairs and burst through the doors into the ground floor hallway, catching the many gazes which darted her way. She clambered forward and gripped the ornate table in the center of the open room with unsteady hands, desperately trying to calm her nerves and stop herself from trembling. Jamie and Hanna rushed to her, but she collected herself and shooed them away rather than draw any more attention to the situation.

Less than a minute later Leo entered the hall from the same doorway, and every face turned to look at him, their expressions fearful or, for some of the women, excited. His body was shaking with rage, and Cassie could see his knuckles were bleeding, making her wonder if perhaps he had taken out his frustration on one of the walls beneath them.

"You two," he called to a couple of blonde women snorting cocaine from the table in the hall. Both of them were clearly ready to party, and they followed him upstairs while the rest of the partygoers watched them with intrigue. He didn't so much as look at Cassie as he passed. It was as though he'd become another person entirely from the soft and affectionate man who had just kissed her so tenderly.

"We're leaving," Jamie said from behind her, and Cassie was grateful when she felt his hand on her hip as he led her and Hanna out the front door toward his car. Within minutes they sped away, and Hanna grabbed her friend's hand, pulling her over the center space in the back seat to hug her tightly.

"What the fuck happened?" she whispered, her eyes wide. Cassie took a deep breath and told them what had gone on between her and Leo.

"You were right not to do anything with him. He would've demanded more, I'm sure of it. You're very lucky he took no for an answer at all," Jamie said from the driver's seat, his words sending a shiver down Cassie's spine.

Chapter 7

Leo Solomon sat in an armchair and watched as the two blondes he summoned upstairs kissed and played with one another to entertain him. He had taken them to a guest room, as was his usual way at these parties. No woman ever, or would ever, share his real bed with him. He tried to enjoy them. He even slid on a condom and fucked them both hard and deep in a bid to release his tension, but it was no good. Cassie had wound him up more than he would ever reveal, even to himself, and he knew it would be a long time before she was out of his system. He kept the girls busy for a while, working up a good sweat while commanding them to pleasure him and pummeling each girl hard until he finally came, but he was still unsatisfied. He made his way upstairs to his bedroom on the third floor after informing his right-hand man, Tyler, to send everyone home.

"Party's over," he muttered, and the burly man nodded but did not say a word. That was one of the things Leo liked most about him. He had worked for

Leo for a long time and earned his place as second-in-command by never asking questions and always doing as his boss asked, no matter what it had been.

Leo retired to his room, pulling one of his many laptops from his bedside desk. He opened up the video file he had been watching from his office earlier of the threesome that had enticed him downstairs to join the party at last. He ignored the other two, the lovers who were enjoying having a third person in bed with them, and focused on Cassie. Her breasts were beautiful, as was her body, and she had the most stunning smile he had ever seen. But the best part of the whole clip, the moment that had turned his full attention toward her, was not during her exploits while pleasuring herself and her friends. It was when she fell back on the bed, laughing loudly and enjoying herself in a genuine and unmasked way. In that moment she was happy, carefree, and quite simply the most spectacular creature he had ever seen.

***

The next morning, after a few hours of fretful sleep, Cassie awoke to the smell of eggs and bacon. She yawned and stretched, pulling on her dressing gown and then heading out to sit with her friends. They were back to being everyday Jamie, Hanna, and Cassie, chatting loudly and joking around while the two lovers openly fawned over one another. Despite the previous night's events, Cassie was not a part of their relationship other than being a friend to them both, and she was happy with that. Last night had been fun and scary, sexy, and even exciting, but she was not ready to re-enact their interlude anytime soon.

She had fallen straight into bed when they got back to the apartment. Her overwrought emotions overtook any other needs, but now she felt rested and at ease. Her pent up sexual tension from the dangerous time spent alone with Leo Solomon was now forgotten, thanks to the anxiety caused by her unwelcome attraction to him that had taken its place.

The three of them ate together before Jamie headed out for work, kissing Hanna tenderly and waving Cassie goodbye.

"You okay, sweetie?" Hanna asked when they were alone. She was washing the dishes while Cassie dried them and put them away.

"Yeah, that Leo guy sure is scary. I'm glad he didn't force me into anything, but he saw right through my façade and called me out on not being a green girl. He has cameras in the bedrooms and watched our little threesome. Leo knew Jamie was lying when he re-told the story of how he fucked us both senseless. He asked me outright why I didn't let either of you touch me. He knew our secret all along. That guy is very clever when it comes to reading people. I bet you any money there's no fooling him."

"I bet you're right," Hanna agreed. "But he is pretty fucking hot too, agreed?"

"Oh yeah," Cassie conceded, grinning across at her friend. "When he stared into my eyes and told me he wanted me to be his, I nearly caved and let him have me there and then!"

"I'm glad you didn't, though. I get the feeling he would not be such a gentleman the morning after," Hanna replied thoughtfully. Much to her dismay, Cassie couldn't help but agree.

***

Over the next few days Cassie kept herself busy between working at the restaurant and more parties for Cyrene's and other escort providers from the city. She enjoyed being back to her normal routine, sleeping late before heading out for her evening at work in either role, and her confidence continued to grow thanks to her newly found prowess at wooing the opposite sex.

The powerful memories of Leo Solomon and her still strong desire for him kept popping into focus, though. Part of her hoped he would reach out to her in some way. She hoped he had taken her refusal as a challenge to be the better man she needed him to be, but she had heard nothing. As hard as it was to accept, he must have considered her unworthy.

"Quit fooling yourself," Cassie told her reflection in the mirror as she finished cleaning up the ladies' bathroom and turned out the light. She knew those types of romances only existed in the movies or in the many romance novels she continued to pore over. Bad boys did not change their ways, they did not repent and offer whores the world in return for their hand in marriage. Leo was not about to come storming into her life to whisk her off of her feet and give her everything she had ever dreamed of. The idea that a lifetime of happiness and a sex life to blush over might be right around the corner was naïve. Those fantasies were exactly that, fantasy.

"Goodnight, Cassie, thanks for covering tonight. You're a star," called her boss, Mrs. Brown, as she left the restaurant. Cassie waved her goodbye with a wide smile from across the room.

"Any time, Mrs. B, see you next week," she called back, grabbing her things and leaving the others to finish off the rest of the cleaning up.

Cassie headed home, her body ready to rest and her mind ready for some much-needed quiet time. When she got back, she showered, put on her pajamas, and then poured herself a large glass of chardonnay. She stood at the kitchen counter for a while, flicking through the pages of a fashion magazine Hanna had left out, while eating a bag of jellybeans she had found in the back of one of the cupboards. It was probably one of Hanna's secretly stashed sweets for her hormonal days, and she promised herself she would replace them.

Cassie hummed as she unwound, allowing her hectic life to fall away as she enjoyed her wine and sweets. After a while, she heard the front door click shut, and Jamie's voice filtered in from the hallway. He was talking quietly to someone she assumed must be her roommate, and she waded out to greet them, stopping dead when she saw who had invited himself into their home along with his employee—Leo Solomon.

"Cassie, you remember my boss?" Jamie's voice was calm and steady, but his eyes were full of apology. Cassie knew there was nothing he could've done to stop Leo from coming here. He would've found any excuse or quite possibly just come alone if he really wanted to, and she could not be mad he had used Hanna's boyfriend as a way into her private life.

"Of course, hello again, Mr. Solomon," she said, smiling at the man who oozed sex-appeal but still scared her to the core.

Leo looked Cassie up and down, taking in her baggy pants and loose fitting t-shirt with a wry smile before staring into her face. She had already removed her makeup and had let her wet hair fall down messily around her shoulders to dry. She hadn't realized she would be entertaining tonight, but she was glad he was seeing her this way. This was the real Cassie, and part of her hoped her pale, natural features might put him off.

"Please, call me Leo," he said with a wicked grin. Cassie shook her head, remembering the words she had last said to him in that dark hallway of his home. She would not call him Leo until she was ready to be his. "I'd rather not, if it's all the same. Can I offer you boys a drink?" she asked, being hospitable, and Jamie shook his head while Leo nodded.

"Hanna's right behind us. We were thinking of heading out to a party, but might just leave it tonight. I'm too tired," Jamie said, clearly not happy at leaving her and Leo alone, and she mentally thanked him. "We bumped into Mr. Solomon here on our way back from the liquor store. He helped us carry the load and even offered me and Hanna a ride home," he added, explaining his presence here somewhat, and Cassie could read between the lines. Leo had given them a ride in order to find out where she lived and to see her again. She guessed maybe she had been wrong about him not thinking of her after all.

"Such a gentleman. That's ever so kind of you, but you didn't need to follow him up," she teased, making Leo smile.

"He needed help with some crates of beer I added to the cart on the way. Hanna is just grabbing the wine with my assistant, and she'll be right up," Leo replied, probably expecting her to be impressed by his generosity.

She just shrugged and wandered back into the kitchen, still hating the fact that she was actually pleased to see him.

"Great, in that case you can have one of your fancy beers then," she called to them, and she returned to her spot at the counter. Cassie flicked through the magazine's pages without even looking at them, her hand trembling as she brought the wine glass to her lips. Her mind was racing, wondering what he wanted from her and if she was willing to even try being with him. Leo was interested in her. She had known it right from that first moment by the poolside, but she had gone about it all the wrong way. Instead of keeping her cool and walking away, she had toyed with him, teased him, and then left him wanting more.

Cassie had known giving him the option of a possible future with her was foolish. Leo was not the kind of guy you fell in love with. Even without the scary and violent way he had about him, the fact remained he was a very powerful drug-lord and his way of life must constantly be accompanied by the threat of rivals and police alike. She was not the sort of woman who could bear a life of fear amidst that kind of chaos. She had only just found herself again and was not ready to give that up for anything. Cassie decided to put an end to their playful games, an end to her teasing. Since he'd shown up at her home unannounced, there was no time like the present.

Leo joined Cassie in the small kitchen, eyeing her thoughtfully. She ignored him at first, finishing off her handful of jellybeans before sliding him the bottle opener from the drawer beside her.

"Thank you." He pulled off the bottle top and took a long swig while she kept her eyes on the magazine. "Something interesting? You've been staring at that same page since I walked in here, and there's nothing but a toothpaste advertisement and an article on bolero jackets." A sly grin curled at his lips. Leo was getting under her skin, and she had a feeling he liked it.

"Yes, actually. I was thinking a bolero would look perfect with some of my little black dresses. Sorry, I thought you were here to have a drink with your friend out there? I didn't want to get in the way, so figured I'd hide out back here. Was there something you wanted, Mr. Solomon?" Cassie asked, her eyes skimming up his tight-fitting t-shirt and over his incredible biceps before landing on those soft, full lips. She remembered their kiss from the weekend before and felt herself blush at the memory. Despite all her reasoning, she desperately wanted him to grab her and kiss her that same way again.

This is gonna be harder than I thought.

"I don't have any friends, Cassie. I thought you knew that, just like you think you know everything there is to know about me," Leo teased her, calling her out on her standoffish demeanor. "I'm a coldhearted, emotionless monster who loves nothing more than business and fucking, and not always in that order," he added, knowing exactly what was said about him behind his back. This man caught her off guard every time she thought she was making some progress in her attempt to pull away from him. He had a strange sort of empathy that hid itself behind his clever and controlling guise, but Cassie could see through all of that now, and wondered if that was exactly what he had wanted. Leo seemed to be trying to get her to delve deeper, to call him out on his behavior and reputation just as he had with her. He was giving her every indication he was ready to bare all, and so she pounced on the opportunity to figure him out.

"Did you come here to see me tonight? Did you set the whole 'need a lift' situation up as a ruse to get in here?" She stared up into his dark brown eyes confidently, despite being so much shorter without her heels.

"Yes," he said, swigging his beer.

"And what exactly did you expect would happen? That I would be instantly at your mercy and fall to your feet because you dared bless me with a second look?"

"That would've been preferable to the cold shoulder I received, yes. But I didn't expect anything of the sort, Cassie. You are not that kind of woman, which is exactly the reason I'm even here," he replied with a smirk.

"Did you ever think that the reason you're here might simply be because I said no? That I'm nothing but an attempted conquest gone awry, and you're here to claim what you believe to be rightfully yours?" Her tone was cool and calm, but deep down Cassie felt far from it.

Leo took a moment to answer her, as though really thinking it through before he answered. "Yes."

"And?" Cassie pressed, taken aback.

"And what? I answered your question. Yes, I did wonder about it."

"Okay, I'll rephrase that then," she retorted, getting grumpy. "Are you here to claim what you believe belongs to you?"

"No," Leo's features softened slightly. "I'm here to ask you on a date."

Cassie laughed loudly, unable to control her startled surprise, and shook her head.

"You really are something else, Solomon. You do know that, right?"

He grinned down at her, his smile wide and his eyes alight. "I do, but I also know what I want and how to get it," he replied.

"Oh, and how's that?" Cassie demanded, one hand on her hip as the other brought her wine glass to her lips again.

"Time, patience, and trust." Leo's body language

had shifted ever so slightly, showing her he was willing to give her what she needed, that he somehow deemed her worthy of an effort to change. She hated how much it made her want him in return.

"I'm not worth it," she mumbled, shying away from his intimidating gaze. "I'm a walking disaster, and I'm not the type of girl who can live in your world without breaking. I'm the cheap wine and jellybeans kinda girl, not the champagne and cocaine hooker. I can't be hanging around with gun wielding drug-lords and their cronies. You'll soon grow tired of me telling you no, and then you'll resent me for having been a waste of your time and effort. It's been wonderful meeting you, Mr. Solomon, but I'm afraid I'm not the girl for you."

Cassie turned on her heel and made her way over to the doorway, unable to look at Leo. She knew she would either cry or cave if she did, and either way she would be utterly disappointed in herself. She had finally set him straight, told her admirer the truth about herself and her needs, all of which they both knew he could not give her.

Leo said nothing as she walked away, but Cassie heard the sound of glass smashing against the kitchen cabinet, and wondered if perhaps her wine glass had just been thrown in his rage. She quickly made her way to Hanna's bedroom and slid between her roommate and Jamie on the bed, grateful they were watching a movie rather than being caught in an intimate moment.

"I'll make sure to see him out," Jamie whispered, climbing out of the bed and taking a few tentative steps toward the hallway of the apartment. The last thing any of them wanted right now was an altercation with his powerful and angry boss, but it seemed he had to be sure the dangerous man had gone. Cassie was glad he went to check, or else none of them would've rested easy that night.

Chapter 8

Weeks passed by in a blur after the night when Leo turned up out of the blue. Cassie kept busy with her waitressing or going along to events with Hanna and the other Cyrene's girls. Jamie had stayed over every night for the past couple of weeks, their relationship unofficially seeming to have moved on a stage without either of them realizing it. One night as they got themselves ready to head into a bustling party, Hanna reached for a yellow band, catching Cassie watching her as she did.

"What?" she demanded, and her friend just gave her a knowing smile. "It's complicated, okay?"

"I know it is, sweetie. You don't need to explain anything to me," Cassie replied, hugging her tightly for a moment. They made their way out into the venue for the evening, a stunning burlesque club that not only entertained the men and women inside with tantalizing shows every night, but also provided special evenings on certain nights when the clients had the option for more than just a show.

Tonight the place had been reserved entirely for

a large record label, the artists and their associates looking to party the night away as well as having some fun with a partner…or two. After donning her red band, Cassie worked her way through the crowd, trying to get a read on the room. She soon made eye contact with a ruggedly handsome man who looked to be in his mid-forties and whose face she recognized from subway billboards and magazine covers, but she couldn't quite remember his name.

He made his way toward Cassie, smiling warmly and seemingly intrigued by her too, even from afar. Despite the promiscuous world she now lived in, Cassie still felt herself blush when men looked at her that way, as though she were still that quiet young woman who first set foot at these parties.

"Well, aren't you just the most beautiful piece of living art on show here tonight," the man said as he reached her, taking Cassie's hand and planting a soft kiss on the back of it. He then let his own hand stroke over her wrist and flicked the red band with his forefinger. "What a shame I cannot have you, but perhaps you would be so kind as to keep me company a while?" he said, his sexy southern American accent catching at his words. He looked effortlessly cool and suave as he offered Cassie his arm.

"It would be my pleasure, Mr…?" Cassie asked, sliding her arm through his and following his lead toward one of the booths.

"Simmons, but you may call me Otis," he replied. "And what is your name, sweet flower?"

Cassie chose not to give out her real name

anymore, just in case. "Savannah," she said, her voice a soft hum, and he leaned in closer to hear her as they made their way through the crowd.

"Well, Savannah, I have a very important question to ask you." His voice was stern, but his expression was playful. "What type of music do you listen to?" He took her hand in his when they were opposite one another in the booth, and she let him. Cassie knew she had seen his face before but still could not place his genre of music within the label. She had the feeling he was not a country or folk singer, seeming to remember seeing his face on one of the rock music channels she frequented, and she decided to give it a shot.

"In all honesty? Indie rock. I love a bit of something deep and melodic but with a powerful bass line and plenty of guitar riffs. Perhaps not your kind of thing," she said, watching him with a delicate smile.

"Oh, and what do you think is my thing?" he asked, smirking back at her. The way he said *thing* came out more like *thang*, and she enjoyed listening to the lilt on his accent. Her only experience with the accent in the States so far had been the Brooklyn tones, and this softer, southern style had a nice sound.

"I'm willing to bet everyone stereotypes you for your style, however I don't think you're a country singer, am I right?" Cassie smiled sweetly and could see by the flash of appreciation that swept across his chiseled face that she had figured him out. Otis clearly thought she had never heard of him, and had assumed she might have thought he must be a country artist like most people did, when in fact he was part of a large and very well-known heavy metal band, The Death Marchers. Otis was the drummer and joint vocalist, famed for his hillbilly style, when in fact he was far from it. Cassie's memory of the articles came flooding back to her. She'd read once how Otis loved to fool people into believing the stereotype he portrayed, and Cassie knew he would appreciate a different impression of the role he seemingly loved playing.

"Very good, flower. Carry on." His smile widened.

"I'm thinking something edgy, different, and yet still melodically beautiful in its own way. I was going to bet you were a guitarist, but judging by these hands, I'd say drummer?" She slid her hands over his rough palms, and Otis stayed quiet, completely mesmerized. "Perhaps not only that. Do you write some of the songs too? I bet you feel the world around you like one long creative spark that inspires and obsesses you until you finally put pen to paper. Am I even close?" She feigned a shy laugh, her voice low and seductive, and she knew without him uttering a sound she had him hooked on her every word. Otis eventually gave her a nod along with a dazzling smile, mesmerizing her too. Cassie felt her core tense, feeling genuinely attracted to this man.

When the party was over and the working girls all made their way toward their awaiting vehicles, Otis was still by Cassie's side and had stayed with her the entire night. He begged her to go home with him, promising he would expect nothing but her company, but she had to refuse. It was not how things were done.

"I'm afraid that's against the rules, Otis. I'm happy to accompany you anywhere publicly that you wish or stand beside you at any event, but home visits are not part of my service, and I must insist upon that rule. If you want to see me again, just call the number on this card and arrange it with my madam, Delilah." She handed him the simple, elegant black card from her purse.

"I will," he replied, kissing her cheek, and she let him, feeling genuine affection for the kind man. "If I lived the rest of my life alone and unloved, at least I could take with me the memory of this night, of you." He stepped back to let her go. "You spoke of inspiration and obsession earlier. Now I truly know what it means to be captivated and stirred into a creative frenzy. You are my muse, Savannah, and I will write you one hundred love songs in the hope you might change your mind and spend the night with me."

***

For the next three weeks Otis reserved Cassie's company for almost every night. She found his attention both flattering and a welcome distraction for her still wandering mind that kept betraying her by thinking of Leo. Being treated to posh dinners or going to gigs as a VIP was great fun, and she had a blast, genuinely smiling and enjoying her time with the enigmatic client. Cassie even changed her shifts at the restaurant to accommodate the man and found herself having a genuine connection with him very quickly.

Otis was kind, gentle, outrageously comical, and fun-natured. He loved showering her with affection, and didn't think twice about breaking into song for her in public places just to see her smile.

They had still never been alone together in private, and Cassie had not yet been inside his impressive penthouse apartment in the city. She maintained her cover, not daring to let herself be alone with him because, despite her past, she was beginning to think she could eventually see herself letting Otis in. She knew when the time came and she agreed to go with him to his apartment, she would no doubt find herself in his bed with Otis before the night was over.

"I often wonder who you are, underneath the mask you must wear in this career," he said one day as they sat having a picnic together under the bright spring sun in Central Park. Cassie had put together an array of nibbles and added a bottle of chardonnay, her favorite, but laughed to herself when Otis turned his nose up at the cheap wine. "I want to know what makes you tick, Savannah. I need more from you. I think I've fallen in love with you, and I need to know if I love the real you." He looked across the field toward some teenagers who were playing with a bat and ball. Cassie watched him, staring at the profile of the kind and tender man who had been the perfect gentleman. She took in his older but very handsome face in the bright sunshine. She had never thought she would go for an older man again after Jonah, but it had turned out that Otis was five years older than her ex-husband, so she was now faced with the prospect of letting in an even older man than she had previously loved.

The only thing standing in her way was Leo. His face still flitted across her mind every now and then, the memory of his bulging biceps and the feel of his soft lips on hers haunting her. The sheer thought of him after so long made her core tense, and she felt herself growing horny. Cassie wished it was Otis making her feel this way, but knew otherwise. She had really hoped to feel more for him, to feel as if she could end up like Hanna and Jamie with this man, or to even leave her life of escorting men for money for Otis, but she was not convinced. Cassie knew the only way to tell for sure was to eventually bare all, like she had done with Leo. If Otis still wanted her despite her haunting past and hang-ups, if he still stared at her the same way without the makeup and fancy clothes, and if he still lusted after her despite her trauma and trust issues, she decided she would let him in. Her decision made, Cassie chose to give him something, starting small.

"My real name is Cassie," she whispered, trailing circles on her thigh with her fingertip. "I love the theater, art, and the movies. I want to travel the world, but I'm scared of flying. Oh, and I'm a terrible dancer."

Otis laughed and took her hand to cradle it in his.

"Thank you, Cassie." He kissed the back of her hand before placing it on his cheek, leaning into her soft touch affectionately. "Do you have any idea the life I want to give you? The world I can show you? I'll even teach you how to dance if I need to…I had noticed your lack of prowess on the dance floor," he added, laughing softly.

"There's more," she replied, her face falling, and Otis peered up at her as though she were an angel sent just for him. "I'm damaged goods, Otis. I have issues, and I won't be able to hide them behind my mask anymore if you make me lower it. I need a little bit of time and a lot of patience."

"I'll give you everything you need, I promise. It will be my life's work to make you happy and help you forget your past, Cassie. I want you to be mine, forever," Otis said, leaning closer to her so their lips were just inches apart. "You don't have to answer me right away. I'll be patient with you for as long as you need. But if you want more, then show me now, kiss me, and I'm all yours. I'll always be yours."

She closed the gap without thinking it through, her instinct taking over as she placed her lips on his. This was exactly what she wanted, and Otis was the type of person she needed in her life. She wanted to be taken care of and loved, respected and treated like a queen. Cassie knew she didn't love him, but hoped one day she would, and that was more than enough to begin with. Their lips parted and their tongues delved into one another's mouths effortlessly. Their kiss was sensuous yet soft, full of need and passion, but also full of promise. She had finally found it. Cassie was sure this was the beginning of something special, something real, and she endeavored to keep it safe.

Chapter 9

From that moment on, Cassie's affections belonged solely to Otis. She agreed to give herself over to him exclusively and knew from now on she would only ever find herself at parties or functions to accompany him. Delilah locked down her contract after a hefty payment from her beau, and she finally found herself at his home the following week, the two of them alone for the first time. They had already agreed they would take things slowly, and Otis had promised not to proposition her.

"Make yourself comfortable, and I'll grab us a glass of wine," Otis said, directing Cassie toward the lounge, and she took a seat in the large, comfy sofa that overlooked the impressive city. He soon joined her, handing Cassie a glass of expensive red wine, and she forced herself to seem impressed when he watched her take a sip. No matter how many times she said she preferred white wine, he still insisted on serving her red, a point that aggravated her, but she never let it show. The pair chatted for a while, Otis telling her about his upcoming session with his band to record some of the new tracks he had written, the tracks about her, and she smiled sweetly, hanging on his every word. Cassie knew they were still playing their roles, that this was not real yet, but she enjoyed the time with him anyway, allowing Otis to hold her hand and even kiss her gently for a while before she excused herself and used the bathroom.

On her way back to the living room, a knock at the front door startled her. It was a loud, booming knock, as unwelcome in this calm home as club music in a library. Instinctively, Cassie made her way toward it and looked through the peephole. She froze in shock when she saw three men on the other side of the door.

For a split second, part of her wondered if the men worked for Leo, thinking he might have sent them over to put a stop to her relationship with Otis. But then she reminded herself she had neither seen nor heard from Leo since that night in her apartment when she had finally told him no. He had backed off and had pursued her no more, a fact she was happy about, but at the same time she was also a little saddened. Cassie felt misled, as though he had lied about his goals of gaining her trust and accepting her troubled past. When push came to shove, Leo hadn't fought for her, but Otis had. She would remind herself of that fact for as long as it took to feel the same way toward her rock star client as she had with the intimidating gangster.

Cassie continued to stare out into the corridor for a few seconds, wondering if she should go and get

Otis, but then one of the men held up a badge as though knowing she was on the other side of the door. This man was not a drug-dealer henchman of Leo Solomon. This man was FBI, and for some reason he was intent on being let inside.

"We have a warrant for the arrest of Mr. Otis Simmons. Please open the door," he said, his voice deep and rang with authority. Cassie immediately did as the man asked and stared wide eyed at the three men, each of whom pushed past her and went in search of their target. She followed, moving toward the living room. Otis was not there, so she led the men down the hall to his office, assuming he must have moved to the back of the apartment while she was in the bathroom. When she stepped over the threshold, a strong, rough hand wrapped around her neck, and Cassie felt cold steel press hard against her temple from the other side. Otis pressed his body into hers from behind, his breath ragged. He held her still, eager to use her as his leverage to get away from the police.

"Take one more step and I'll blow her brains out," he said, his voice harsh. The three men raised their hands, none of them having drawn a weapon, evidently hoping to negotiate with him before making a move.

Cassie was surprised with herself. Rather than breaking down, she remained perfectly calm. Each second that passed felt as if it were going in slow motion, and she allowed herself to move with Otis as he pulled her backward, distancing themselves from the agents. She took long, deep breaths, and her mind was alive. What shocked her most was that even with a gun pressed against her head, she was not afraid. If anything, she was excited and found her body tingling with heightened sensitivity.

"Are you going to kill me, Otis?" she whispered, her hands sliding behind her toward his hips, pushing back into him as she ran her fingers over the contours of his slim waist and down over his hipbones. "You said you loved me. I thought we had a deal, you and me?" Cassie pressed on, turning her head so she could look back at him.

"Yes, we did. Didn't we?" he replied, pushing Cassie down with his free hand on her shoulder so she fell to her knees, still looking forward. "This is the only way to make you truly safe, to stop anyone hurting you ever again," Otis added, and she heard the gun cock beside her temple.

Cassie gasped, her fear finally grasping her when the almighty sound of the shot came crashing through her ears. She immediately flinched and fell to the ground, but the shot was not for her. Another body hit the ground just behind her, and she realized what had happened. Otis had lifted it to his own temple in that split second and taken his own life.

She was glad she had not seen him do it, and that she didn't have to look at his lifeless body. Cassie was content to bury her face in her hands and keep her eyes closed until well after one of the three FBI agents lifted her up in his arms and took her with him into the living room.

"You were very lucky, miss," he whispered as he wiped her face with a tissue from a small packet in his pocket.

"What do you mean?" Cassie managed to ask. It

felt like hours had passed, when in fact the backup hadn't even arrived yet, so she knew it must have only been minutes. There were no sirens or officers ready to lock down the crime scene. There was still only her, the three agents, and now a very dead Otis.

"We came to arrest him on suspicion of multiple homicides. We were given an anonymous tip that led us to conclusive evidence that Mr. Simmons was responsible for the deaths of more than ten prostitutes from all over the US. He fell in love with every one of them, promised them the world, but then when they weren't everything he had expected them to be, he turned on them. Whoever provided that tip, they saved your life today," he told her, smiling down at Cassie with a warm expression and compassionate eyes.

In that moment she knew, or suspected she knew, exactly who her savior might be, and she immediately calmed down. Her tears stopped, and she composed herself quickly.

"Thank you. I need to call my people," Cassie told him, indicating she was talking about her agency, and the man nodded. She chose not to correct him about his assumptions she was a prostitute, wondering to herself if that was exactly what she had become. Despite not actually having sex for money, Cassie now knew how quickly the experience changed from having fun at parties and enjoying the attention, to downright reveling in one man's adoration of her. She had done everything she could to keep his affections on her. Any sane woman would have seen the signs early on, the control, the obsessive nature, and the desperation to have her as his own. Cassie knew she had rebounded from her dismissal of Leo's proposal straight into Otis's arms, and she had let herself believe it was all okay, that Otis was good for her, when evidently he was a more dangerous predator than Leo ever had been.

She was collected within minutes and taken home, Delilah arriving in person to speak on her behalf and assure the officers Cassie would provide a full statement in due course, but they had no reason to hold her. The agents agreed and let the two women leave.

"Hanna's on her way. Do you want me to come up and stay with you?" Delilah asked as the car pulled up outside her dark apartment building.

"No, I'll be fine. Thanks." Cassie climbed out and made her way up in stunned silence. The events of the night replayed through her mind over and over again, but she was still not scared, just numb. She was also more determined than ever to keep men away, convincing herself she was happier without them, just as they were better off without her drama. But at the same time Cassie felt hornier than she had been in ages. She would've welcomed the proposition from a lover right now, or just some genuine affection, and suspected it was her subconscious need for comfort.

She made her way into her apartment and flicked on the lights, her eyes quickly drawn to the dining table before her where a bottle of chardonnay and a big bag of jellybeans sat waiting for her. Cassie laughed out loud, giggling almost maniacally as she pulled out a small note that sat beside her gifts and read it aloud.

"I tried to stay away, really I did. But how can I choose between pain and pleasure when you bring me both? How can I let you go when I cannot live in a world without you in it?

Yours patiently and honorably, Anonymous."

Cassie read the note over and over, feeling her heart flutter in her chest as she realized all the thoughts she had been having about Leo Solomon and his affections for her had been right. He did care, he cared enough to let her go when she asked him to, but he also cared enough to keep her safe all the time since.

Harsh, forceful sobs began to claim her as the emotion finally flooded her system, the fear and anguish from the last few hours affecting her at last. Cassie fell to her knees, clutching the note to her chest as tears forced themselves out of her. When two powerful arms gripped her tight and enveloped her from behind, Cassie didn't even flinch. She turned to face him and let herself fall deeper into Leo's hold, and then unashamedly fell apart.

"I told you I couldn't stay away. Don't ever ask me to leave you again, because next time I'm putting my foot down and saying no," he whispered, wrapping his legs around Cassie while she curled into a ball. Her hands gripped his bicep, and Cassie knew she didn't want him to let her go ever again. A wave of uncertainty swept over her, though.

"I'm not the girl for you, Leo," she whispered, sobbing harder.

"Yes you are, and you just called me Leo, which

tells me you're mine at last," he replied, reiterating the words she had said to him in his basement that night oh-so long ago.

Chapter 10

Leo held Cassie for a long time, seeming not to care about the uncomfortable floor beneath them or the tears and snot that now covered his t-shirt from her breakdown. She hoped he was glad to have stayed after taking her the silly gifts. Cassie couldn't bear the thought of having potentially been so broken all alone, and she was happy to hold on as long as he let her.

"How did you do it?" she eventually asked, lifting her head, but still not moving from Leo's tight cocoon. "Did you know he was a murderer?"

"No, not at first," he replied, stroking her hair. "I've been keeping tabs on you since the very first day we met, Cassie. I'm going to be honest about it, because you must surely have realized that already."

"Yes, I had a feeling. But I wasn't completely sure, until tonight," she replied, grateful he hadn't chosen to lie or cover up his intrusive protective methods.

"I was glad when you two met, at first. He seemed nice. He was taking you out to fancy restaurants and being a gentleman. I was crazy jealous, I'll happily admit that. But I was trying to let you go, trying to forget about you, and if that was going to happen I had to know for sure he was going to be good to you." Leo pulled Cassie's chin up so her gaze met his. The pads of his thumbs began tracing the contours of her cheeks, sweeping across the dark circles under her eyes in a bid to wipe them clean.

"I hired a private investigator to look into his past. Otis had a string of relationships in his younger days that led nowhere, followed by a few shorter ones as he got older, nothing to report about. But then I learned his penchant for prostitutes went as far back as his late teens. He also happened to be playing gigs in cities where women were found beaten and murdered. When I took a really good look, it was all too much of a coincidence. I had a deeper delve, and lo and behold, he had not only beaten many women, but had also paid off one or two pimps as recompense for accidentally murdering their girls."

"You've gotta be kidding?" she mumbled, shaking her head.

"I wish I was, love. He wanted to find the perfect girl, but each always turned out not quite good enough, and he would get violent. As soon as I was sure, I sent the information to the police anonymously. I knew he had paid for you exclusively, and he was progressing with his affections for you. I assumed he might turn, and you could be his next victim," Leo said, his long explanation shocking Cassie to her core. "I obviously could not allow that, Cassie. I couldn't let him hurt the only thing I've ever truly cared for, the only woman I have ever loved," Leo added, making her jump.

Cassie wiped her face on her sleeve. The tears had long since dried, but she was still puffy and had a headache from hell. She looked up into his handsome face, noticing how relaxed and innocent his features were after their tender time wrapped in each other's tight grasps. Leo looked younger, more delicate now, and it was hard for her to picture him as the same intimidating man she had met at his party. His words sunk in, and she felt her resolve completely melt. He loved her. She remembered the words so clearly and couldn't help smiling.

Cassie leaned up and trailed soft kisses over his strong jaw up to his lips, climbing onto her knees so she was level with him and grabbing his stubble covered cheeks with her palms.

"You love me?" she asked as she pulled back, her hands resting on his shoulders before she slid them down to take his hands in hers.

"Yeah, I guess I do," he replied, peering into Cassie's eyes solemnly before gathering her up in his arms and carrying her toward her room. Once inside, Leo unzipped her dress and let it tumble to the floor.

She instantly clammed up, but he made no move toward her underwear, so she relaxed and stood watching him while he wandered over to her chest of drawers and pulled out a set of pajamas for her to climb into, helping her move her tired body as he went. Cassie smiled up at him, planting another kiss on his lips when she was changed, and he welcomed her affections, wrapping her tightly in his bear-like grip as he kissed her back fervently. Leo gathered her up and carried her over to the bed, placing her delicately on the duvet before retreating, a dark look of regret on his face.

"Don't leave me, Leo, please. I couldn't bear it if you left me alone in this bed tonight. I know I'm a mess and a tease, but…" She tailed off when she felt the tears welling at her eyes again.

"I'm not going anywhere, love," he replied, smiling down at her. "I'm just going to ask Jamie if I can borrow some comfy clothes. I didn't bring any PJs."

"Are they back? I didn't hear them come in. I thought Hanna would've come to check on me," Cassie replied, feeling sad, but Leo's face said it all, and she felt better for having looked up at his sheepish grin.

"Yeah, they were already here before you came back. I convinced them to let me take care of you. I needed you to know how much I would do to keep you safe, that I meant what I said." He leaned down to plant a soft kiss on her forehead. She grinned back up at him, loving him this way. She knew it had taken her complete meltdown for his own layers of armor to come away, but she didn't care. This was the Leo she needed to see. Cassie needed to know him this way in order to accept the everyday version of himself she knew would be back again soon, the hardened criminal who cared for no one and sat atop his throne bought and paid for by drug money.

She wanted to learn how he'd gotten there, and hoped one day he would tell her, but there were big changes they each needed to make for one another first, and she was determined to get it right.

Cassie followed Leo toward Hanna's room, and he took her hand in his, the affectionate and protective gesture not lost on her one tiny bit. She knocked, giving it a few seconds before popping her head around the door, but hoping they'd been expecting to see her after knowing the terrible ordeal she had gone through.

"Oh, Cassie! You look terrible," Hanna cried, grabbing her tight while Jamie shook his boss's hand awkwardly.

"Thanks very much," Cassie murmured, looking back at her friend, and she managed a half smile. Leo asked Jamie if he could borrow some clothes, and the two of them headed over to his drawer in Hanna's huge chest. He produced a pair of tracksuit bottoms and a t-shirt, handing them over without a word, and Leo headed to the bathroom to change. Cassie could tell Jamie felt uncomfortable in Leo's presence, and she hoped he would feel more comfortable as time went on.

"Did he tell you about Otis?" she asked, sitting down beside Hanna on the bed. She didn't stop her when Hanna hugged her tightly.

"Yeah, he also promised me that he would take care of you from now on, better care that is, seeing as it appears he never stopped. He seemed really sincere, as far from that man we met in his house as I could've ever imagined. Even Jamie was surprised by how much he cares for you, otherwise neither of us would have let him in here, much less let him be the one to comfort you when you got home," Hanna replied, and Cassie knew she was feeling guilty for not letting her know earlier they were home.

"It's okay, I'm glad he was here," she replied. "Wow, Leo must have been really convincing for you to let him in here?"

Hanna shrugged, leaning closer, and she whispered in her ear so as not to be overheard. "He's Leo Solomon, he doesn't need to be convincing, Cassie. Don't ever forget who you are dealing with, and don't get complacent just because he's swooped in to save you in your hour of need, sweetie."

"I won't, Han, don't you worry. If he wants to be with me he already knows I won't make it easy on him." Cassie laughed out loud, giggling uncontrollably when Leo came back into the room wearing Jamie's clothes. The tracksuit bottoms seemed a decent fit, but the shirt was far too small, showing off his incredible body, but also reminding Cassie of the shirts she used to regularly catch Liam trying to squeeze himself into back at the theater to try and impress the objects of his affections. Leo's muscular arms bulged beneath the cotton sleeves, and Cassie wondered if they might be about to rip, a thought that made her core tense at the sheer fantasy of it. His huge pecs and thick collar muscles were stuff of dreams, and both girls' mouths dropped open as they took him in.

"Something tells me it's a little too snug?" Leo laughed along with her and Hanna. Jamie smiled but stayed rooted to the same spot he'd been in, thoughtful and clearly uncomfortable at having Leo here. Cassie noticed his unease, and felt a flutter of doubt sweep over her, but ignored it. This bad-boy lover was exactly what she needed, and wanted, in her life. She couldn't fight her feelings for him anymore, even if he was bad news.

Leo slipped off the t-shirt and tossed it back at Jamie with a grin. The girls' giggles silenced instantly as they devoured the sight of his naked torso. Hanna stared at him, and Cassie was sure she was taking a mental picture of the gorgeous man.

She grinned, biting down on her bottom lip as she too let her eyes roam over Leo's impressive physique, and her mind wandered to some wonderful places.

Chapter 11

After a few more cuddles from Hanna, Cassie finally pulled away and followed Leo back to her room. He had been waiting patiently for her beside the still quiet Jamie, and she loved that he was doing everything he had promised her he would. His entire demeanor was so calm and patient, putting her very much at ease.

"Even in your darkest moments you brighten up my life in a way I could never have known possible," Leo told her once she was safely wrapped in his arms under the covers on her bed. Cassie felt her cheeks burn at his random sentiment but let herself enjoy his tender words, needing them in a way she would never have openly admitted to him. Despite being strong and independent, she sometimes needed someone to see through her layers and find the truth in those still waters that ran so deep inside of her. Leo seemed more than capable of doing so. He had even done it the night they met, and she wondered if he was something out of this world. Surely an ordinary man could not possess such powerful empathy and an effortless insight into the minds and feelings of those around him.

Cassie tilted her head, and Leo immediately took her mouth with his, sliding his tongue between her lips and conducting her own into submission. Her body went limp, her senses overwhelmed, and she reveled in the all-consuming passion she was filled with for the first time in so long. She climbed on top of him, and Leo happily lay on his back. His arms gripped the pillow beneath him while Cassie straddled his half naked body and ran her fingers down his ripped torso. She soon slid her mouth from his, moving down onto the hairless chest, taking time to caress each of his nipples with her tongue, enjoying his groans as she did so.

Cassie continued south, and she pulled back the covers so that he could watch her in the dim light. As she found her way blocked by the hem of his borrowed tracksuit bottoms, she grinned up at him. She wanted Leo to know she was enjoying this, needing to see as she pleasured him. He remained calm and let her do as she pleased without moving a muscle.

When she tugged at the cotton and pulled the pants down, he obliged. Cassie slid them over his thick thighs toward his feet, and she savored his groan as he watched her stare down at his huge hard-on and lick her lips in anticipation. She quickly pulled off her t-shirt and kicked off her own pants, leaving on her panties, as always. Cassie started to speak, to warn him not to take anything further than she was ready to, but he shushed her.

"I'm completely at your command Cassie, I'll keep my hands up here, and I won't push you into anything. You can trust me," Leo said, his voice a harsh whisper.

She wanted to trust him, and hoped Leo would fight any urge to take the prize he so readily might've snatched up if he were with anyone else. Cassie slid her mouth over the tip and down his long shaft, almost gagging as she took Leo as far back as she could. Her mouth explored him inch by inch, and she grew wet as she caressed him with her tongue. One hand held him in place, the other gripping his thigh as she moved, keeping herself steady. When he came, she swallowed down every drop, desperate not to waste even a bead of his pleasure. She then kneeled back on the soft bed and watched as Leo panted in elated defeat. She owned him; Cassie knew it in that moment. Despite everything he was and would no doubt continue to be once they were away from the privacy of her room, Leo belonged to her in a far more powerful way than she ever had, or would, belong to him.

Feeling more turned on than ever before, Cassie slid her hand inside her panties toward her already swollen clit. She wrapped two of her fingertips around the tender nub and began working it in a circular motion, building her climax quickly. Leo watched her with a hunger in his eyes that scared her, and she nearly stopped, but instead commanded him away.

"Don't move, stay there," she whispered through trembling lips, and watched as Leo gripped either side of her mattress firmly in his strong hands while lifting his shoulders off of the bed for a better view. He followed her request, though, his breath coming fast and heavy until he eventually held it. Her orgasm hit, and as soon as she began bucking and moaning her release, he let out a deep growl full of raw lust and savage need. Leo flung himself forward when she pulled her hand away, pinning Cassie to his powerful body while the wonderful aftershocks still reverberated through her, and he kissed her deeply.

"That's the sexiest thing I've ever seen," Leo whispered, his kisses ravaging her face and neck as he ran his hands through her long hair. "I would die a happy man if I got to see you do that for me every night."

Cassie laughed, but she lapped up his passionate words and savored his touch as they lay down and their bodies intertwined on the bed.

***

The next morning Cassie woke with her face pressed into Leo's chest. His hands were tangled in her hair, holding her so tightly it was almost as though he was terrified of not having her close. It had taken them hours to fall asleep, their bodies buzzing. They had just chatted quietly, whiling away the hours with easy conversation before finally drifting off to sleep. Leo stirred as she roused, releasing his grip, and he peered down into her eyes apologetically.

"It's okay," Cassie whispered, nestling her face into the crook of his neck and enjoying the warmth that spread over her when his thickly muscled arms wrapped around her small body, pulling her tighter.

"I love this," Leo murmured, clearly not ready to put his armor back on yet, and she was glad. Cassie groaned in affirmation, unable to say much in his tight hold, but she leaned into his embrace, enjoying their closeness. "I've always longed to have this. I hate being alone, but I've always been my own worst enemy when it comes to addressing my feelings. I think I always thought I was better off not feeling at all, but now I know better." Leo kissed her softly.

"Promise me that no matter what happens we'll always remember this, how we are now, and we'll try to find our way back here if we ever lose it," Cassie said as he stroked her hair out of her face. Leo climbed over her on the bed, pinning her to the mattress with his powerful body.

"How can I ever forget? Of course, I promise," he answered before finally climbing out of bed. He started dressing in the clothes he had worn to the apartment the night before.

"Do you have to go?" Cassie asked, hating to watch him leave.

"I have to, I'm sorry," Leo said, sitting down on the bed beside her. His features turned stoic, and she knew he was slowly going back to his usual demeanor. "My job isn't exactly nine-to-five. In all honesty, it is more like twenty-four-seven. I'm always busy, always needed, and I cannot change that, Cassie. We will have to find a way to slot you into my world. We'll figure it out eventually, but please know I will never intentionally put you in harm's way. There may even be times I will have to push you aside for your own safety, and I would rather do that than ever see you get hurt because of me. But in the meantime, I want us to share as many nights like this as we can, okay?" He wasn't looking at anything in particular, just gazing thoughtfully across her room as he buttoned up his shirt.

"Of course, we will both have to find a way to accept and take care of each other as best we can. I know you're not the hero, Leo. But you aren't the villain, either, and I'm more than willing to find our happy medium." Cassie climbed up on her knees behind him and wrapped her arms around his shoulders. He stroked her hands and kissed each palm before standing again.

"Me too. But, there is one thing I will ask of you now. I would like you to consider ceasing your contract with Delilah permanently. I won't pay for you. I want you to be my girlfriend, Cassie, not something I own." His entire demeanor was commanding and intimidating again, but she could see the softness behind his cool features. "I've already programmed my number into your phone. Will you call me later?"

"I'll ring to let you know when my contract is over with. Why would I ever need the attention of the men at those parties again when I belong to you?" She smiled up at him, and he scooped her up for one more bear hug and a deep, lingering kiss.

***

Leo left without another word, pulling his phone

from his pocket and he waved goodbye to Hanna as he made the call to his driver. Jamie walked out of the bathroom as Leo passed, smiling at him timidly, and his boss stared at him for a moment before stepping closer and sliding his cell back in his pocket.

"Don't you dare think this means you've got something on me, Jay, or that we're best mates now," Leo warned, his voice low and fierce. "You do not tell another soul my personal business, or I might have to terminate your contract, is that understood?"

"Yes, Mr. Solomon. I would never tell anyone your private business, and I would never expect special treatment. My lips are sealed, as ever, sir," Jamie replied, his eyes wide and his expression fearful. Thanks to his reputation among his men, Leo knew he had delivered no idle threat. He meant every word, and would stand by his promise to terminate Jamie's working arrangement in the only way people in his business knew how, by quite literally terminating them.

"Good." Leo stared him down for a few more seconds. "Because if this goes sour thanks to you, I will procure your little whore of a girlfriend over there for a night of my most depraved fantasies. After I finished, I'd make it a matter of utmost importance that my sickest men had their fun too. You know she'd never be the same once we were done with her. That's why you shit yourself that night when I honed in on the pair of them. You were more concerned I was going to try and fuck her than you were for Cassie's safety." He stepped closer to his trembling employee and dropped his voice. "I think you actually breathed a sigh of relief when I chose her instead of Hanna, so don't pretend you're the good guy," he warned, sealing Hanna's fate with a terrible promise. Jamie just nodded in understanding, staring at his feet while Leo grabbed the last of his things and left without another word.

Chapter 12

Leo worked out for two hours at his home gym later that morning, forcing the excess tension out of his body, and then lifting weights with his personal trainer, Ivan. Leo was in his prime, and he was now bench-pressing impressive weights thanks to Ivan's strict regime and round the clock motivational tactics. In his past life, the guy had been a Marine, a cage fighter, thug for hire, and everything in between. But now Ivan belonged to Leo and had been well worth the investment.

Fitness had become Leo's obsession the last few years, and he was only happy when he had hit the gym and worked his body hard, constantly checking his weight, eating well, and putting his physical limits to the test. Leo knew he had an obsessive personality at times; his intrusive methods with Cassie were testament to that, but he didn't care. Without those intense sides of himself, Leo would not be the man he was today, and Cassie would still be in the company of a killer.

"What's up with you today? Am I pushing you

too hard, little girl?" Ivan shouted, picking up the pace during their run, and Leo sprinted after him, his taunts having worked in spurring him on.

"Do you want someone waiting for you?" Leo's assistant, Tina, asked as he made his way back inside the mansion following his run around the vast grounds. She was used to procuring women for her boss to help him release those tensions the hours at the gym could not relieve.

"Not today. Get me Javier," he said. He needed his driver for an errand. Part of him wanted to instruct Tina to tell Javier to go over to Cassie's with flowers and chocolates. He felt all gooey inside, and he hated it. Leo Solomon was not the warm and fuzzy type. Regardless of the part of himself he had shown Cassie last night, he still had no idea when it came to romance.

He decided instead to put a tail on her, needing to know where she was and who she saw. He also knew he still had needs, and soon he would need to have them seen to, but Leo hoped Cassie would come around before he had to go elsewhere to scratch his itch.

"Of course, I'll make sure he's ready. You have a meeting later, but it's not until eight o'clock this evening," Tina replied, reminding him of his itinerary, and Leo nodded, heading inside for his much needed shower and protein shake.

After he was washed and dressed, Leo sat at his desk and grabbed his laptop from the locked drawer. He opened it and loaded his surveillance software, reeling with excitement at what he knew he would find on there. He knew at some point he would need to come clean about just how involved he had become in Cassie's life. He had given her a little bit of a confession on his hired investigator regarding Otis, and that he had been keeping an eye on her, but he hadn't let on how much.

As he sat and waited, tapping his hand impatiently, he remembered her with a smile. The way Cassie had touched herself so gently, yet she knew exactly what she needed, and she delivered it without even breaking a sweat. Her stunning body and beautiful face would remain forever in his memory, but he was also glad he had hidden cameras all around her apartment so didn't need to keep it as just a memory. He couldn't wait to watch it again.

Leo clicked back through the previous night's recordings and watched the highlights, from the moment she had found his silly little gift right to when he had threatened Jamie in the hallway. Cassie's bedroom feed was fantastic. He watched her moment of self-satisfaction with a flutter in his chest and bated breath, growing hard at her stunning display. Leo knew it was wrong to have planted the cameras. He was wrong to do a lot of things, and he was not sorry about it. He needed to know what she did and what she said to Hanna.

Leo's insatiable need for control was evident in everything he did, but it had also earned him his place atop his vast empire and the fantastic lifestyle that came with it. He enjoyed having power over others and used whatever tools he had at his disposal. He had gotten a great deal of satisfaction from delivering Jamie his little warning this morning, and enjoyed watching him squirm on the screen.

Leo pulled up the live feed, finding Cassie and Hanna sitting at the kitchen counter having coffee together. He plugged in his headphones and listened in on them, and wasn't ashamed at all.

"So, you let him spend the night. Does that mean…?" Hanna cradled her coffee in her small hands as she peered across at Cassie expectantly.

"No, we fooled around a little, but you know it'll take a lot for me to finally be ready. I need to trust him completely, but I'm also scared he will be put off," Cassie replied. Leo couldn't be sure what she meant by it, but Hanna seemed to understand.

"If he's telling the truth about how much he cares, then he'll love you no matter what. He seems really different with you, far from that scary man we saw at his party," Hanna said, smiling wickedly. "Hot as fuck, but still terrifying as hell, don't get me wrong. He seems real when he's with you, though. It's as if he really does let down that mask a little. You need to be careful, Cassie. I can't tell you enough how much it worries me that you have somehow charmed the most powerful and intimidating man I've ever known, and I've met a lot along the way."

"Me too. I was terrified last night that he might try something. Even after I'd sorted him out, I could tell he was far from satisfied. I know I'll need to let him have more of me eventually, but I'm not sure he's ready for my baggage. He says he is, but how can I trust it?" Cassie asked, and Hanna shrugged.

"Because he says so," Jamie said, joining the two

women. Leo immediately stiffened, hoping his employee would follow his warnings. The girls looked over at him questioningly, and he topped up their mugs with coffee from the jug as he spoke. "Leo Solomon is many things, but he is not a liar. He says what he means, and he would never make promises he couldn't keep. I know I clammed up last night, but that was out of respect as well as fear. I wouldn't work for him if I didn't think he was trustworthy. In our line of business you always need to know someone's got your back, and that's what he delivers. Yes, he calls the shots and makes the rules, but do you really think thousands of guys would follow his lead if he continually screwed them over? You both know I wouldn't have let him in here last night if I thought he might hurt you, Cassie. Give the guy a chance."

"Good lad," Leo whispered to himself, watching as the girls mulled over Jamie's words, and both of them softened.

"I guess so. I hadn't thought about it that way," Cassie conceded. She took a long swig of her coffee and looked over at Hanna again. "He wants me to close my contract with Delilah. He refuses to pay for me because he wants me to just be his girlfriend. I like it that he doesn't see me as his property."

"That's a good idea. This life was never one hundred per cent for you anyway, sweetie. It will be a lot better if he doesn't see you as something he owns. He will no doubt treat you better and with more respect," Hanna said, eyeing Jamie as she did so, and Leo detected it might be a sore subject between the two of them. He could use that against

Jamie if it ever came to having words with him again.

"I'm gonna ring her now, get it over with, and then I'll call him. I don't even know when we're seeing each other again. I've got a shift at the restaurant tonight, but could change it if he wants me to," Cassie replied.

"Don't, he needs to know you already have a life and commitments that do not involve him. Don't forget, Cassie, if he doesn't own you, he has to respect that," Hanna said. "Make him work for you. He seems to like the chase. I get the feeling he'd make a good predator."

"I know, sometimes he looks at me like he's getting ready to pounce." She took a deep breath. "Talk about bittersweet," Cassie said, taking a final sip of her coffee while staring off into space dreamily, and Leo grew hard again as he watched her.

She was right, he was not fully satisfied, but he also was stubborn enough to force those urges away for now. His self-control and keen instinct had helped out a lot over the years, and he would use them to his advantage now. Leo closed the laptop and pulled the headphones from his ears, grabbing his cell phone and ringing his assistant.

"Tina, I want you to book me a restaurant for our meeting tonight, rather than having the boys here. It's called Brown's. I think it's Italian food. I want the entire place reserved. Pay the owner well over the odds if necessary, but make it happen. And play nice," he barked, hanging up once Tina confirmed she would get right to it.

Leo opened the laptop again, finding the live feed still running, and he overheard Cassie's telephone conversation with Delilah, informing the madam she would not be returning to work, and he grinned widely. "Mine," he said, sliding his finger over her face on the screen before closing the application and opening his emails to get some work done at last.

***

"Thank you Delilah. I'm glad you understand, and thank you for your help last night. Goodbye."

Cassie hung up the phone and grinned, feeling freer than she thought she would. She really enjoyed her time as an escort, and would miss the parties and the flattering men, but now she had the attention of a man far superior to any of them and couldn't wait to tell him the good news. She grabbed her phone and began pulling up Leo's number from the phonebook, but stopped. She decided to let him wait a little longer. Hanna was right, and if she was his girlfriend rather than his property, Cassie was determined to be strong and bring her entire self to the equation, not the bought and paid for attention she normally would give to her clients. She threw her phone down onto her bed and headed for the shower, unable to stop from pleasuring herself while she was in there, the wonderful memories from the night before driving her to climax alongside her fingertips.

Chapter 13

"Bye, see you later," Cassie called as she left the apartment, heading to the subway. She called Leo on her way, having managed to wait an extra few hours. She was pleased with herself.

"Ah, there she is," Leo said on the other end as he answered. "I was beginning to think you'd changed your mind."

"Of course not," Cassie replied, unable to hide her swoon at hearing his voice. "I've been busy, that's all."

"Okay, I'll let you off then. I hope you have some good news for me?" Leo asked.

"I do indeed. You are now officially dating Cassie Taylor, waitress," she told him, enjoying his gruff laugh. "I still need a job, you know? I've grown accustomed to the luxuries of the escort business and need to pay for my designer handbag addiction somehow," she teased.

"I'll buy you one hundred handbags, and the shoes to match. Am I gonna see you tonight?"

"I'm working until midnight. You can come and

collect me after my shift if you like?" she offered, wanting to see him too.

"I don't know if I can. Let me check my schedule, and I'll let you know. Okay, love?"

Leo seemed aloof, and Cassie wondered if he was playing games, so she swallowed her pride, not wanting to push him away by foolishly playing with his affection.

"Okay, I really want to see you, though, Leo. I miss you already," Cassie replied, her voice softening.

"Me too. I'll make sure we see each other tonight, don't you worry."

After a short subway ride, Cassie arrived at the quiet restaurant and made her way inside, surprised there weren't already customers at the tables. She went straight into the kitchen to find Mrs. Brown.

"Hi, everything okay?" she asked, and the middle-aged woman nodded happily.

"Yep, we've had a booking for the whole place tonight. Some kinda party, and they had to change venue at the last minute. The girl on the phone said they loved this place and were wondering if they could reserve it for the evening."

Cassie stared at her employer and searched her mind. "You've never done that since I've worked here. Have you before?"

"I know we don't usually do it, but she seemed desperate and I figured, why not? I'm just putting together some canapés to serve. She's arriving any minute to set up, and then the guests are arriving at eight o'clock," Mrs. Brown replied.

Cassie quickly got to work, helping put the

finishing touches on some bruschetta while her boss bustled out to the dining hall in preparation to greet the generous party hosts. Cassie remained in the kitchens, oblivious to anything other than her workload. When she started to hear the sound of tables being moved outside, she quickly changed into her uniform and poked her head around the doorway.

A young businesswoman had entered the quaint restaurant with two burly men. Together they were moving around the tables to open the room up. That accomplished, they set up a small area toward the back with one table and twelve chairs.

"Tina O'Brian. I'm pleased to meet you, Mrs. Brown. Thank you for accommodating us at such short notice," the woman said. Cassie watched as she went over their requirements for the evening, but then headed back into the kitchen to finish her prep.

Before long the restaurant began to fill up. With two trays held high, she entered the now open-plan room, and smiled warmly as she offered the canapés to the guests.

"Cassie, come and help me," Mrs. Brown called, waving her over, and Cassie left the canapés to one side so she could go and help her. Mrs. Brown was filling flutes with expensive champagne, but they were disappearing quicker than they could be filled. Cassie put her experience of such parties to good use, remaining level headed and calm despite the chaos.

"Do you have any chardonnay? I'm not really one for champagne," said a voice from behind her.

Cassie immediately turned on her heel, knowing the voice's owner before she saw him. She laughed, shaking her head. "Oh dear, you really are full of surprises, aren't you, Mr. Solomon?" She was genuinely surprised he had orchestrated this entire thing without her having figured it out. She had thought it strange a small Italian restaurant had somehow ended up being booked for a party, but had assumed it was one of the regulars who enjoyed the food and had decided to call upon Mrs. Brown in their hour of need.

"I promised I would make sure we could see each other tonight, didn't I?" Leo replied, leaning in to give her a kiss on the cheek.

Cassie smiled but pulled back, eyeing him shyly. "I'm not comfortable with people seeing us together like this. I don't like being seen as the hired help. Maybe I'm not a whore, but I'm no servant either," she said, handing him a glass of champagne. Cassie couldn't bring herself to meet his gaze, but his silence forced her to. She expected to find an angry stare, but instead he seemed sad.

Leo took the glass and gave her an uncomfortable smile, thanking her quietly. "Shit, I'm sorry, I have never done this before. And now I've completely belittled you by expecting you to serve me and my employees canapés and wine," Leo replied. "I'll stay away until we can be alone tonight, and I'll never bring my business here again. I understand if you're angry with me."

"I'm not angry. Please don't worry. I know what you were trying to do. Let me get on with my job, I'll see you later. Just make sure you leave me a very generous tip." Cassie winked before busying herself with the champagne flutes again.

"Okay, I'll use tonight as an opportunity to see how my men act around you. Let's see how many pass my secret test," Leo said, winking back at her over his wine, and he wandered back off through the crowd toward his cronies.

The rest of the night went smoothly. Cassie stayed behind the bar serving the drinks, while Mrs. Brown and a couple of the other staff moved through the crowd with the food. She was glad not to be among them, and even enjoyed people watching as she took in the variety of men and women employed by her dark and dangerous new boyfriend.

Cassie blended in so perfectly to this homely little restaurant that none of Leo's men knew she was the girl they had watched kissing her best friend at Leo's house party just a few months earlier. None of them put it together, and she had to laugh, realizing how shallow some men were.

"Vodka on the rocks," said the woman, Tina, who had come to speak with Mrs. Brown earlier. She didn't fit into this party in the same way the scantily clad hookers who were on the arms of all the men did. She wore a designer pantsuit that showed no cleavage, and Cassie got the impression Tina was as different from the other women as she was.

Tina had barely even looked at Cassie as she barked her request, and she couldn't resist pushing the woman a little, intrigued by who she was and what she might mean to Leo. Cassie purposely forgot to add the ice to her glass, sliding the woman neat vodka, and she stalked off without a word of thanks. Cassie watched as she approached Leo, about to hand him the drink, but then she pulled it back again when she realized there was no ice in the glass. The woman's face was in a hard, cold stare, and she bristled as she stormed back over to the bar, slamming the tumbler down in front of Cassie.

"You forgot the ice," she said, eyeing her with a look of sheer disgust. "Remind me not to ask you for something more complicated like soda next time, otherwise I'm sure I'd be left disappointed again." Tina was clearly disgruntled at having her time wasted. Cassie wondered if she was really angry at her, or whether this woman was more annoyed at being expected to serve her boss drinks rather than the waiting staff doing it for her.

Cassie sneered but said nothing, grabbing the tongs and sliding a cube of ice into the tumbler as she sized up the woman, making a mental note to knock her down a peg or two as soon as she could.

When Leo's meeting in the corner with a group of his best dressed and obviously highest paid cronies was over, he began saying his goodbyes. Cassie watched as he grabbed the arm of the woman who had been rude to her earlier and practically marched her out of the restaurant and into the cool night air. He didn't look over at the bar as he went, so Cassie couldn't be sure if he was taking her off to chastise the woman for her behavior toward her or not.

The crowd eventually dispersed, and Cassie set about cleaning up, grateful when the men who had helped move the tables earlier reappeared and helped speed up the tidying process. Cassie saw Tina come back inside, handing Mrs. Brown an envelope no doubt stuffed with well over the amount they had offered her, and the woman beamed. Cassie wondered if she had ever taken so much money in one night before, and was glad Leo had asked her to close the place to the public tonight.

At just after midnight, Cassie stepped outside, having changed and freshened up. A black limousine was at the curb a little way down from the entrance, and one of the back windows slid down as she reached it. Cassie peered inside and saw Leo's dark brown eyes staring back at her.

"Can I offer you a ride?" he asked, his tone friendly yet businesslike. She wondered for a moment why he was acting so strangely, but then she saw Tina over his shoulder, and she was now sure she must be Leo's assistant.

"That would be lovely, thank you," Cassie replied, stepping back a little when the door opened, but instead of her climbing straight inside, Leo stepped out to join her on the sidewalk. In less than a second she was wrapped in his arms, his mouth finding hers, and she swooned. She leaned into his strong hold and gave in to his overwhelming prowess. Every one of her senses obeyed his silent commands, and she was sure she heard herself purr from somewhere deep within.

"I'm sorry, I couldn't pretend any longer," he said when he finally pulled away, stroking her cheek gently before guiding her inside the limo, where Tina was sitting in stunned silence.

"Hello again," Cassie said, enjoying watching her squirm.

Leo gave her a knowing smile. "Cassie, this is Tina, my assistant. I employ her because she is meticulous, insanely clever, and her business instincts are fantastic. Her manners, on the other hand, leave something to be desired. I know she would like to take this opportunity to apologize for the way she spoke with you earlier, especially after I expressly insisted she remain polite with the staff."

Tina snapped back to reality, looking down at her feet. Her entire body language was different than she had been at the party. Her demeanor was now timid and even scared. Cassie quickly began enjoying this much less than she had earlier.

"I'm sorry, I was stressing about one of the clients' dietary needs, but I know it's no excuse. I shouldn't have spoken to you that way, Miss Taylor. Please accept by sincerest apologies," Tina said, not looking at Leo as she stared past him toward Cassie.

"You're forgiven, of course. I purposely forgot the ice because I was being bitchy. I wanted to know who you were, so I thought I'd wind you up and see who you went running to. Let's hear no more about it. As far as I'm concerned, the matter is closed." Cassie hoped Leo would see they were both to blame and move on from the issue, but she could still sense that he was angry. "So, your place or mine?" Cassie asked him, trying to pull his attention to her, and it seemed to work. Leo smiled and held her cheeks in his hands, his face softening a little bit at a time.

"Yours, I can't take you to mine yet. Not until you're ready," he replied, and she knew he meant until she was ready to have sex. She grinned back at him, nodding in understanding, and he kissed the tip of her nose. Leo gave the details to his driver and they made their way toward her apartment in silence, their hands entwined and their lips locked for the duration, while Tina sat in silence beside them.

Chapter 14

Leo spent the night with Cassie again, their bodies tangled together on the bed and their mouths never far from one another's. He left the next morning, having enjoyed her delicate mouth on his body as she slid it up and down his hard cock again, but he felt far from satisfied.

When Tina greeted him at the door of his mansion, her usual coolness exuding from her as she welcomed her boss, he immediately asked her to procure him a distraction for the afternoon. He was annoyed his resolve hadn't lasted long, but it was too difficult. This was all very new to Leo, and he couldn't just switch off those old urges the way his heart wanted him to.

"No Cyrene's girls, though," he insisted, knowing it might get back to Cassie if he fucked one of her previous colleagues or someone who knew Hanna. He didn't want to have a row with her so early in their relationship over sex, but his patience was wearing thin, and he knew he would press the issue soon if he didn't have his release.

"Of course. You're free from noon until three o'clock. Shall I have someone ready?" Tina asked, maintaining her business-like demeanor. She had worked for Leo for a long time, and he trusted her to do everything he asked with professionalism and respect. The pair of them had attended college together long before he began his ascent to drug-lordliness, and had stayed together ever since. They had never been intimate, and never would be.

Leo respected Tina simply because she was a clever, considerate, and discreet subordinate who had supported him right from the start of their friendship. Tina had tutored him through college, and in return he'd helped the shy, timid girl change into the powerful and unashamedly intellectual woman she was today. She'd stuck around as Leo rose to power, and he appreciated her years of service.

He'd had Tina maintain his workload and ensure that his accounts and business dealings were kept out of sight from both the American authorities and tax office. She never attended his sordid parties—his men wouldn't respect her if she did—so her personal life was kept completely separate from her work. The two never overlapped, and Leo had worked hard to keep it that way. He didn't like to share, and Tina was his most valuable asset, even if she could be a pain in the ass at times.

"That'd be great. Make sure she has long, dark hair and brown eyes," Leo told her. "Big tits and a skinny waist." He knew Tina would never ask him why he needed extra relief from his sexual needs after spending the last two nights with Cassie. She knew better than to question him.

"Consider it done." She made a small note on the corner of her note pad.

Leo nodded to her and then stepped closer, pinning his employee to the wall behind her. "Good, and you ever pull something like last night again, and I will be forced to punish you. You've always been a good girl, a perfect assistant, and I would hate for that dynamic to be ruined now," Leo said, stroking her cheek in an affectionate manner, and Tina trembled before him, nodding profusely.

For a long time during their younger years, he knew Tina had considered herself his only friend, until he had made the transition from drug-dealer to drug-lord and no longer had any friends, only employees. Their relationship had stayed strong, though, and he had afforded her many benefits for staying loyal and trustworthy during his rise to power.

Their dynamic had then taken a darker turn a few years ago when she had drunkenly propositioned him one night, and he had quickly put her back in her place. After that night, Leo had played on her embarrassment and manipulated the usually strong woman to serve his needs better, effectively creating a dominant/submissive relationship between them that he openly enjoyed.

Tina's rewards were never sexual. Instead he rewarded her with gifts and generous cash bonuses, knowing she enjoyed the materialistic things in life, and she lapped it up despite it being a somewhat chauvinistic approach. But with that dynamic also came the punishment side of things. He had only had to do it a couple of times but had made it quite clear he was more than willing to do so whenever necessary.

"I'm sorry. Please don't punish me," she whimpered, staring down at the floor.

"I won't unless I have to, you know that. You disobeyed my orders last night. Do you think you deserve to be punished?"

Tina shook her head again.

He remembered the first time he had done it. Leo had called her over to him while he was at his office desk to discuss her attempt to hide one of his dealers' discrepancies in his takings. The dealer had been beaten and robbed one night outside a club, the culprits had been found and dealt with, but the earnings were short until his takings could be found. Tina had neglected to inform Leo only because his second in command, Tyler, had assured her the cash would be there in the next take. Without a word of warning Leo had slapped her hard across the face, just a backhander, but her cheek had been red for days.

The second time, he had shut her in one of the panic rooms of the vast house, keeping her locked up for only a couple of days, but it was more than enough to set off a panic attack. Tina was claustrophobic, a fact he had known all along.

She clearly didn't want to be punished again, and stood silently as Leo pinned her to the wall. He kept her there for a few seconds, and then wandered off in search of Ivan, eager for another training session.

At noon, Leo was at his desk, watching his movie files of Cassie in both her apartment and in the guest bedroom of his home. He was already hard, watching his delectable lover as she pleasured herself, her friends, and Leo on the screen, and by the time he heard a quiet knock at his office door he was more than ready to pounce on whoever was on the other side of it.

"Come in," he barked, watching as the door slid open. In walked a stunning woman, just the right likeness to Cassie. Leo smiled. Tina had outdone herself and was well and truly forgiven.

"Good afternoon, Mr. Solomon. Where do you want me?" the woman asked, sliding off her dress and revealing her naked body. Leo stood and pushed back his chair, creating room for her on the desk before him.

"Bend over," he commanded, and she quickly moved in front of him, sliding her torso down onto the desk. Leo unbuttoned his pants, sliding them down with his shorts, and removed them along with his shoes. His shirt came off next, leaving his naked body on show, but he didn't let the woman look at him. He was not hers to enjoy.

Leo muted the laptop and pressed play, ensuring that his favorite scenes continued to play for him as he slid on a condom and pushed his throbbing hard-on inside his substitute for the real thing. The woman groaned as he pressed himself inside of her wet cleft. He slapped her ass cheek, ordering her to stay quiet while he proceeded to achieve the satisfaction he so desperately craved from the woman he watched on the screen.

Leo was tender, gentle, and even considerate with the woman, as he would endeavor to be with

Cassie when the time came. He used this time as practice so when he finally slid inside his lover's ready body he would not be tempted to push her before she was ready. When he was finally satisfied, Leo pulled out, discarded the condom, and got himself dressed.

"You may leave." He snapped the laptop closed so she couldn't see what was on the screen, and the woman immediately stood and climbed back into her dress. "Come back the same time tomorrow," he added, barely bothering to look at her.

"As you wish," she whispered before leaving him there alone.

Leo's phone made a low chirping sound that indicated he had a text message. He fished it out of his jacket pocket and checked it, finding a message from Cassie, and he smiled broadly. In some strange way he had an ecstatic, excited feeling as if he had just been with her, rather than inside some faceless, nameless substitute, and he had to contain his afterglow in case he gave himself away.

It just so happens I'm now free tonight. Fancy dinner at my place?

The message read.

Absolutely, I'll bring Chinese food.

Leo sent back, before sliding his phone back in his pocket and settling down to do some work.

Chapter 15

Within a few weeks, the pair of them grew closer. Leo let himself be genuine and comfortable around Cassie in a way he had not been with anyone in years. He told her he thought about her day and night, more than ready to take their relationship further, but he was being a perfect gentleman and respecting her boundaries.

He took her along to all of his social gatherings now, and every one of his men knew Cassie as his girlfriend and treated her with respect and even a little hint of fear. They all knew their actions toward her were watched by their all-knowing boss, so maintained their friendly demeanors and kind guises with her at all times.

She enjoyed the gentler way of them, despite knowing full well she was in the company of henchmen, drug-dealers, and pimps who would act very differently if she were just another of Leo's whores. Cassie soon grew used to being in the company of criminals, though. Her ease came quicker than she would have anticipated, and soon began getting to know Leo's closest men by their first names, enquiring after their wellbeing, and even chatting with some of them when she saw them. This group of bandits and bad guys soon became her group of friends, and it surprised Cassie how desensitized she had become to their trade.

After a night on the town with his handpicked cronies in the VIP area of his nightclub, Odyssey, Leo escorted Cassie home. Their mouths were locked the entire car ride, and she offered no resistance when his hands slid inside her bra to caress her nipples. Cassie felt more alive than ever, ready to move things along a little at last. She readied herself for her final admissions, grateful he had taken her out drinking and dancing so she felt carefree, and was glad of the Dutch courage she felt coursing through her veins.

Once inside her apartment, Leo turned back to the caring, gentle man he had been on so many nights before, and he immediately ran Cassie a hot bath. He filled it with far too many bubbles, concealing her body from view completely. When he returned to the small bathroom with a glass of wine, Cassie didn't even flinch at being naked with him there. She knew with each passing moment of sexual tension and every intense conversation, their bond was cementing even more firmly.

"Don't go, we need to talk," she whispered, her tone fraught with fear and pent up emotion, but he seemed to know she had important things to offload.

"Sure love, of course I'll stay," he said, closing the lid of the toilet and taking a seat beside her.

"What's on your mind?" Leo waited as she took a sip of her wine and composed herself.

"I need to tell you the whole story about what happened with Jonah," Cassie replied. She watched as he tensed up, but Leo didn't say a word. He was clearly ready to hear more at last. She knew he would hate hearing it, but his loving gaze spurred Cassie on. She took a deep breath and began, her eyes on everything except Leo.

"In those awful days when Jonah had succumbed to his addiction and let it overpower every inch of his body and mind, he became a different person. He was a completely feral man. He had been using crack, and I had no idea about any of it. Apparently he'd been snorting cocaine for years to keep him alert because, in his words, caffeine wasn't cutting it anymore. I couldn't reason with him. He didn't sleep, and in those awful few days he lost everything about him that I ever loved." She paused to take a long swig of her drink and a deep breath. When Cassie finally looked to her left, she caught Leo's eyes on her.

"Carry on, love. I'm ready."

"Well, we started out just going at it like mad in the bedroom, more intense and harder than ever before, and I let him. In all honesty, I enjoyed it, but then after a while I had to tell him enough was enough. I only needed to use the bathroom. That was all it took to send him over the edge. Jonah snapped and beat the shit out of me. He handcuffed me to the bed, gagged me and did all the depraved things his tormented mind could come up with, not just rape," Cassie said, trembling. She finished off her wine and placed the glass down onto the floor beside her.

Leo stayed quiet, seemingly lost in his own thoughts as he fiddled with the button on his shirt.

"He cut me," Cassie said, continuing with her story again, breaking Leo's reverie with the hard truth. He stood and began pacing the small bathroom with his head in his hands. "Jonah said he wanted to make sure I was hideous. He wanted it so no one would ever want to touch me, or look at me again. I've had surgery, but there are still scars. I can't even bring myself to look at them, let alone anyone else. I know I should've been honest from the start that it was more than just the ordeal holding me back, but how do I tell someone this terrible truth? How can I let you see when I know you'll just pity me and walk away? I'm so ashamed. I hate him, and I hate myself for becoming a victim." Tears fell as she despaired over the constant reminder of her past.

For a while Leo said nothing. He stopped pacing and sat back down, staring at his hands thoughtfully and rubbing at his eyes. Cassie climbed out of the hot water and quickly wrapped herself in a towel, dressing in record speed before standing in front of the still somber man. She stroked his hair, desperate to know what he was thinking, and she gasped when he peered up at her with tears in his eyes.

"You are not a victim, Cassie. You told me that the first night we met, and I believe it. I only pity victims, so I would never pity you." Leo grabbed her around the waist and pulled her closer to him, burying his face in her stomach. "I'm a man of my word. I never make promises I cannot keep, and I promise you right now that I will never walk away. If we end, it'll be because I've fucked up somewhere down the line, or hurt you. Either way, it'll be you who leaves me, because I know with all of my heart I could never leave you. I'm not strong enough to keep my distance, and we both know that."

Cassie's walls came crumbling down.

"How do you do that, Leo?" she asked, drawing his gaze back up to meet hers. "How can you take my crazy and make it sane, when no one else before you has managed it? How do you see me at my worst and then somehow make it better?"

"Because my crazy is ten times worse than yours, Cassie, and I'm terrified you're gonna find me out. I've never answered to anyone, never had to feel guilty, because I've never cared before. But now there's you, and in your eyes I see myself laid bare. I'm ashamed at what I see. This is killing me, but I cannot get enough," Leo murmured, a single tear breaking through his barricades as he spoke.

Cassie fell to her knees, kissing away the droplet that now lay on his top lip before covering his mouth with hers. Neither one could bear how exposed they felt at revealing all, but the freedom was also enlightening. Cassie felt hopeful for the first time in over two years, excited and ready for more at long last.

She took Leo's hand and led him toward her room, stopping only when they were inside. She switched off the lights, engulfing them in complete darkness. Cassie traced her fingers over his lips, following her fingertips with her mouth, and Leo followed her lead, seemingly eager for more. Her hands found the hem of his shirt and lifted it over his head, their mouths apart for only a second before they found each other again, and she pushed him backward. Together they took slow steps and stopped when they felt the side of her bed press against his calves.

***

Leo let her take the lead completely, following every one of Cassie's silent commands. He delighted in the touch and taste of her while temporarily blind, as though his other senses were heightened due to the darkness. Her hands ripped open his fly and pulled his pants down, freeing his hard-on, and she gripped it, pulling rhythmically before sliding down to take him in her mouth.

He groaned, a low, guttural sound he could tell drove Cassie crazy. She sped up, spurred on by his need, and swallowed him down as he came. After, she pushed Leo back onto the bed, and he laughed. He kicked the bunched-up jeans and boxer shorts from his feet, sliding higher on the bed in anticipation of whatever might come next.

Cassie pulled off her nightdress and panties before she climbed on top of him, leaning over her lover with her knees either side of his hips. Her wet opening was just inches from his barely satisfied member, but he made no move to push her down onto him. Leo sensed her trepidation and slid his hands down her sides, gripping her ass cheeks and pulling her closer, needing her kiss, but not going anywhere near her forbidden treasure. Cassie grabbed one of his hands, closing it into a fist before allowing his index finger to slide free, and Leo gasped when he suddenly felt her wetness on the tip.

"Only touch what I let you, Leo," she whispered, sliding his finger in deeper. He stayed as still as possible, completely enthralled by the woman he wished he could see, and the body she was opening up for him. Cassie stopped, pulling him out of her. He groaned in protest, but she just laughed. She pulled his middle finger free of his fist, and performed the same move as before, holding onto his balled fist tightly as she slid the two fingers into her wet, hot cleft.

Cassie moved her hips back and forth on his fingers, driving him wild. She came quickly, her body pulsating around him, and as she slid him out of her one last time, Leo finally felt some of her scars. They were just thin lines either side of her opening, but he didn't say a word or do anything other than lick his fingers clean of her delicious juices, unable to help himself.

Chapter 16

When Leo awoke the next morning, the dawn light was pouring into Cassie's room, and she lay next to him, naked. His hands were around her back as she slept, rather than fisted in her hair, and he was glad this night's sleep had not been as fretful as their others. Each of them had fallen into an easy, restful sleep following their climaxes, and he grinned as he remembered how it had felt when she came around his deeply delving fingers.

Her words replayed in his mind, and Leo stared up at the ceiling as guilt washed over him for the first time in his entire adult life. The abuse she'd suffered was terrible, but Leo knew it was nothing he hadn't almost done himself in his past. He'd never consciously set out to hurt women, nor had he wanted to do it. Things had just progressed the wrong way during his past exploits, and had ended badly. He had no excuse for any of it, but he'd never needed to explain his actions either. He had never considered their effect on the woman on the receiving end.

Leo hated the way he felt right now, realizing at last how awful he'd once been, and while he was angry with Jonah, he was even angrier with himself for having taken so much for granted.

Cassie groaned as she roused. She was still naked, Leo realized. He knew she would panic when she woke up, so when he felt her stirring he pretended to still be asleep. Leo softened his grip and remained still when Cassie slid away and pulled on some shorts before climbing back into his embrace. She seemed satisfied that he hadn't caught sight of her, and snuggled into him. Leo let her enjoy a few more minutes of dozing in his arms before he yawned and kissed the top of her head, pretending to have just woken up.

"Oh no, look what you did," he mumbled, pressing his erection into her hip, and Cassie giggled.

"I did nothing!" she replied, feigning surprise.

"Yes you did. I was just dreaming about you fucking my fingers again, and I got hard just thinking about it." Leo traced his hand from her chin to her nipple, tweaking it gently and refusing to let her go coy on him. "I seem to remember you owing me a shot on these," he added, stroking her breasts, and Cassie raised an eyebrow.

"Oh really? Well in that case..." She leaned down to suck his hard-on. He groaned loudly as she swirled her tongue over the tip, trailing her mouth up and down his thick shaft, and taking him as far back as she could. When he was nearing his end, Cassie quickly pulled it out and let his hot offering spurt onto her bare breasts.

"That's what I'm talking about," Leo whispered when he was finished, smiling down at her as she grabbed his t-shirt and used it to wipe herself clean with a cheeky grin. "I'd forgotten how good it feels to do that, especially on tits as beautiful as these." Leo kissed her forehead and lay back down on the bed, drawing Cassie into his arms and pulling her on top of him. She followed his lead, his bulge pressing into her mound as she straddled him, but thin material of her shorts restricted his pressure from penetrating any higher than her folds. Cassie groaned, kissing him deeply, and she pushed down onto him, her cheeks turning a delicate shade of rosy red as she gyrated.

"Touch yourself for me," he murmured, feeling her wetness through the shorts, and Cassie immediately followed his order. Leo watched her unravel atop him with a satisfied smile. He loved that she did as he commanded without hesitation or fear, and wondered if perhaps he should be more persuasive with her pleasure in the future. Part of him wondered if Cassie enjoyed the dangerous side of him as well as fearing it. She openly enjoyed being alongside him when he was the fear-inducing Leo Solomon at his gatherings. He had noticed she was quicker to bed on the nights she had seen him exert his power over his men. The two of them had barely made it into the limousine one night when he'd had to be tough on one of his guys in front of her before she had released and devoured his cock with her eager mouth. Cassie had also confided in him how she had grown excited rather than scared when Otis had first held that gun to her head. Leo enjoyed thinking that perhaps her past trauma had left her with a lust for the powerful, forceful lover he knew he could easily be, and he hoped that time would prove him right.

His reflections were derailed when Hanna burst into the bedroom a few minutes after Cassie had finished, her hands covered in blood, and her eyes wide with shock. Both Cassie and Leo stared at her in surprise before Leo sprang from the bed, grabbing his pants as he did, and sliding them on.

"Hanna, what the hell is going on?" he asked, stepping over to the frightened woman. She jumped, as though having zoned out for a few seconds.

"Jamie. He's been shot," she replied, the color draining from her face. Leo pushed her aside and raced out to the living room where Jamie lay sprawled on the floor. The pale man was gripping his side while writhing in pain. Leo grabbed the cell phone from his pocket and dialed Tina.

"I need a doctor, quickly," he barked, pausing to listen to her reply before he turned fierce. "No, not for her, you presumptuous bitch. It's for Jamie." Leo hung up the phone and turned his attentions on his employee, propping him up on one of the pillows from the sofa. Cassie and Hanna joined them, Cassie having pulled on a t-shirt, and they had cleaned up Hanna's hands before heading back out. Leo had hoped she hadn't heard his call to Tina, but her face said otherwise, and although she was trying to hide it, she was clearly a little taken aback that his assistant would assume he needed a doctor for her following a night together.

***

Cassie shook it off, focusing instead on the matter at hand, and she deposited Hanna beside her barely conscious boyfriend before running to the kitchen for water and towels. As she came back, Jamie was talking to Leo, both of their faces pained.

"The deal went sour. Victor said Luis decided your offer wasn't good enough. He said you should've thrown in extra for their efforts," Jamie said, likely being careful not to say too much in front of the girls.

"Looks like he's going to be a problem. I'll take care of it Jay, I promise." Leo applied pressure to his wound while Cassie held a water bottle to his lips. The doorbell rang, and after Leo giving her the go-ahead, Cassie quickly answered it. On the other side were two of Leo's men and a tall, wiry man who dragged a small suitcase on wheels behind him. He nodded to her and made his way inside, his sights set on the patient.

"Mr. Solomon. What do we have here?" he said, looking down at the two men.

"Bullet wound to the abdomen, looks clean but no exit wound," Leo informed him, stepping back so his two henchmen could take over.

They lifted Jamie and placed a plastic sheet beneath him, which was no use as the rug was already soaked with blood, but Cassie was sure it meant they were planning on him losing more in the process of his care. His shirt was cut open, and the doctor injected Jamie with an anesthetic. He was out cold within seconds, and the bloody scene before her enthralled Cassie. She sat down on the armchair, wrapping Hanna up in her embrace, but watched with interest as the man slid a scalpel across Jamie's entry wound and pushed his gloved hand inside. Hanna yelped and buried her face in Cassie's chest, unable to watch, but Cassie's eyes remained fixed on Jamie while Leo watched her. She could see him from the corner of her eye, and he seemed surprised, intrigued, and almost beguiled by her lack of fear.

Blood poured out of the wound, making it impossible for the doctor to see, but Cassie got the sense he was simply feeling around at the moment, checking for damage and seeking out the intruding bullet. When the man finally pulled his hand free, the small piece of metal was clasped between his fingers, and he placed it on the plastic sheeting beneath them.

"He's clear. I'll patch him up, but it's fifty-fifty. He needs rest, ideally in a hospital, but I guess that's out of the question?" The doctor looked up at Leo, who nodded.

"These two are his friends, they'll take good care of him," he assured the doctor, and the man looked over at the women with a warm smile, addressing Cassie as she was clearly the only one ready to hear his instructions.

"The dressing will need changing twice a day at first, then once every day. Keep him comfortable, warm, and try to get him to drink plenty of water. I will put in an IV, and leave you with antibiotics and saline. You will know within a few days. If he improves by day four, he'll make it. Otherwise, he's a lost cause," the doctor said, not bothering to sugar coat it, and Cassie nodded, grabbing the now sobbing Hanna tighter.

"Very well, if you'll excuse me a moment," Leo said. He moved toward the kitchen, and Cassie assumed he must need to make some phone calls, but he didn't leave without first placing a tender kiss on her forehead, silently telling her he was here if she needed him, and she was grateful.

It seemed to take hours, but eventually Jamie was sewn up and cleaned before being placed gently on the sofa to rest. His IV was in, and Cassie was given her instructions again along with the necessary bandages and bags for the drip. Everything was ready, and the doctor left with the two cronies. Leo also left them for a while, after the many terse phone calls she'd heard from the kitchen. Cassie knew whatever had gone down last night was serious. It was all over his face, and she hoped he would have it cleared up soon.

Even when they were finally alone, Hanna still could not bring herself to look at Jamie. Her face stayed buried in the sofa cushions. As soon as Cassie had said her goodbyes and checked on Jamie, she quickly scooped her friend back up in her arms and held her tightly.

"He's gonna be okay, he'll make it through this, I just know it," Cassie mumbled, unsure of her words, but she wanted to help her friend cope, so she tried to remain positive.

"I was going to stop, we were going to be together properly," Hanna replied, finally looking up into her friend's face. "He asked me to marry him."

"You will still have all of that, sweetie, I know it. He needs you to be strong for him now, though." Cassie kissed her forehead affectionately. Hanna snuggled into her, her sobs and tears having ceased for now, and she held onto her dear friend as though she would fall apart if it weren't for her. Cassie found herself thinking of Leo and this world he had drawn her into, a world where deals went sour and his employees ended up with bullet wounds. It was all still very scary when she let it all in.

In an attempt to swallow her fearful thoughts, Cassie instead mulled over her wonderful evening she'd had in Leo's arms the night before. She remembered his hands on her body, and the way he had tasted her after she had finished using him for her release. It was the first time since Jonah that she had let anyone touch her, and she felt like a weight had been lifted from her shoulders thanks to the trust she now felt in Leo.

Hanna seemed like she was dozing in her arms, but then stirred, breaking Cassie's reverie. She peered down at her and Hanna planted a deep, sultry kiss on her lips. She slid her tongue into Cassie's mouth before she could resist. Hanna gripped her tightly, her hands stroking Cassie's hips and breasts.

"No, Han. This isn't what you really want. You're just confused, and scared," Cassie said, pulling back. She didn't let go or stop Hanna's hands from touching her. They had been intimate with one another the night of the party, and she didn't feel uncomfortable with her advances, but this felt very different. Hanna was looking for some affection in the only way she knew how, sex.

"I just want to feel good, to feel happy. Please Cassie, I need this," she replied, blushing at her request, and kissing her lips again lightly.

"This won't solve anything, trust me," Cassie replied, pulling her mouth away but being careful not to reject her harshly.

"Fine, I'll just go and book a client who will," Hanna snapped, still angered by her refusal, despite Cassie having been gentle.

"That'll be even worse, sweetie. Jamie needs you here. He deserves for you to keep your word, and if you let him down now he'll never trust that you can be faithful. Show him you meant every promise you made, and you'll be a good and loyal wife to him. Show him how much you love him and will always take care of his needs, in and out of the bedroom."

Hanna burst into tears, cuddling back into her friend. She didn't say another word or try to proposition Cassie again, seeming to have taken her words on board, and she appeared willing to at least try and follow her advice.

The two of them sat quietly and soon fell into an exhausted sleep, still wrapped in each other's arms while Jamie slept soundly on the sofa, the rhythmic sound of his breathing bringing both girls comfort.

Leo returned hours later and found them that way. Cassie woke to the sensation of his fingers lightly stroking her cheek. She smiled up at him, but was not pleased to see how rough he looked.

"Hey. I've got a nurse coming to look after him," he told her. "She'll be here in a couple of hours, and will stay as long as he needs."

Cassie smiled up at him in thanks. She had been more than willing to help Jamie recover, but was glad the responsibility had been placed into more capable hands.

"Thank you. How are the other men?" Cassie asked, and her concern appeared to take him by surprise. No matter who his men were, and what line of work they were in, she cared for their wellbeing. But she had a feeling Leo saw them as expendable.

"They got off much better than Jamie did," he replied casually. "I need to sort this out, and I cannot have you distracting me. I'm sorry, but I have to step away for a few days. I need to have my boss-head on, otherwise I'll make mistakes, and there's no room for error in my line of work. I'll be back when it's over. I hope you understand?" Leo asked, his face serious but clearly saddened by his words.

"I tell you what, when you're off being big, bad Mr. Solomon, I am nothing to you, just as he's not anything to me." Cassie climbed out of the seat carefully so as not to disturb Hanna. She stood before him, peering up into Leo's eyes as she spoke. "When you come back to me, you come back as Leo, and that's when we have this." She kissed his mouth gently.

"I like the sound of that," he replied, smiling at last. "The two people cannot safely overlap, except for the parties and stuff, but we can figure that out over time."

"Good. It'll be easier this way. I'll be me, waitress or otherwise, but you need to know I won't be at your beck and call. I have my own life, Leo, and that will include you, but will not revolve around you. I won't stop living my life, just as I'm sure you won't stop living yours. I know fucking hookers might be part of that life. You have needs I cannot fulfill, and I'm no fool."

Leo's face paled with shock. He seemed genuinely caught off guard. He stroked her cheek and pulled her mouth up to meet his own, devouring her.

"Mr. Solomon fucks whores, Cassie, not Leo," he promised, not looking into her eyes as he admitted it to her. "Leo is going to worship this waitress who stole his heart for the rest of his god-dammed life."

"Good to know, and Leo's girl is only going to let that one man touch her. I will give myself to you fully eventually, and when I do, I want you all to myself. But in the meantime, we will have our happy medium. It's hard for me to share you, but I know your reasons why." Cassie felt sad, but she was determined to let him know she was on to him, and that it was okay. Lots of men used prostitutes to fulfill their sexual needs in a way their partners could not, she knew that all too well from her short time as an escort, and she had seen the signs in him early on in their budding relationship. Sharing Leo had never even occurred to her at the start, but as long as she was denying him his satisfaction, Cassie knew she needed to understand he had to release that need in other ways. As long as he was taking faceless women to his bed rather than someone else to kiss and touch the way he did with her, Cassie was determined to be okay with it.

"I'm going to look at working back in the theater, obviously not with my ex-husband, though. I need my life back the way it was before Jonah ruined it. If I'm to let you have your life, I will need my own. I will be me, I will earn my own living while you go be the big, bad drug-lord and earn yours. When we are together we will just be us, Leo and Cassie." She felt more settled with this idea than she had ever thought she could be.

"That's a wonderful plan. I'll let you go back, but only if you promise to stay safe, and don't get close to any actor types," Leo said, plainly annoyed she wanted to go back to that world.

She nodded. "I'm all yours. I promise."

"Good. And I promise to send Leo back to you as soon as I can," he said, stepping away from her, and she saw him growing colder, his mob-boss façade creeping back in.

Cassie watched him go, feeling lost despite their agreed compromise. She had hoped, deep down, that she was wrong about the hookers, but he had told her the truth, a fact she both respected and hated.

"Is it just me, or did that feel like he was saying goodbye?" she mumbled after the door had closed, knowing full well that Hanna was awake, and had been listening to them.

"Kinda, but he's right to push you away. He needs to keep his head straight. Having you around has affected him, and when you think about it, you're actually a liability. Those who don't like him, which is likely to be many, might try and use you to hurt him. It's either separate the two lives he's living, or he goes crazy with paranoia, and you both could get hurt in the process. Jamie and I went through this. He would go mad with jealousy, or worry himself sick for me, and I couldn't stand it. His feelings nearly drove us apart, but eventually we found our way." A sob caught in her throat as she spoke of him, and she was finally able to take a look at her frail, motionless fiancée. "I love him, no matter what, that's all I ever need to know."

"Damn right, sweetie," Cassie replied, laying a gentle hand on her shoulder. "I guess I can try and lead a double life. He'll do it with ease, I have no doubt, but at least this way I can still be me. I can find my way to being the person I was before all of this, at least he didn't disapprove of that."

Chapter 17

By the next day, the nurse, Imelda, had settled in and was taking great care of Jamie. Hanna stayed by his side and even helped to feed him ice cubes when he roused. His throat was terribly dry, and he was desperate for water, but couldn't sip it properly, so they had settled for her giving him ice chips. Cassie was sure she caught a wry grin on his face as Hanna tended to him, letting her know he was enjoying having her full attention for a while.

In those solemn few days, Cassie decided the time was right to start out on her own, and rang around all the theaters she could think of, skipping the one where Jonah worked, of course. She managed to get a few interviews set up, and was so excited to get back to the job she had loved more than anything else in the world. Art was her calling, and Cassie vowed never to let it go again.

After setting up her appointments, she grabbed her old portfolio from her drawer and flicked through the pages. They were pictures of her set designs and costumes from London, as well as her first few years in New York City. They brought back many memories and were a stunning and accurate portrayal of the shows she had worked on. Cassie also found a few old photos of her and Jonah inside. They were snapshots of a time when they were very much in love, happy, and so carefree. She immediately threw them away, unable to look at them for more than a second, and she knew she never would.

Within a few days Jamie was on the mend, a clear sign he would pull through, and they all calmed down a little. Imelda did her work while the girls kept him company and fussed over him, much to his enjoyment. None of them had heard from Leo, not even Jamie, so Cassie kept her promises and waited patiently for him to make contact when he was ready. In the meantime, she had a lot on her plate and busied herself with planning her next move back into the world of set design.

After just a few interviews she was offered her pick of theaters, her reputation preceding her. Cassie reveled in their praise and generous offers of work. She eventually decided on one of the larger venues New York City had to offer, catering to anything from operatic theater productions, to strippers and traveling circuses. The variety was what swayed her final decision. The prospects there were limitless, and Cassie knew her portfolio of work would dramatically increase during her time there.

She immersed herself in the forgotten world she had left behind. Her creative spark quickly returned, and it wasn't long before Cassie truly found herself on that stage again.

***

When Leo returned over two weeks later, his face was deeply tanned, and his hair incredibly scruffy. He had dark circles under his eyes and was obviously exhausted, but he was otherwise the same man who had left her after Jamie's mishap. He wouldn't let on what he had done or where he had been, only telling Cassie he spent the time away sorting out a misunderstanding between his men and their suppliers in the south, hence his tan.

"I came straight here from the airport. I've missed you," Leo told her as they sat together in her kitchen, and she poured coffee, grabbing him some protein bars to replenish his lost energy.

"I've missed you, too," she replied, and meant it. Despite her busy days at the theater and the few evenings a week she still worked at the restaurant, she still found time to be lonely, to miss his kisses and the feel of his hands on her body.

"Will you come and stay at mine tonight?" Leo's face was calm, but his eyes were alight and excited. Cassie contemplated it for a moment, feeling surer than ever that she was finally ready for more, and so she nodded, smiling shyly and noticing the wide grin that spread across Leo's handsome face.

Less than an hour later they arrived in the back of his limousine. The place was alive in preparation for his return. There were members of his staff already inside, eagerly awaiting Leo's arrival, and many greeted him, but he shooed them away. Cassie counted more than a humble few; he had over a dozen people milling around doing one job or another. There were also numerous guards and even dogs patrolling the grounds, a fact that scared her, but Cassie didn't let on.

Inside his home there were more guards, maids, a butler, and just inside the door waited Tina. Leo's assistant greeted them both warmly and peered up at her boss as he quickly skimmed over his mail and caught up with her on the important things, leaving Cassie to wander around the vast hallway. She didn't mind leaving him to work for a few minutes, understanding he must have some catching up to do, and happily took a look around.

Cassie recognized most of it from the night of the party, easily finding her way over to the pool and its impressive terrace where two employees were tending to the flowers and cleaning the pool with a netted pole. Her hand came up and she smiled a polite greeting, which was returned. Cassie thought how she'd love to dive in there, to feel the cold water hit her skin. She loved to swim, but hadn't in years, her busy schedule always taking precedence over a trip to the local pool.

"Shall I give you the tour?" Leo asked, his voice right beside her ear. Cassie jumped, not having heard him approach. He laughed, burying his nose in her hair and taking a deep breath. "You smell wonderful, like shampoo and coffee. But there's something new." He inhaled again. "You smell of paint!"

Cassie giggled. "Wait until you see my fingernails. No amount of scrubbing seems to be getting them clean anymore."

"I don't care, I love you and your dirty nails. I can't wait for you to tell me all about your new job." She turned and peered up into his deep brown eyes, utterly transfixed, and she felt herself getting weak at the knees under his intense gaze.

"I'd almost forgotten how good it felt to be in your arms, Leo Solomon. Is there a way for me to enjoy my independence but belong to you at the same time? I don't think I can give up either," she whispered, stroking his cheek, and he shrugged.

"Perhaps. I'll tell you what," he replied, holding her tightly. "You tell me exactly what you want me to do to you, and I'll obey your every command. That way you're in charge, but you belong to me at the same time, and we'll both get everything we ever wanted." He was giving her the chance to take the lead, and Cassie jumped on it.

"I like the sound of that. Well, show me your bedroom. I want to watch you strip for me while I lie naked in your bed, in your own sheets," Cassie said, eyeing Leo and feeling cheeky. He immediately gathered her up in his arms and carried her upstairs, their mouths devouring one another's passionately.

Leo flung open the door to his bedroom. "I've never taken a woman in here, but it feels so right bringing you here."

He placed her on the bed and then stepped back, removing his t-shirt as he went, and she did the same, but didn't stop there. Once she was completely naked, panties and all, Cassie watched Leo like a predator ready to pounce, thinking to herself her analogy when she had spoken to Hanna had been correct. However, the tables were now well and truly turned, and she loved it. Cassie felt as though she was someone else, far from the timid victim she had once thought she was. Cassie felt powerful, commanding, and fiercely beautiful. Her entire demeanor had changed, and showed Leo she was ready to have him at last.

He slowly slid out of his clothes and awaited her command. A sudden flash of fear swept across her face, but she wouldn't let it linger. She couldn't let herself lose the incredible prowess she had gained in the last few minutes. Leo seemed to sense it too. He flung himself into her embrace, kissing her lasciviously and running his hands over every inch of her body, including her cleft.

Leo touched every inch of her as though he didn't care about her scars. She realized perhaps he had never cared about them, but let Cassie move at her own pace because he was scared of frightening her away. Now, though, she knew she needed to give him full control. By trusting him, she might finally be free of the restraints Jonah had put on her mind and body.

When his mouth closed over her throbbing clit and his fingers slid inside her wet opening, Cassie cried out for him, whimpering as tears rolled down her temples while she lay her head back on the bed and let go at last. Leo was not gentle, he was not being careful, and he certainly didn't seem to pity Cassie for her scars. This man was a ferocious lover. He touched and nibbled her body into submission with an expert touch, never once giving her a moment to hesitate as she writhed beneath him. Leo's mouth commanded her body effortlessly, and he soon orchestrated her most intense orgasm ever, his eyes sliding up her body to watch her come undone for him at long last.

Leo slid his fingers over her scars, delicately tracing the contours of the thin lines before kissing each one with a tenderness that nearly sent her over the edge again. Cassie watched him in awe, her tears gone, and her heart pounding in her chest, beating for him as though he were the only being that existed in the entire world. Leo was the air in her lungs and the blood in her veins. Cassie knew she belonged to him now and forever, and she didn't care who he was or how he made a living one little bit.

"No matter what you are, Leo, you're beautiful to me, do you know that?" Cassie whispered, her mind and body raw from their closeness, and he smiled as he climbed up over her.

"Don't you get it? You're the beauty, and I'm the beast. We were destined to fall in love eventually." Leo grinned at her, and she laughed. Cassie arched her back, inviting his mouth to caress her tender nipples, and he obliged. Leo's lips ran circles around each hard nub in turn before trailing up toward her neck and face. His erection lay against her folds, the tip nestled cleverly at just the right spot to dive in when she gave the word, and she gyrated a little, taking just the very tip of him inside.

"I'm ready for you to have the rest of me," she whispered in his ear, and felt him shiver in response.

Leo immediately leaned in, pushing his rock hard length inside a little at a time. He pulled her hips up to meet his, opening her up even more, and held her gaze. He watched Cassie as she finally let go, and then kissed the last tear away she would ever let herself shed for those old wounds.

***

Leo knew he was done for. This enigmatic woman had not only revealed the last of her secrets to him, but had given him her trust. Leonardo Solomon, the unrepentant drug-lord who hadn't earned an honest cent in the last ten years. He was gobsmacked she had given him this amazing gift.

Leo gave her a silent vow as he made love to Cassie to never betray that trust. He had been away the last two weeks, having been given the go ahead to sleep with prostitutes behind her back, but her acceptance had worked only as a sort of reverse psychology. Whores had surrounded him the entire time while visiting his disgruntled associate, Victor Sanchez, and his even more powerful cartel brother, Luis, in central Mexico. They had out-and-out insisted he take as many of their girls to his bed as he wanted, yet he had not touched a single one of them. He didn't feel the need for them that he felt for the woman who waited for him back home, and he was so glad he had resisted. This was the most perfect reunion he could have ever imagined, and Leo didn't want Cassie to leave his bed ever again.

When he felt her body pulsate around him, her

deep muscles clenching his cock, it drove him over the edge. She cried out, kissing him as her orgasm rippled through her body, and she held him close as he pushed himself deep and emptied into her. Leo collapsed on top of Cassie, their bodies still connected, before he slid himself out and lay to her side, pulling his lover close. Neither of them spoke, but their bodies lay wrapped in one another's for a long while.

"It's a good thing I started taking the pill, isn't it?" Cassie mumbled into his hold, and Leo laughed. He had known she was taking contraception in preparation for their being together, just like he knew everything else she did, but he could not reveal himself or his intrusive protective methods to her just yet, if ever.

"That's good. There was no stopping me from you today, not even to grab a johnny. I was gonna get you the morning after pill, but it seems as though I don't need to worry now," Leo replied, pulling her in for a deep kiss.

"Fiend," she retorted, climbing up and running into the bathroom to clean herself up. Leo laughed, wandering after her to wash up too.

***

The pair spent the rest of the afternoon in bed. Leo was attentive and gentle, taking time to touch and kiss Cassie all over her trembling body, including her scars again, as though he wanted her to know just how much he loved every inch of her body, no matter what.

Cassie had been so scared to show him, and was glad now that she had gone for it. There had been a moment when she first stripped off that her confidence faltered, but she was grateful Leo had quite literally forced her to forget about her insecurities and not to hold back anymore. She'd needed that push. This had been the most wonderful day of her entire life, and when she was ready for him again, Cassie didn't hesitate to proposition her lover, her confidence well and truly back where she needed it to be.

"I hope you don't have any plans tonight, Leonardo Solomon, or you'll have to cancel them," she said, climbing on his lap and straddling him. She ran her hands over the rippled curves of his pecs and abs. Leo was so strong, she could feel it in every controlled movement his body made, and he effortlessly moved her slim frame as though she weighed nothing.

He lifted her up, positioning his already hard member beneath her wet opening, and then let go, both of them gasping as he slid inside her, and she began moving instinctively. Leo gripped Cassie's hips, pulling her into him so each thrust nestled his hard-on perfectly into her g-spot. Her movements were primal, her body commanding his without words or force.

"God, I love you," he moaned.

"I love you, too. Forever." She tilted back, gripping his thighs as she moved, goose bumps rising on her skin while a contrasting bead of sweat trickled down between her breasts. Her nipples hardened, the tension almost painful, and Cassie welcomed Leo's hands as they slid up her stomach and grabbed her heavy breasts. He squeezed them, hard, rolling each now softened peak between his fingertips. The movement sent a wave of pleasure down to her core, and Cassie teetered on the edge of her release.

A deep growl escaped Leo's lips as she came for him, her hips bucking and her panting breath driving him to climax within seconds of hers.

Chapter 18

Cassie and Leo slept in each other's arms that night, finding comfort in one another. When she finally drifted off, she did so with a contented smile on her face.

Cassie dreamed of Leo, the two of them walking hand in hand through the streets of London, just like she had done many years ago with another man she had once thought she would be with forever.

In the dream, she was happy, carefree, but before long she became scared, sensing crazed eyes on her. Suddenly rough hands found her throat, and cold steel pressed against her temple. When she looked back, she found Leo holding the gun to her head, not Otis. Cassie could tell he was frightened, terrified she would leave him, just like Jonah had been.

She winced as he whipped her with the cold barrel of the gun, and she fell to the ground, her cheek burning. She tried to cry out, but there was no sound. As she lay on the cold floor, Leo ripped off her clothes and forced his hardness inside. Her body trembled as he moved over her, and Cassie jolted awake as a very real orgasm shuddered through her body, waking her from the terrible dream.

She was aware how awakened she felt following the combination of fear and arousal inspired by the dark dream with its climactic ending, even if the combination did confuse her.

Cassie took a moment to calm down and get her bearings. Leo had her wrapped safely in his arms, his hands twisted in her hair again. She couldn't move, but didn't want to. She loved his tight grip, finding herself wanting more, and she nestled deeper into his embrace. As she lay there awake in the early hours of the morning, she wondered if some of her darker thoughts had turned into something far more unnerving than mere fear. They seemed to have turned into a strange sort of sexual fantasy during that dream, and had manifested themselves in a very real physical reaction.

She eventually drifted back to sleep, waking up a few hours later in exactly the same position. This time, however, Leo seemed to sense her rouse, and immediately awoke, letting go of the fistful of her hair as he stirred.

"Sorry, Cassie. I honestly don't know why I do that," he mumbled, smoothing her hair. His eyes were only half open in the early light, but he still looked amazing. Leo's stubble had come in, his rough cheeks just begging to be stroked, and Cassie couldn't resist sliding her fingers over his strong jawline.

"I love it how even in your sleep you want to keep me close, that you need to feel me next to you," she replied, smiling up at him. "I feel safe in your arms, Leo. Don't ever let me go."

Leo smiled. He slipped his hand into her hair again and gripped it tight. He pressed his huge body against hers, and she snuggled deeper into his hold, willing him to own her. He accepted and glided his free hand down between them to stroke her clit. Leo then slid the same hand down to her no longer forbidden opening, groaning when he stroked it.

"You're very wet," he panted, his need showing on his face, and she giggled.

"Yep, I had a very sexy dream about you." Cassie tilted her hips up to invite his fingers inside. He accepted, delving two at first, and then three, as she opened up for him even more and began grinding back and forth.

"Tell me," Leo whispered, kissing her lips before moving to her neck while caressing her tender cleft with his fingers.

"You'll laugh, or maybe even be a little bit disturbed. I don't know," she replied, groaning with pleasure as his fingertips pressed into her g-spot.

"Nothing you say could shock me. Tell me this, then. Did you like it?"

Cassie's body and her resolve melted beneath him as he pursued her. "Yes, I did. That's what was so disturbing." She kissed him with a feverish passion that made him hard for her. He pressed it into her hip, and she giggled.

"Tell me, and I'll do it," he teased her. "I don't

care what it is."

"You forced me," she replied, expecting shock and horror on his face, but Leo didn't seem fazed.

"I've had my suspicions for a while, and I'm glad you've proven me right." Leo took a deep breath and kissed her intensely. "I won't lie to you, I like it rough in the bedroom. Making love to you last night was the most amazing experience of my life, but I am definitely up for some good old-fashioned fucking. I'm ready to do whatever you ask of me to fulfill your needs. Tell me what you want," he whispered, pulling his fingers out from between her legs with a dark look that stirred her senses. "Show me."

Cassie peered into his eyes, looking for the monster she'd been warned about so many times, but there was just her Leo. She flipped onto her stomach and pulled her legs closed. Leo seemed to know exactly what she was getting at, and he straddled her. He locked his knees firmly outside of hers and kissed her neck. His body pressed into hers, and she could barely breathe.

"I want you Leo, I want it hard and deep. I want you rough and animalistic. Don't stop even if I ask you to." Cassie shocked herself at the words that left her mouth. Leo literally growled as he nibbled on her earlobe, gently at first, and then he gave her one hard bite before grabbing her hands and holding them tight behind her back.

Cassie tested his hold, attempting to wriggle away, and playing the prey while her predator held her in his unyielding grasp. She bucked her hips, crying out when Leo delivered a hard slap onto one of her exposed ass cheeks. Cassie thought she might explode in orgasm from that alone, never having realized how satisfying that type of pain could be.

She had no time to recover. Leo forced his thick length between her tightly closed thighs and straight inside her soaking crevice. He thrust into her hard, making Cassie gush, and she came within seconds of his relentless pressure on her g-spot. He didn't stop, though. Leo merely held onto her wrists tighter and kept going, pummeling Cassie until a second orgasm forced her into complete submission. She lay before him, limp and spent, while Leo released his own tension with one last, deep thrust. He fell onto her sweat-dappled back and gasped for breath. Cassie did the same beneath him.

"Wow," she mumbled, her body still reeling from her multiple orgasms, and he laughed, sliding off her and then pulling Cassie close.

"Yeah, I know."

***

The pair had barely recovered from their intense role-play when a quiet yet urgent knock at the door made them jump. Leo pulled the covers up around Cassie and climbed out of bed, grabbing his shorts as he went. He strode over to the door, pulling it open impatiently. Tina stood on the other side, clearly worried, but it seemed she didn't have any choice other than to disturb her boss.

"What is it?" Leo barked.

"It's Victor. He's here," Tina replied. "He's at

the gate right now, asking to be let in. What do you want me to do?" she asked, her face pale. Leo's body tensed up immediately, going from an impatient pose to one of clear foreboding.

"Tell the guards to let him in. I'll head down to meet him at the front door," Leo replied, running through the options in his head. This was very unusual. They had left things on good terms the day before, Victor and his brother having been satisfied with their new deal, and even if it were otherwise, you did not simply turn up unannounced.

"Let Victor in. Mr. Solomon will meet him at the house," Tina said into her cell before sliding it into her pocket.

"You stay here with Cassie. Keep her safe, use the panic room if you need to, and watch us over the cameras," Leo told her, looking back at his wide-eyed lover.

"Leo, what's he doing here?" Cassie asked. She looked as though she was trying her best to stay relaxed, but she was clearly terrified.

"I'm not sure, but I intend to find out. Stay here with Tina. I mean it, Cassie. This is not a joke, it's an order," Leo replied, stepping back into the bedroom with Tina in tow while he slipped on some pants and a shirt. Cassie wrapped the sheet around her still naked body and stood on her tiptoes, laying a soft kiss on his lips.

"I'll do as you ask, Leo. I'll always do as you say when it comes to this stuff. I promise I'll stay here," she replied, and he nodded. Leo was glad she was not trying to be stubborn or petulant about the issue. This really was a meeting he did not want her present for.

He gave Tina a look full of dominance and silent command, and she nodded up at him timidly. He was tasking her with keeping Cassie out of sight from Victor, but also to try and get her out of the house without the Mexican drug-lord knowing she'd even been there. Tina would do her job, as always, and Leo was glad to have her.

Leo pulled one of the laptops out from his dresser and typed in his personal login. He accessed the house's cameras and pulled up the live feed from downstairs. Tina sat at the desk with the laptop while Cassie quickly dressed behind her. After giving Leo a quick kiss, she stood to watch the screen over Tina's shoulder. The two women barely knew each other, but they had a common interest, Leo, and right now he knew they were both desperate to see whether he was going to be okay.

"The inside cameras record sound, but not the outdoor ones. You'll be able to watch us the entire time," he told Cassie, and after a couple of clicks, the screen was filled with the image of the front steps.

Leo left without a word, heading downstairs to greet his impromptu guest, but not before taking a lingering look at his lover as he went.

***

By the time the black sports car pulled up and Victor Sanchez stepped out, Leo was waiting patiently with a coffee in one hand, trying to seem casual. Victor removed his sunglasses and peered up at his host with an interrogative stare. He wasn't as tall or muscular as his colleague, but Victor was a fearless, highly trained gangster and assassin, who was clever and incredibly intuitive. Leo hadn't underestimated Victor once in the years they'd been associates, and he certainly wasn't about to start now.

"Leonardo," Victor said, smiling broadly at him. His Spanish accent accentuated every syllable of his long name, and Leo hated the way he rolled the r.

"Victor, to what do I owe the pleasure?" He reached out a hand to him, and the Mexican shook it with a strong grip. This was a good sign as far as Leo was concerned, and he quickly ushered his visitor inside.

Doing a quick sweep with his trained stare, Leo saw Victor's trusty knife was in his belt, as always. He seemed otherwise unarmed, and Leo was glad. He had not wanted to seem intimidated by Victor's sudden appearance, so had not grabbed a weapon en route to the door, but knew that in doing so he was vulnerable to a potential attack.

"I know we only said our goodbyes yesterday, but I needed to have a break from my brother. I was hoping you might entertain me for a couple of days?" Victor invited himself into Leo's life, and presumably his home, without any embarrassment at being so forward.

"You're welcome here any time, old friend. Please, come and have breakfast with me. You can tell me all about it." Leo led the way to the dining room where a table had been laid with fruit, cereals, coffee, and tea. Victor helped himself to a mug of coffee, grabbing a slice of melon along with it.

"Always so healthy. I guess it shows with your physique, but I have never been able to resist the carbs and the chocolates," Victor told him, his smile still present, and Leo eyed him cautiously. He maintained his pleasant expression, but kept a close eye on his guest.

Victor winced as he sat down at the table, and caught Leo watching him. "Luis and I had a disagreement after you left yesterday. We had a tussle. He shot me, and I stabbed him. Just a graze, nothing to worry about. Brothers, sometimes we need to have a fight to offload, but we'll be back to normal again by the time I go home." He shrugged nonchalantly, as though it meant nothing, but Leo knew full well the Sanchez brothers never fought, unless it was over something extremely important.

"I'm sure you will. I will admit, I don't have any brothers or sisters, so have never had to endure sibling rivalry. I'm sure you had your reasons. Nothing to do with my visit, I trust?" Leo replied, joining him at the table.

"Well, actually, it was. He still thinks you should have accepted his offer to begin trading girls alongside our other operation. His nose was, how do you say? Out of joint, because of your refusal. He's not sure if he wants to continue doing business with you after all." Victor's expression turned serious. Leo knew Luis called the shots, and Victor always followed his command. He was part of the Sanchez cartel by both blood and service, but rarely made decisions without his brother's authorization.

Luis was five years older than Victor. From what

Leo had heard, he'd let him be a part of his drug-running crew when he was a teen, and their organization had grown incredibly since then. Victor had trained to become both a businessman and a cold-hearted killer, his place as Luis's second in command was his by right.

Leo chose his words very carefully, eager to get straight to the point, but not wanting to offend his associate.

"I see. So my compelling arguments that the States does not have the same market for human trafficking that Mexico enjoys, or the penchant for the younger girls, went completely amiss? Did I not give him reason enough to let it go?" Leo sipped on his coffee and forced himself to remain calm. He knew Victor had the upper hand, and wondered if he'd been sent here to terminate their business dealings in the only way these hardened gangsters finished anything, a hit.

Victor took a bunch of grapes from the bowl between them, popping one into his mouth, while Leo grabbed the jug and topped up his coffee.

"I was convinced by your strong opinion, but my brother, on the other hand, not so much. I put my foot down, and eventually we came to a compromise. I told him I would come here and see for myself the women you prefer to the pussy we had on offer back home. I knew they must be of high caliber for you to resist the companionship of our girls. I wanted to give you the opportunity to settle the issue, once and for all." Victor took a long sip of his strong drink while eyeing his host with a fierce expression.

Leo knew he would have to appease Victor on the subject at last, or risk another incident. He began planning the ways he might do so while they ate their breakfast and chatted with a strange air of forced relaxation.

There was one thing he had to do first, though. Leo needed to get Cassie out of his house safely. He would then set about showing Victor the time of his life with the best hookers New York had to offer. Leo also knew he would have to partake of their company to show Victor he'd not meant any offense by not taking any of his girls to bed with him in Mexico. He mentally kicked himself for not considering how his actions may result in their suspicions, but it was too late to worry about that now. Just like many times before, Leo would do whatever it took to come out on top. It wasn't in his nature to accept anything less.

***

Up in the bedroom, the two women watched Leo and Victor's conversation with silent stares and open mouths. Cassie had heard the comment Victor made about Leo not having taken any girls to bed with him while he was visiting. The realization made her heart pound in her chest. He hadn't done it, even though she'd given him the go-ahead. Despite the tense situation playing out downstairs, she had to smile.

Victor seemed just as powerful and intimidating as Leo, but she knew the real man now, and had seen the softer side to him, so was no longer scared to be alone with him. Victor, on the other hand, was someone she knew she would not like to be around if she could help it. He seemed cold from the inside out, more than just another hardened criminal.

"What do we do now? If he's staying with Leo, how can I hide up here?" Cassie whispered. She was being quiet, despite knowing they wouldn't be able to hear her.

"I don't know. For now we'll have to stay here until he tells me what to do. I've met Victor many times, and I doubt he'd try anything. You're a little bit old for his taste, if you know what I mean." Tina raised one eyebrow, and Cassie knew exactly what she meant.

"Yuck. So, he's trying to get Leo into trafficking girls? As in, young girls?" Cassie's interest was piqued, but she didn't really want to know the sordid details.

"Leo's always been in the business of women, Cassie. He owns Cyrene's, as well as many other lucrative call-girl agencies over here. He also has numerous nightclubs and a porn business. Did you think all of his money was in drugs? It's none of your business anyway. Don't forget you're supposed to leave his work out of your dynamic as a couple. I thought that was the deal." Tina snapped, letting Cassie know she was well aware of their agreement.

Although it angered her, Cassie let it go. She was shocked to hear the truth about which pies Leo had his fingers in, but then again she knew it shouldn't surprise her how easily available he had wanted his women. Owning them must've surely been cheaper than paying handfuls of hookers every week, if the stories about Leo had been true, of course.

Cassie shrugged and stepped back from the laptop, climbing onto the bed and lying back on the pillows in a huff. She took a deep breath and enjoyed having Leo's smell envelop her again. Tina left her to it, watching the screen and observing in silence.

Chapter 19

"So, explain to me just how an American hooker in her twenties can rival my teenage girls and their tight pussies?" Victor asked as he accepted a thick, Columbian cigar from his host, and Leo lit it for him while smirking.

"Because my girls don't get into the business until they are older in the first place. By the time your girls are twenty-five they've had anywhere from fifty men, if they're lucky, to five hundred. They're used up. Their bodies are a mess, and their heads even worse, my friend. Surely you agree?" Leo spoke so coldly of the girls he knew were often forced into a life of prostitution after being beaten and raped by their pimps.

"Perhaps. Go on." Victor took a long drag on his cigar and rolled the smoke around his lips. He seemed to enjoy the flavor of the hand-rolled tobacco, and took another drag while he waited for Leo to respond.

"Luis wanted me to take those girls and sell them here? They're nothing but trash, and my clientele wouldn't go for it. There are some who like them young, but the Manhattan socialites definitely prefer class, beauty, sexual prowess, and a hot body. Only the locally sourced or stringently interviewed girls can provide those things. You've seen for yourself how different it is here. Forgive me if I'm wrong, but that's why *you* agree with me, Victor." Leo's business-head was back on, and his argument clear.

"It is true. Luis never leaves the complex unless absolutely necessary. He has no idea of the real world outside of Mexico, or the economics behind the deals I make for us. I will give him a couple of days to calm down, and I will return home to inform him again that you are not our man, as far as girls are concerned." Victor leaned across the table, his arm outstretched. Leo shook his hand, glad to have reached an accord.

"Wonderful. I'll tell you what," Leo said, leaning closer with a cunning smile. "Why don't I get some of my best girls over here, and you can see for yourself just what I have to offer?"

"Now, that really would sweeten the deal," Victor replied, his eyes bright at the promise of trying out some of the girls. Leo grabbed his cell phone and dialed Tina. She answered immediately, her voice was low, which was good. He didn't want her side of the conversation being overheard by Victor, just in case.

"I need some of our best girls at the mansion as soon as possible. I want the sweetest and youngest talent we've got, plus a bit of variety. You know what Mr. Sanchez prefers," he said, winking at his associate.

"Yes, Mr. Solomon, I'll get right on it. Should I take the other work away with me?" She was clearly wondering if she should try to get Cassie out of the house now.

"Yes, you do that, and give me progress reports," Leo retorted, hanging up and grinning to Victor. "Let me take you for a tour." He stood and led him out toward the pool for a lap of the gardens. He was intent on taking him as far away from the house as possible for a few minutes so the girls could escape unseen.

***

"We need to go," Tina said, grabbing Cassie's hand and pulling her down the hallway toward her room. Inside she handed her a pantsuit and blouse. This outfit would cover Cassie from her chin to her ankles very formally, but Cassie guessed the reasoning behind it.

"I bet you look very different out of your work clothes, don't you?" she asked, sliding into the clothes.

"You probably wouldn't recognize me." She grinned. "One of the ways I manage to stay in my line of work is by never being seen as one of Leo's girls for his men to prey on. I keep my body covered, my hair and makeup plain, and none of them even give me a second glance. Don't get me wrong, I've had a few close calls, but Leo has always saved me from ending up in the wrong place at the wrong time. I trust his judgment. I always have, and you should do the same. He's asked me to get you out of here, and this is the best cover in case we bump into Victor on our way." Tina twisted Cassie's hair into a plain bun and then added some thickly rimmed glasses. She took a look in the mirror, and Tina was right. She looked like a librarian, and was sure no one would look twice at her right now.

Within minutes the two women walked down the stairwell that led to the kitchen and out into the hall. They rounded the doorway and stepped out into the bright sunshine, and a voice boomed from over Tina's shoulder.

"Señorita Tina. So wonderful to see you again," Victor called. His tour of the gardens hadn't lasted long enough.

"Señor Sanchez." She stepped away from Cassie, leaving her at the step, and shook his hand. "The pleasure's all mine. Mr. Solomon, I have your order ready, and it should be with you in less than an hour. Let me just finish up here, and I'll be right with you," she replied. Cassie could tell they were talking in code. She wondered if perhaps it was Tina's attempt to make Victor believe she was an outsider, and he grinned. He looked over at Cassie with intrigue.

"And what have we got here?" he asked, looking her up and down before his eyes settled on her breasts, then lips. He stepped around Tina to get closer so he could greet her personally, reaching out his hand, and Cassie shook it. She smiled politely and relied on her experience from her escorting days to help her nerves stay calm under this scary man's gaze. The sunshine was hot on her back, and she could feel herself sweating in the suit jacket. It was uncomfortable, and although she wanted to remove it, she didn't dare show more. Cassie was careful not to look at Leo. She could see his face over Victor's shoulder, his contorted features far from the face he had watched her with just a couple of hours before, and even he scared her.

"Sandi Smith, pleased to make your acquaintance." Cassie spoke eloquently and pronounced her words carefully to give a posh air to her British accent. She also used a different variation of her first name with Jonah's surname to avoid giving Victor anything real about herself.

"Well, well, well. Your accent is divine, my dear. And may I ask how it is that you come to be at Mr. Solomon's fine home this morning?" Victor asked. She got the impression he was hoping she might be one of his prostitutes, so Cassie wracked her brains trying to think of something she could tell him to dissipate his interest in her.

"I'm organizing a party for Mr. Solomon in a few months' time. Tina was kind enough to let me see the house so I have a clear idea of his requirements before putting together the plans." She was doing her best to look business-like and intellectual in the hope of deflecting his intrigue.

"What party? I don't remember receiving an invitation," Victor said, still staring at Cassie, but it was Leo who spoke.

"My birthday party next summer, to which invitations have not yet been sent out, my friend. Of course you'll be invited," he said, his eyes on Cassie. "Thank you for making the time to come and see us, Miss Smith. I'll have Javier take you back to the city."

"No, no. I won't hear of it. I wish for you to tell me all about this party. Please, Miss Smith, you can spare five more minutes, can't you?" Victor held out his arm for her to take. Cassie knew, just as she had known the night Leo had asked them to stay at his party, Victor would not take no for an answer.

"Well, I'm envisioning Medieval England. King Henry the Eighth," she began, taking his offered arm. "Shakespearian tapestries, scantily clad maidens serving ale and wine." She walked back up the steps into the house with Victor while still holding his arm. He led her around, asking what ideas she had for every room's decoration and entertainment. She tried to keep it simple, using her knowledge of Shakespeare from the theater as a rough guide, but she pretty much made it all up as she went. Leo played along, as did Tina, but they were just improvising until Victor made his next move.

"I cannot wait for this party. I look forward to it, and to seeing you again, Miss Smith. I do hope you will attend?" Victor asked when Cassie had finished her creative ramblings.

"I very much doubt it. I shan't be a guest, just the planner. It was very nice to meet you, Mr. Sanchez, and I hope you enjoy the party when the time comes." Cassie checked her watch and looked over at Tina. "I'm afraid I really must dash. Mr. Sanchez, Mr. Solomon." Cassie smiled warmly at the two men, but didn't let her gaze linger on Leo for more than a second. She stepped away and made it only a few feet before Victor came after her again, grabbing her arm gently so she turned to face him.

"I would love to hear more. Perhaps you would let me take you to dinner tonight so we can get to know one another better?" he asked, seemingly a genuine gentleman, but she knew better than to trust his kind front.

"I'm afraid that's not a good idea, Mr. Sanchez. I'm married."

"I don't see a ring on your finger," he pressed, looking down at her hands.

"You're right. We're separated at the moment, but are not over yet. The answer is no, but thank you," she insisted. Cassie smiled up at him, but could tell her response didn't faze him at all, just as she feared. Victor pulled one of his cards from his pocket, handing it to her, and Cassie took it.

"In case you change your mind," he said with a wink before he wandered back over to Leo and finally let the women leave.

Chapter 20

Cassie spent the next few days constantly looking over her shoulder in fear of being followed by one of Victor's men. She was sure Leo wouldn't let the man himself out of his sight, but she couldn't be sure whether or not the powerful man had brought any of his men with him on his travels.

"Just lay low. You didn't give him your proper name, and fingers crossed Leo procured all sorts of women to keep him occupied after you left," Hanna told her when she explained what had happened.

Jamie lay quietly in his bed, resting, but Cassie knew he wasn't asleep. His silence had scared her, but she hoped it was his foreboding of the man, seeing as he had shot him a few weeks before.

Cassie had done just that. She stayed in the apartment with Hanna and Jamie during her downtime, and took cabs to and from the theater or restaurant for her shifts. By day five she began to relax, trusting in Leo and his ability to read his fellow drug-lord.

She arrived at the restaurant in plenty of time to

start her shift that evening, and quickly set about preparing for opening time. Mrs. Brown soon joined her and greeted Cassie warmly, as usual.

"Don't worry about the prep tonight. We've been booked out again," she told her, and Cassie stared at her boss in shock.

"What, for a party like last time?" she asked, but Mrs. Brown shook her head.

"No, table for two, but the guy wants the place to themselves. He said he's got big plans for the object of his affections, and has chosen tonight to ask her the ultimate question. He was a bit odd with his wording, but I think he means he's planning on proposing to his girlfriend. Hard to tell with his strong accent."

"Please tell me the guy's not Mexican?" Cassie asked, her stomach turning.

"Yeah, he is. He's out in the dining room now waiting for her to arrive."

Cassie felt cold all of a sudden. She couldn't hide her panic-stricken look, and Mrs. Brown seemed worried about her unease.

"What's the matter, dear?"

"I need to get out of here," she replied, thinking about which exit to run from. Then the realization dawned on her that Victor might do something to Mrs. Brown if she left her here, or he might burn the restaurant or something if they both sneaked out and left him alone. "Shit. You stay here. Please don't come out there. I'll get rid of him, so he won't be needing any food."

"Cassie, you're scaring me. Do you know this man? What's going on?" Mrs. Brown pressed, and

Cassie hugged her tightly.

"My world is falling apart, that's what. I don't want you getting involved. I'm asking you to stay put because I want you to be safe. Please, promise you'll stay back here until he's gone," she begged, her eyes wide, and she knew they must be full of fear.

"I will, I promise. But then you've got some explaining to do." Mrs. Brown folded her arms and eyed Cassie with a disappointed look.

She didn't care, Cassie knew she had to face him, and was happier knowing Mrs. Brown would be safe. She removed her apron and took a deep breath before heading out into the dining room, finding Victor at the small table he had reserved in the eerily quiet restaurant, smiling at her like the cat that got the cream.

"Miss Taylor, so wonderful to see you again. Please sit," Victor said, his mouth moving over the sound of her real name with a satisfied smirk as she joined him. He poured her some wine from the bottle Mrs. Brown must have opened for him before she had come into the kitchen. Cassie accepted it, taking a sip to help moisten her dry throat.

"Mr. Sanchez, this is not appropriate. I would like you to leave," she managed to say after a few seconds of awkward silence.

"But you haven't heard my proposal yet," he replied, pouting playfully.

She shook her head, remaining stoic and hiding her fraught feelings as best she could.

"Aren't you at least a little bit interested how I tracked you down?" He twirled the stem of his wine glass with his fingertip, watching Cassie intently, while her eyes looked everywhere except into his.

"Of course, but at the same time I'm well aware this liaison is not what either of us should be having right now. I'm willing to remain clueless. Regardless of your proposal, I'm not afraid to say I do not believe you would be a good influence on me." Cassie realized she sounded desperate, but she didn't care.

"But Leonardo Solomon *is* a good influence? You are willing to be his, but not mine?" Victor completely caught her off guard. Her mind was racing. How did he know about her and Leo? She wondered where Leo was now, and what steps Victor had taken to get here.

"You have my attention, Mr. Sanchez," she said, causing a flash of satisfaction appear in his eye, and she mentally kicked herself for letting him gain the advantage.

"He tried to distract me, my goodness did he try, but I soon noticed all the girls he took to his bed came back not having been thoroughly fucked. He had them sucking his dick, touching each other for his entertainment, but he didn't fuck a single one, except the one who looked like you, of course." Victor took a sip of his wine and let that sink in for a few seconds, his expression making Cassie's skin crawl. She felt physically sick at the sheer thought of Leo with all those women, and fought to hide her pain.

"I very much doubt a man like Leo Solomon refrained from enjoying his women fully. He took me as quite the predator the one time I met him," she said in an attempt to fool Victor, but it was no use. He laughed loudly, his powerful voice booming all around the empty restaurant.

"One time?" He sniggered, making fun of her, and Cassie pursed her lips to stop herself from pouting. "He loves you, doesn't he? Don't bother lying, I've already found you out. I know *all* your secrets, Cassie. I found Tina to be very forthcoming, especially when I was holding a knife to her throat. She gave me every sordid, dirty secret."

"What do you want, Victor?" Cassie demanded, fearing the worst for both Leo and Tina, and ready to hear his demands at last.

"Feisty, aren't you? I hope you're the same in the bedroom."

"I'm not a whore. Leo has never paid me for sex, and he has never demanded it from me. I will not open my legs just because you tell me to, Victor. Now get to the fucking point, will you?" She knew she was pushing her luck talking to him this way, but didn't care anymore. Cassie was so terrified, she had gone past the point where her fear made her tremble. She just felt that strange numbness again.

Victor leaned forward in his chair, eyeing her like a trophy he couldn't wait to get his hands on, and he sneered. "I gather you're already aware of the purpose for my visit? That my brother, Luis, is not happy with Leo for refusing to trade our whores with him, and I came up here to see for myself the clientele he says is not into young girls." Victor slid his hand forward to take hers, but Cassie quickly pulled back, resulting in more gruff laughter from him. She could tell he was enjoying this game.

"Yes."

"Well, that's not really the mission. Luis asked me to kill Leo for causing him such offense, unless I could change his mind. I still intend to carry out my task, one way or another, but now I have another agenda I wish to bring into negotiations first," Victor said, leaning closer to her and staring into Cassie's eyes as he spoke.

"Victor, please," she whispered, not sure where he was going with this, and hating how she was already begging him.

"A certain feisty, beautiful woman has caught my eye. She has somehow won the heart of the man I have known for many years as a ruthless heartbreaker and merciless leader, and I want some of it."

Cassie shook her head, her breath catching on the sobs she tried to stifle.

"I could tell from the moment I laid eyes on you that you were his lover. He stunk of sex, reeked of it, despite his best efforts to appear relaxed. I knew right away he had refused my girls in preference of something very special back here. When I leaned in and smelled your hair as you took my arm, I knew I was right. I smelled him on you. I had a, how do you say it, light bulb moment? I knew you were a precious treasure indeed, Cassie, and one I wanted to take from Leo."

"He doesn't own me. I'm not something you can take for your own," she replied, her voice quiet and her eyes low. Cassie felt very lost all of a sudden.

"Perhaps not, but I can be very persuasive.

You'll come willingly, Cassie, have no doubt about it. I'm only in the kidnapping business for the money, not when it comes to my private life." He laughed at his sinister joke and finished off his wine, while she continued to look down at her hands on the table.

"Where's Leo?" she asked, looking up at him at last.

"At his house. Here, I'll show you." Victor seemed almost cheery as he pulled a tablet computer from the inside pocket of his jacket. He punched in a passcode and then loaded a video. He had somehow hacked into Leo's home camera feed. With a satisfied smile he showed the tablet to Cassie, and she shuddered. The feed showed Leo in the center of his hall, tied to a chair, while a brawny man stood over him with a gun pressed against his head. He was gagged, severely beaten, and his head hung down between his shoulders. It bobbed as though he was breathing, but was either asleep or, more likely, unconscious. Cassie gasped and held her hand over her open mouth in shock and disgust.

"You monster," she whispered.

"Yes, but I'm no worse than your lover, Cassie. Make no mistake the types of men you are surrounding yourself with." Victor closed the app and placed the tablet on the table. "I have lots more footage I could show you, things that would make you think again about placing your trust in that man, but it can wait for now. I haven't finished telling you my offer, have I?"

"I could never love you, Victor," she said, unable to help herself, and stood, wishing she had the guts to storm off, but didn't dare. Cassie paced the few feet of space between the tables and tried desperately to hold back her tears.

"I don't want you to love me. I want you to surrender to me. In return for your cooperation I will keep you safe and give you everything you desire. You have two choices." He stood and stared her down, challenging her to try something, but Cassie stood her ground. "You can walk away from me and I will return to Mexico, but I will kill Leo before I go. Or you can choose me, and I will spare his life. As a gesture of goodwill, I'll kill my brother in Leo's place, and our business will continue as usual, thanks to you." Victor's voice was calm, his entire demeanor suave and determined. "You have until noon tomorrow to make your decision. If you run away, I will not only kill Leo, but everyone you care about, including Mrs. Brown and your hooker roommate. I'll be at Leo's house when you're ready to talk." He stood and watched her with a cunning grin. The game had begun, and although she hated to admit it, he was already winning.

Chapter 21

Victor sauntered away without another word, throwing a handful of bills onto the table closest to the door before he left. Cassie fell into a heap on the floor, sobbing uncontrollably as she clutched at her aching stomach. Her mind was racing, terrible images of Leo and his suffering at the forefront of her fraught contemplations, followed by her predictions for the fates of her friends. She imagined them all lying dead in a pile at her feet, their empty eyes peering up at her, knowing she had sacrificed them for her own freedom. Cassie couldn't let that happen. She would have to give in to him.

There was no other choice, she absolutely could not let Leo die for her, and even if she did, she didn't trust Victor would stand by his word. Without Leo around to protect her, Cassie couldn't be sure he would let her go after he'd sealed Leo's fate and their apparent deal.

Mrs. Brown locked the front door and came to comfort Cassie, gathering her up off the floor. She sat her back down at the table before taking the seat opposite.

"You need to go to the cops, or run. Don't let him win," she said, clearly having been listening in on their conversation, and Cassie stared at her wide-eyed.

"I can't. He'll kill everyone I love, including you! If I ran, he'd find a way to track me down, and then he'd take me anyway. I couldn't live with your death on my conscience." Cassie rubbed her chest, which was aching so badly she felt as though she'd been punched. "I can't think straight right now. I'll have to go with him. I'm sorry, Mrs. B, but there's no other choice." Cassie took a large gulp of the wine before she grabbed her things and hugged the woman goodbye, unable to say another word for fear of breaking down again.

When she hit the cool night air outside, Cassie took a deep breath and peered up at the dark sky for a while, feeling broken. She went over every possible scenario in her head and still didn't know what to do. She knew with absolute certainty she could not let Leo die.

During his proposition, Victor had given away the real reason for his visit. His brother had sent him here to kill Leo. If she could stop that from happening, Cassie knew it would be worth it.

Victor had sworn not only to save Leo, but also to kill his brother as proof of his new allegiance to him if she chose wisely. This terrible promise showed her how much he was willing to do for her. Victor was apparently willing to betray his brother, and not take the life of his target, in return for her affections. Cassie hoped that meant his fondness for her might put her in good stead. She still didn't trust him, not wanting to think too far ahead to what impact making that decision would have on her, but hoped he wouldn't abuse her acquiescence when the time came.

Cassie stared at the smoggy sky until the cold started to creep in, and her body began complaining via strong shivers and the chattering of her teeth. She composed herself and set off toward the subway, realizing she hadn't called a cab.

Cassie then noticed a black car which was slowly following her. She turned and stared into the driver's seat, seeing Victor. She waited, climbing into the passenger seat when he pulled to a stop beside her.

"Can I offer you a ride home?" His eyes skimmed over her entire body appreciatively, but she shook her head.

"I don't wanna go home. Do you really know everything about me, Victor? About what I went through, and how fucked up I am because of it?" She turned to look at him, and he nodded.

"I know what your ex-husband did to you, and I know how long it took for you to get over it, yes."

"Then you should also know I never took my revenge on him. Can you understand my need for closure? If the people I love are in danger because of you, you at least owe me one favor." Victor grinned, as though he knew what was coming next. "If you really meant what you said about keeping me safe and giving me everything I desire, show me. I want to watch as you beat the shit out of my ex-husband. I want to see him suffer. Can you do that for me, Victor?" Cassie asked calmly, and he nodded. He put his foot down and sped off toward Jonah's apartment.

Cassie pressed the buzzer on the wall, feeling strange that this was once her home, and now she needed to be buzzed inside. Upon hearing her voice, Jonah unlocked the foyer and came to the door to greet her with a shocked expression on his face. She knew he would be able to tell she'd been crying, but Cassie remained quiet and followed him inside, leaving the door ajar.

"What's going on, honey?" Jonah took a seat on the sofa they had once picked out together. She sat beside him and peered into his soft blue eyes. Cassie saw nothing but warmth, and even a lingering hint of love still in them. She shuddered as the memory of his contorted face reappeared in her mind, but hid it. She needed to stay calm, so she pushed away her fraught emotions.

No matter what, this needed to happen. Cassie had the idea to have Victor beat up Jonah for her while she'd peered up at the dark sky outside the restaurant. She would no doubt be wanted for questioning following the beating. Even if he didn't press charges, she would still be the only person with definite motive, and the police would surely come looking for her with assault charges.

Cassie was very aware that in twenty four hours' time she might well be locked up in some Mexican mansion at the behest of her new master. If she were a wanted woman, at least the police would discover her missing, and hopefully begin a deeper

Laura Morgan

investigation into her whereabouts.

This was the only way Cassie could think to involve the police without physically contacting them herself. Jonah would have to pay the price for her plea, but she could think of no other way. In order to have a Plan B in place, this had to happen, and part of her did want to punish her ex for his crimes. Time had healed many of her wounds, but not all of them, and Cassie was sure in some awful way she might actually enjoy this.

"How many times have I told you never to call me honey again?" she replied, angry, but she remained composed. She took a breath. "Look, Jonah. I've really fucked up. I've gotten involved with the wrong people, and I have to go away. I'll be gone a while, maybe even forever." She stood to leave, and he caught her hand in his.

"Don't go. We can figure out how to help you. Who is it you've gotten involved with?" Jonah asked, clearly still worried about her even after all this time.

That was the moment Victor stepped out of the shadows. He approached and wrapped his hands around Jonah's throat and started to squeeze. "Me," he whispered, pressing down hard on his windpipe before throwing him back down onto the sofa in one fluid movement. His fists met Jonah's handsome face over and over again until he fell silent, blood oozing from the cuts. Only Jonah's gurgling breath let Cassie know he was still alive.

She hated seeing him this way, but a strange sort of satisfaction for doing karma's job appeared deep within her gut. She hadn't thought she would need

178

so much closure after so long, but it was truly liberating. Cassie felt completely calm at seeing her ex-husband in such a bad way, knowing he deserved a good dose of payback for what he had done to her.

"Okay, Victor. Let's go," she said, stepping back toward the door.

"One last thing," Victor replied with a sinister smile, pulling a knuckleduster from his pocket and sliding it onto the fingers of his right hand. The metal had sharp spikes protruding from it, and Cassie finally felt sickened by her dark request. She watched as he placed a handful of punches to Jonah's crotch. The semi-conscious man writhed in pain as the powerful blows rendered his manhood useless, at least for a while, and he was quickly out cold. Cassie was glad he hadn't been awake to endure Victor's extra level of punishment, and hoped he would seek medical help as soon as he came to.

She said nothing more as she wandered away, heading out to the street in stunned silence, where she emptied the contents of her stomach into the grate on the sidewalk. She climbed in Victor's car beside him, staring out at the empty street through the windshield.

"Now I'm ready to go home. Thank you," she told him, watching as he wiped his hands and face of blood with a wet wipe from a packet stashed in one of the driver's door pockets. He then drove to her apartment without a care in the world, arriving several minutes later.

"You have twelve hours, do not keep me

waiting," Victor told Cassie as she climbed out of the car. She nodded, unable to speak, and headed to her apartment to get cleaned up. She wasn't sure whether to tell Hanna what had happened or not, knowing she would get the same advice from her that Mrs. Brown had given. At the same time, though, she needed her best friend to know what was going to happen to her when she left the next morning. Hanna had to know the truth. She had to know Cassie had been forced to leave, rather than having chosen to run off to Mexico with Victor over a life here in New York with Leo.

"Hey, sweetie, fancy a cup of tea?" Hanna called from the kitchen as she came inside.

"Yeah, please," she called back on her way to her room. Cassie climbed in a quick shower, slid into some pajamas, and joined Jamie in the living room. He was sprawled on one of the sofas, resting, but did a double take when he saw how pale she was.

"What's happened?" Jamie asked, clearly having noticed her fearful numbness as she took a seat in the armchair, and Cassie took a deep breath. Hanna came in and sat beside her boyfriend, handing him a cup of tea after depositing one for Cassie.

"Victor happened," she replied.

Both Jamie and Hanna sat up, their attention fully on her, and they stared at her expectantly.

"What?" Hanna cried, and Cassie shrugged.

"He's gonna kill Leo if I don't go with him. I haven't got a choice. He's not letting this drop, and his demands include you guys, too. He'll kill you if I run, and he'll kill Leo if I don't choose him. I'm so sorry. What the fuck was I ever thinking getting involved with Leo? He always said he'd be bad news for me, and there we were, thinking we'd managed to keep things separate." She hung her head, feeling lost.

Hanna jumped up and wrapped Cassie in her arms. "Take a gun stashed in your knickers and kill him before he gets the chance, sweetie. Do whatever it takes to stop him from dragging you off to god-knows where as his slave. He's not like Leo. Victor won't be gentle, patient, or kind," Hanna yelled, her pain coming to the surface. Cassie wanted to laugh at how her British wording had somehow rubbed off on her friend, but now was not the time. Hanna stared at Jamie, seemingly in shock that he hadn't yet offered his opinion.

"He cares for me enough to orchestrate this whole thing. I'm hoping he'll stay that way. He even beat up Jonah for me, no questions asked. There's no other choice, I've gone over and over it in my head. You have to let me go." Cassie took a deep breath and stroked Hanna's face. "I can't do this without you, both of you. I need you to take care of him when I've gone, don't let him do anything foolish," she added, talking about Leo.

"She's right, baby," Jamie told Hanna, much to her apparent disgust. "Guys like Victor Sanchez don't stop until they get what they want. We're all collateral damage, so don't think for a second we're safe from him. You're doing the right thing, Cassie. In time we will try to negotiate your return, but right now he has you cornered."

As much as she appreciated his truthful response,

Cassie broke down following Jamie's damning words. She pulled Hanna back over to the sofa and slid between them, holding tight to her friends for a while before eventually going to pack up her essentials.

Chapter 22

Jamie loaned Cassie his car the following morning. None of them had slept, so rather than wait, she'd set off for Leo's mansion around eight o'clock. When she pulled up at the entryway, the gate stood wide open, ready for her without her needing to buzz in. Cassie was shocked to find none of the staff or guards there. It was eerie outside the huge home, sending a shiver down her spine, and she wondered where everybody might be, or if they were even still alive.

She made her way inside, finding Tina alive, but either asleep or out cold on the hard floor in the hall. She was covered in what seemed to be a mix of her own blood and urine, bullet wounds to each of her thighs rendering her immobile.

Leo was in the same chair she had seen him in via the video feed the night before, and Cassie ran over to him, shaking him awake. He peered up at her with terrified eyes, shaking his head. She pulled the gag down from his mouth, and he stared up into her face with a mixture of anguish and anger on his face.

"What the fuck are you doing here, Cassie? Please tell me you aren't seriously thinking of doing as he asks?" Leo growled.

"I have to. I can't let him kill you. I can't live in a world where you don't exist, even if we can't be together." She ran her hands over his broken nose and shattered cheekbone.

"I'm not worth your freedom. Don't you dare put my life before yours. I knew all along this was how my sorry life would end. Don't go with him. I don't care what it takes, say no. You have to say no." Leo's torment was seeping out of him in his ramblings, and Cassie suddenly began to doubt her decision to go with Victor. She yelped as hands grabbed her hips from behind and pulled her away from him.

Victor's gun pressed into her temple, reminding her once again of Otis, but this time she froze in fear. She was unable to focus on anything other than the words Leo had just uttered. Cassie trembled, the weight of her world coming crashing down on her all at once, and she felt more terrified than ever before. Victor's free hand ran across every inch of her body, checking for a weapon. When he found nothing, he lowered the gun from her temple and stashed it in the back of his tan colored chinos.

"Best check everywhere, you might have a gun stashed in your knickers," he whispered, having somehow known the exact words Hanna had said to her the night before. Cassie inhaled sharply, her mouth dropping open in shock as he thrust his hand down inside her jeans and straight under the hem of her panties. He unashamedly slid his fingers over her opening, while gripping her tightly by the waist with the other hand and staring at his captive host over her shoulder. Cassie couldn't take her eyes off Leo, a stray tear falling down her cheek as Victor touched her so intimately. The sight of his tormentor touching his lover unmistakably affected Leo, and he fought against his bonds.

"Get your fucking hands off her," he groaned, his voice deep and almost animalistic. Victor's hand was already sliding back up, but he taunted Leo further, licking the tips of his fingers with a smile. Cassie squirmed away from his grasp and fell to her knees.

"So sweet. I can't wait to have more," Victor groaned, his smile never faltering. "Speaking of which, I think it's time you made your choice, Cassie."

She looked back at Leo, seeing the pain in his eyes, and she began shuddering uncontrollably as Victor walked around to stand at his side. He placed the gun to Leo's temple and stared down at her with an expectant glare.

"Don't kill him, please," she begged.

"Say it."

"No, Cassie. Don't do it!" Leo cried.

After a few short, panting breaths, she stood and composed herself. Her mind was made up.

"I choose Victor. I'll go with you now, but you leave him alone," she replied, screaming as Victor silenced Leo's angst-ridden response to her decision with a swift whack across the face with his weapon, rendering him unconscious.

"He's still alive, come on." Victor grabbed Cassie's arm and dragged her out to his car. He flung her in the passenger seat and climbed in. He started the engine without even looking at her as she fell to pieces beside him. Cassie soon began hurling abuse at him and writhing in her seat, both unwilling and unable to calm down. Her outburst forced him to slam on the brakes a few moments later. He turned to face the screaming woman, and she slapped him across the face, hard.

"I hope you're fucking happy. I hate you!" she spat. Victor returned the slap, which knocked Cassie's body into the dash. He watched icily as she sobbed and clutched at her burning cheek.

"Don't ever hit me again," he said, and then delved into his pocket, producing a small vial, seemingly prepared for her meltdown. Victor grabbed Cassie's dark ponytail and pulled her head back, the force of it opening her mouth, and he flung a tablet inside. He held it closed until he was convinced she'd swallowed the pill.

"Get your hands off me." She pushed him away, putting as much distance between them as she could in the small sports car.

"Well, I'd hoped I wouldn't need it. But I can't drive with you attacking me, can I?"

Cassie started to go limp, so he pushed her back in her seat and secured the seatbelt, leaning her head back against the rest. She tried to speak, but could only mumble due to the sedative he had given her, and she soon stopped her sobs and violent tears.

She didn't fall asleep as they drove, simply watching through the car windows while her limp body sagged back in the seat. The world around her whizzed by in a blur as he drove them away, her thoughts jumbled yet somehow calm. Deep down, she prayed for a miracle, or even a dose of her own karma to come crashing down on them. She would take anything she could get, as long as she walked away safe and free.

She was aware of being lifted out of the car a short while later, everything still in a haze, but she soon realized they were about to board a plane. She panicked, in spite of the sedative, and tried to move against the lethargy. Her attempts were fruitless, though. Her head fell to the side as the arms beneath her knees and shoulders held onto her tighter. Her senses were filled with the smell of a man she didn't know, and she groaned.

Inside the huge private jet, Cassie was placed on a large bed and tucked under the sheets by gentle hands that didn't feel as though they belonged on the huge henchman who'd carried her inside.

"Gentle giants are nice," she mumbled, making the man laugh, but he said nothing, simply watching over Cassie as she drifted off to sleep.

***

By the time Cassie awoke, they were airborne. She stirred and looked out the small window at the bright sunshine that streamed in. For a minute, she hoped the last day might have been a terrible dream, but knew better than that. Her fear reappeared in her gut, making her feel as though she might be sick, but a few deep breaths thankfully cleared her nausea.

She'd always hated flying, but now the feeling of dread in the pit of her stomach was far from the normal fear of turbulence or engine failure. This was a genuine sense of sheer dread. It welled up inside of her as soon as the sedative wore off. Cassie didn't cry or break down, she simply lay there for a while gathering her thoughts, knowing in her heart she'd done the right thing. In spite of her own fears, those she loved were now safe, and she would do everything she could to keep it that way.

Other than the horrid taste in her mouth and her disorientation, Cassie felt quite rested. She had no idea how long she'd been asleep, but thought she might actually be willing to take a sedative again to help her sleep should her fears overwhelm her in the future. She even felt strangely at ease as she stood and wandered over to the small bathroom, taking in the luxurious private jet as she went.

After using the toilet, Cassie brushed her teeth and fixed her hair and makeup, having found the bag she had packed from home on the floor of the mile-high bedroom, and was glad Victor had let her keep the home comforts. She wished she'd packed some protein bars or something, though. She was famished.

A few minutes later Cassie tried the door, her hunger getting the better of her, and was surprised to find it open. She peered around the other side and spotted Victor sitting at a desk a few feet away. Several hulking men were also aboard, all of them Latino, and she could hear them talking to one another in Spanish. Some were sitting down, while others milled around making drinks and food for their boss.

"Sit," Victor said, looking up and pointing to the chair opposite him at the table. Cassie wandered over, catching the many eyes on her as she went, and he seemed to sense her unease. "Don't worry, they all know if they so much as look at you in a way I don't like, I'll cut off their dicks." He grinned, closing his laptop.

One man delivered them two coffees and a plate of wraps filled with chicken and avocado. Cassie wanted to grab one and devour it whole, feeling ravenous, but she didn't dare. When she finally looked up from the plate at Victor, she caught a wry smile on his lips. She sat back in her chair, eager to get away from the sight and smell of the food before her, despite her stomach's protest at being made to wait. A few more plates piled high with different foods were delivered to their table, but neither of them made a move to eat anything. He continued to stare at her, his eyes roving over every inch he could see, and in spite of her clothes, Cassie felt exposed.

"So, what's next?" she asked, hoping he might finally say something. Victor took a long sip of his coffee, his eyes still on hers.

"I'm taking you to my home in Mexico, where I will require you to do everything I ask of you," he answered, laughing to himself, but Cassie just stared blankly back at him. "I will take care of the situation with my brother, then I will come to you. I understand this is going to be hard for you at first, but you'll get used to it," Victor added dismissively.

He obviously didn't care about her feelings, or her hang-ups from the past. Cassie knew he would not respect her boundaries like Leo had, so she mentally prepared herself. When Victor demanded she sleep with him, she knew she'd better be ready to do it willingly, or else endure his forceful advances.

"I'm not your whore or your servant, Victor. All I ask is you remember our deal. I chose you over Leo. You asked me to surrender to you, which I have. At no point did I ever agree to be your captive, or a slave. I am yours, you needn't be so cold," Cassie replied, drinking her own coffee.

"You'll soon learn to control that feisty temper of yours, Cassie," he warned, glaring across at her, and she just shrugged in response. "I want you to submit to me, fully and willingly. Submission takes work, though. It also requires punishments where they are due. I hope you're ready for this?" Victor licked his lips provocatively. She simply nodded, her demeanor softening as a knowing grin curled at her lips.

Cassie decided then and there to treat this whole situation as a role, like she had when adopting the necessary persona to woo her clients back when she was an escort. She had a character to play, and would for the rest of her miserable life if she had to, and quickly set about pushing all thoughts of her old life away. She knew clinging to the past would only hinder her progress in obtaining Victor's much-needed affection. Cassie did not want to know what punishments he had up his sleeve, so set her sights on the rewards he had promised instead.

"Absolutely. I seem to remember you promising

to not only take care of me, but to give me everything I desire. Submission also requires rewards, so I assume there are rules to our agreement?" Cassie asked and Victor nodded, his dark brown eyes boring into hers from across the table.

"Clever girl. Well, first is you'll have to do everything I ask of you, and I mean everything. You are to speak to me respectfully at all times, no more outbursts." He paused, and Cassie nodded in understanding. "You only speak when spoken to in the company of others, and you are never to deny me my sexual gratification, no matter where or when," Victor told her, laying the obvious ground rules. The escort side of herself that Cassie had said goodbye to, but had certainly not forgotten, picked up on the frighteningly specific commands in his words.

She was mindful they were already playing their roles, and looked down at the huge array of foods that still sat on the table between them. Victor hadn't touched any of them yet, so she peered at him for a few seconds before finally gathering the courage to speak.

"So, you mean like how there's all this food here, and you know I must be starving because I've not eaten a thing since yesterday morning, but you've yet to offer me any?" Cassie asked, relishing his surprise at her clever assumptions.

"Perhaps. Tell me, what do you think I want before I will allow you to eat?" Victor stared at her lips, and Cassie knew without him asking. Swallowing her pride, she slid beneath the table and kneeled before him, unbuttoning Victor's fly and pulling his erection free from his shorts. He had clearly been enjoying their interaction, as there was already a small bead on his thick tip, and despite her fear and hatred of the man, she immediately licked it clean.

Cassie licked, sucked, and nibbled his shaft, sliding her head up and down as she listened to his quiet groans from beneath the table. When he came, Victor grabbed the back of her head and pressed his tip into the very back of her throat, making her gag, but she didn't fight. The muscles clenched around him, only spurring him on more. Only when he was finally spent did he let her go. Cassie climbed back up in her seat, panting and barely stifling her gags.

Victor pushed the plate with the wraps toward her as she smoothed down her ruffled hair. "Help yourself," he said with a wide grin.

Chapter 23

They arrived in Mexico a few hours later, Victor having been a much gentler host for the rest of their journey. Cassie wondered if the change in him was thanks to her gratifying methods and much calmer demeanor. Despite her inner turmoil, she played her part well. Cassie smiled sweetly while Victor chatted, telling her stories about the life of a Latino gangster, and finally of his exploits from the last few days with Leo in a clear attempt to rile her. She couldn't let it show how much his talking of Leo that way bothered her, so paid extra attention to her food and drink as he spoke.

Cassie devoured as much as she could in the time they had, glad of the nourishment, and offered very little in the way of conversation herself. She really didn't feel like partaking in idle chitchat, and hoped she might use the time to figure him out before they arrived. She'd learned a little more about Victor as a person, but less of his past. As they interacted, she watched his preferences with food, making a mental note of how he'd removed the onion from his wrap before eating it, and that he had chosen beef enchiladas over chicken. Cassie also noted he drank strong, black coffee without any sugar, before then moving on to tequila on the rocks. He never once asked what she might like to drink.

One of Victor's henchmen brought over bottled water for Cassie when she refused more coffee. She appreciated the gesture, but only took a sip when Victor gave her the go-ahead. She hated that this was her life now, being his subordinate, his submissive. But she endeavored to stick it out for as long as she could. The hopes of being saved by Leo, or pursued by the police for Jonah's beating, stayed firmly hidden in the farthest reaches of her mind.

The journey from the airport was quiet. Victor talked on the phone in Spanish, his hand on Cassie's lower thigh the entire journey. He curled his fingers around the back of her knee, rubbing her through the skinny jeans, and laying claim to his new whore in front of the men who rode with them.

After a few hours their group reached what Cassie assumed must be the cartel's massive complex. It was a compound filled with many different buildings around a huge, white mansion in the center. The setup reminded Cassie of a small town, rather than just one family's home. She half expected to find a shop on site, and a post office, but knew it would more than likely just be a group of whorehouses and dorms for the Sanchez brothers' employees to live and work under their bosses' constant control.

The land around the complex was arid, the

temperature stiflingly hot, and the air so dusty that Cassie's mouth ran dry within seconds of being outside the cool, air-conditioned car. The huge man who had lifted her into the plane led Cassie inside with a strong hand on her elbow, leaving Victor to head off in search of his brother. They walked through the quiet house, the deafening silence making Cassie feel even more lost and alone after being so used to the noise of the city. Victor's home rivaled Leo's in size and lavish decoration, but also had the added benefit of the hot weather and its fully air-conditioned interior. Cassie tried to take it all in as they walked, but was hurried along by her guard before she could take time to appreciate her luxurious new prison.

The man took her inside the room and stayed, rather than leaving her like before, and Cassie immediately tensed up.

"Don't worry, you're safe with me. Mr. Sanchez has tasked me with being your personal bodyguard. I will never touch you, nor will I let any harm come to you," the man said, blocking the doorway with his body, even though he had locked the door. "This is your bedroom. Through there is the bathroom, which leads through to Victor's room. The door that joins the two stays locked at all times, only Victor has the key," he added, pointing to a door on one side of the room.

"Oh, okay," was all Cassie could reply. She took in the huge room and the locked windows, with their dainty lace curtains and awnings. It was all white and pink, not to her liking, but she could appreciate somewhere along the way that a woman had been allowed to try and make this room look pretty. She had a good look around the large space for a while, opened the door to the bathroom, and checked out the huge bath, waterfall style shower, and double basin sink. Back in her room, Cassie spotted another door and pulled it open. Inside she found hundreds of designer dresses with shoes and lingerie to match. They would easily rival those of any high-class socialite she had met back in New York.

"Nice, they for me?" she mumbled, closing the door, and he nodded. "So, what do I call you?" She figured she had better stay on good terms with this man if he was the only thing standing between her and any potential threats here. She still had no idea how many men and women lived in the complex, or whether she should be afraid of them.

"My name's Joaquin Grayson," he replied with a nod. He had the look of a Mexican, with his dark skin and hair, but his accent was flawless American English. Cassie guessed he might have lived in the States for a while, or perhaps he'd come here to work for Victor and Luis. She wondered if their henchmen were procured the same way as their girls, ultimatum or kidnap. "You can call me Grayson, or GG if you like. I liked it when you called me a gentle giant back on the plane," Grayson added, smiling across at her, and Cassie felt her face flush, suddenly remembering her slurred words. She laughed, glad he was trying to put her at ease.

"Okay, I like it. GG it is." She smiled at him as she sat down on the bed and stared out the window.

"So, what do we do now?"

"We wait for Victor's orders. That's all we ever do, Miss Taylor. I suggest you get used to being at his beck and call from now on." Grayson's round face was stoic and completely lacking the smile he had shown her a few minutes before. He was back to business.

"Yeah, I suppose. I'll have to get used to being a glorified whore, sitting up in her room all day while awaiting her lover's visits," Cassie replied, forgetting her act for a moment, but he didn't answer her anyway. She lay down on the bed, curling her body up into the fetal position as she let the events of the last day wash over her. She wouldn't cry, but let her mind wander, hoping both Jonah and Leo had been found, and were already being cared for. She also thought about her friends, hoping to god Hanna was holding it together without her.

***

It was just a couple of hours later when a key turned in the lock of her door, and Grayson stepped toward it, watching the door intently. He quickly relaxed when Victor entered the room. He was white as a sheet, his features soft and almost pained. Cassie climbed up off the bed and walked slowly toward him. He didn't seem to notice her at first, walking forward in a daze. When they were standing just inches apart, he suddenly grabbed Cassie's face, and pulled her to him. He kissed her lips feverishly, and she kissed him back, knowing she had no other choice. Victor soon turned things up a notch and began grabbing at her, unbuttoning Cassie's shirt, before finally taking his lips off hers and peering across at her with a cold, hard stare.

"Get on the bed," he told her, cupping her breasts roughly, and she couldn't reply as his lips found hers again. When she could, she pulled back, eyeing him cautiously.

"No, Victor, not like this," she pleaded, pushing him back, careful not to come across as dismissive. Cassie peered up into his eyes, attempting a tender, earnest look in her own. She sensed his anger, but pressed on. "Not like this, baby. You promised me, remember?"

Victor looked at her, seeming to snap back to reality, and his callous stare softened just a touch. His mouth opened as if he were going to respond, but he said nothing. Cassie kissed his lips gently, and took his hands in hers, noticing there was blood on them. He had it on his clothes and neck too. She knew he had done it, Victor had killed his brother, and he clearly wasn't dealing with it very well.

"I'll leave you to it. I'm outside if you need me," Grayson said from behind them, taking his leave. Cassie didn't respond. She kept hold of Victor's hand, still staring up into his deep brown eyes.

"Let's get you cleaned up, okay?" She walked him slowly toward the bathroom. Cassie ran the water and emptied his pockets, pulling the huge knife from his belt, but she left it in its sheath and kept her eyes on his as she placed it carefully beside one of the sink basins. She climbed inside the huge shower and pulled him in with her, both of them still fully clothed.

Cassie began delicately peeling off Victor's clothing, dropping the soaking shirt and chinos to the floor, along with his boxer shorts. He soon stood before her, naked and silent, but his eyes were on hers. Cassie stepped closer, kissing his wet lips softly. They were almost the same height, which made it easier to remain close, no stepping up onto her tiptoes like with Leo.

She slipped off her own clothes and kicked the sodden pile aside, timidly stepping closer. She pressed her trembling body into his, feeling his response to her almost immediately. She continued in her pursuit of his tender touches, knowing she would take anything soft over his aggressive hands on her still fragile body.

Even in his softer moments Cassie was not attracted to Victor, but she closed her eyes and pictured Leo in her mind. She imagined his hands on her body, and the feel of him inside of her when they made love. Her body flushed and her core slickened thanks to the one thing Victor couldn't take away, her memories. His thick chest hair tickled her cheek as she hugged him, his body toned and slim, but nothing compared to Leo's sculpted frame and bare chest. Everything about Victor seemed alien, and it took everything she had to take a mental step back from her real feelings. She immersed herself even more fully into her new role, and mentally gave her body to him, preparing for the physical ownership she knew would soon come.

After a few seconds of quiet, gentle embrace, Cassie took Victor's hands and lathered them up.

She cleaned away the blood before she slid her own soapy hands over his torso and neck. Victor groaned and leaned into her touch, seemingly enjoying their closeness, and she kept on. She washed him all over and cleaned away the remnants of this bittersweet day. When the blood was gone, and the water ran clear, Cassie kissed his palms. She played the doting lover as best she could, and readied herself for what was no doubt about to happen next.

"All clean, that's better," she whispered, kissing Victor's lips and pulling his arms around her so he enveloped her again. Cassie leaned into his embrace for a second time, acting as though she enjoyed their closeness. They stood like that for a while, the hot waterfall cascading down over their heads, and Cassie closed her eyes, trying again to imagine it was Leo holding her.

When Victor's hand slid around from behind Cassie toward her cleft, no matter how much fantasizing she did, it didn't stop her from clamming up. She trembled as he stroked her folds, running his hands over her scars, before pushing two fingers inside.

"Relax, Cassie. I won't hurt you. It's time for your reward," Victor whispered into her ear, evidently having come back to himself. He slid his fingers deep inside of her, his thumb rubbing on her clit, and she groaned. Cassie was surprised he felt so good, having expected it to feel so forced that she would not enjoy herself, but it wasn't long until she came for him. Victor's hard-on pressed into her hip as he strummed a little longer and watched her unravel. When Cassie had finished, and her body had stopped tensing around him, he finally withdrew, letting the water clean the juices from them both before he shut off the shower.

They grabbed two towels and dried off, Cassie wandering into her bedroom in the hopes of getting dressed, but Victor was clearly not finished with her yet. He yanked the towel away and grabbed her naked body from behind. His still rock-hard erection pressed into her, and he trailed kisses over her shoulder up to her neck. Cassie yelped when he bent her forward, her hands grabbing at the frame of the bed to hold her steady. Victor entered her from behind in one swift, hard thrust that made her cry out.

"Victor," she groaned, trembling, but he just shushed her.

He was a slow, passionate lover, and Cassie was surprised he didn't seem in any hurry to finish and be on his way. She assumed powerful men with countless whores around to service them day or night wouldn't be interested in languid lovemaking. Victor was proving her wrong with every deep thrust. He glided effortlessly in and out of her, pressing his length into the tender spot that made Cassie gush for him, surprising herself again at her body's responsiveness to his touch.

She followed his every lead, sliding forward onto the bed after a while and letting Victor push her legs closed as he continued conducting her pleasure. She cried out as an orgasm claimed her. When he flipped her over and kissed her lips gently, Cassie truly fell apart beneath his intense gaze and tender touch. As Victor came, he held her close, seemingly unable to pull away, but when he did, he stared down into her eyes as she trembled, watching her intently as though she were a piece of heaven sent down just for him.

***

"You really shouldn't worry about your scars, I think it's all in your head," Victor said a little while later as they lay wrapped in each other's arms in Cassie's new bed. "I expected much worse following Tina's explanation."

Cassie wondered if perhaps Leo's assistant had over exaggerated to try and put him off pursuing her, assuming he wouldn't be interested in a mutilated lover. By then it was likely he already had his sights set on her, and Cassie got the impression nothing would've changed his mind.

"That's good to hear, but it'll still take me a while to feel comfortable with you. It's just who I am, I can't help it."

"Many whores bear scars, Cassie. In fact, most of the ones I've been with have them. It comes with the territory."

"I'm not a whore, Victor. My husband did it to me." She flinched, wanting to glower at him and tell him off, but forced herself to keep calm. "As soon as someone touches me, I just freak out. I know it's in my mind, but I can't forget the trauma. It takes everything I've got not to scream and run, but I'm much better than I used to be. I didn't have any sexual contact at all for nearly two years after Jonah," Cassie replied, tailing off.

"How many men have you been with?" Victor asked, his hand stroking her back as she lay with her head on his chest. He seemed to have ignored her 'woe is me' routine, and Cassie let him lead the conversation away.

"Three. Jonah, Leo, and now you," Cassie replied, groaning when he began laughing at her.

"Wow, Leo was right. You're older than all the other women in this compound, but they've had hundreds of men by the time they're twenty years old. Most are single moms and drug addicts, not exactly what I'd call sexy," Victor said, pulling Cassie's face up so he could look at her. "Not you, though, even with your scars. You're very tight and wet despite your age. I can see the appeal at last."

"Gee, way to make me feel old. Thanks," she retorted, and Victor laughed. He kissed her nose, the gentleness making her feel awkward. She felt far from ready for all this lovey dovey routine, but Victor seemed intent on being softer, and she knew it was preferable to the cold mobster routine he was no doubt very capable of.

"I think I wasn't looking in the right place, or even the right country for a proper lover before. I'm glad you chose to come with me. Tell me you don't regret it?"

"You're a kind man, and a gentle lover, Victor. I don't regret a thing" she replied, choosing her words carefully. While she didn't regret saving Leo, there was no way she was ready to declare her love to Victor and forget about everything he had done to get her here.

"You're the first woman I have ever made love

to, Cassie. Keep this up and you'll win my heart, English girl." He bestowed a kiss on her forehead. His tone was soft, so genuine. Cassie wondered if her dealing with his pain so lovingly after he'd killed his brother might have helped her gain the advantage. She hoped he would now see her as someone who helped soothe him, to chase away his pain and guilt, rather than blame her for being the one who caused it.

Cassie couldn't reply to Victor's heartfelt words. She smiled, fluttering her eyelashes in an attempt to hide her shock. She was glad he seemed to have already begun seeing her differently than the other girls, but he still scared her, and she hoped this side of him would stick around.

"I'll keep being everything you want me to be, Victor. I made you a promise. As long as you keep yours, I'll keep mine," she said, kissing his lips. "Oh, and I'll need to keep taking my contraceptive pill. We don't want any surprises."

"Of course, we can wait for the patter of tiny feet until after we're married," Victor told her with a wry smile, and her stomach dropped. The sheer thought of it made her feel sick.

"One step at a time, baby," she replayed, having noticed he seemed to like her calling him that. He kissed her, pulling Cassie up onto his lap so she straddled him.

"Until then, keep taking your pills, and tell Grayson when you need more. All my girls take contraceptives, but I still use condoms with them. Never with you."

"That's good to know."

"Sí, I'm clean. There are many things I want from you, Cassie, many things indeed. But the first thing I want is your sweet pussy again," he said, watching as she followed his request without hesitation and lifted herself over him. She closed her eyes and pushed his hard-on inside of her, riding his thick length while he sat back and watched with a satisfied smile.

Chapter 24

Victor slept in Cassie's room with her that night, his arms around her tightly in a far more possessive way than Leo's had ever been. She felt as though he was already obsessively protective over her, his hands pressing into her skin almost painfully. As he held her, Cassie knew she was a prized possession, and it scared the hell out of her.

Victor roused early and woke her for a quick fuck before he headed off to his own room through the en-suite. He came back in his suit and expensive shoes, looking every inch the powerful cartel boss.

"Stay here. Grayson will attend to you. He's allowed to leave to get you food, but will otherwise remain here, and you're to stay in your room until I come back," he informed Cassie.

"Is there anything I can do while I'm in here?" she asked timidly, already dreading the boring day ahead. Victor climbed onto the bed, seeming not to care about crinkling his suit. He kissed her deeply, pressing his body into hers, and she went limp beneath him, acting every inch the subservient lover.

"I want you to stay out of sight from the other girls for now. They will be jealous of you, and probably very mean. Today you can lie back and dream of me, and be ready for when I return," he said, not really having given her an answer, but she just smiled and winked.

"Sure thing, baby," Cassie replied, watching as he left, and then diving back under the covers for a little bit more rest.

Grayson woke her up with coffee and a blueberry muffin around nine o'clock. His whole body exuded kindness and warmth, and Cassie wondered if she detected a hint of protectiveness toward her. She also got the impression he might be gay. Having spent a long time in the theatrical world, her gaydar was pretty good, and she definitely got a sense from him. She also wondered if that was why Victor asked him to be her full-time guard.

"Good morning, Miss Taylor. I hope you slept well?" Grayson asked, taking a seat in the armchair a few feet away, and she nodded. "Great. Mr. Sanchez has informed me we are to stay inside while he's working today. I thought I'd see if there's anything you'd like to do. I can find us a set of cards, or how about a word game?"

"No games, thank you. Some conversation might be nice, though, seeing as it appears we're going to be spending lots of time together. Are you allowed to tell me more about Victor? Or perhaps give me a rundown of this place I'm now to call home?" Cassie gazed at him hopefully. She was desperate to take a walk around, to see the complex for herself, but in the meantime she would settle for as much information as she could get.

Grayson was skittish, looking around the room with the careful expression of someone who knew he was being watched, and Cassie made a mental note to be mindful in case of hidden cameras. Victor and Leo were very much alike, and it stood to reason the Mexican gangster would be just as paranoid as his friend farther north.

Cassie took a bite of her muffin. It was still warm from the oven, and she groaned in appreciation. Grayson smiled and took a breath. He told her enough to keep both her and any prying eyes happy.

"Sure. We're in central Mexico, in the middle of nowhere, and far away from any coast. There are a few large cities close by. Victor has access to shops, bars, nightclubs, and restaurants—you name it. The life here can rival any you might have been used to in New York."

They chatted for a while longer, and she didn't press him for details. He wouldn't give her any city names or information regarding their exact location, but she understood why, and was grateful for anything he was willing to provide. Cassie stayed quiet as he offered her his little pieces of information.

"The Sanchez brothers have been in business for a long time, ever since Luis was just a teenager. He fought his way to the top by being ruthlessly successful, and anyone who crossed him usually wound up dead. Victor was initiated into the cartel at the age of fifteen, and Luis trained him personally. No one has ever gone up against the pair of them and won."

"Whoa, that's kinda hot." She grinned, and he let out a gruff laugh before turning serious again.

"Such a shame Luis had his accident last night. He'll be greatly missed." His voice was low and somber, but his expression lacked the emotion it needed to seem genuine. Cassie had to wonder how many of his men might have secretly rejoiced in his demise.

"Yes, a terrible shame."

"I met Leo a few weeks back. He was well mannered and honest, but Luis was offended. He hadn't let on until after Leo left. He and Victor had a fight, and then Victor left. He asked me and a few of the other men to accompany him to New York, which of course we did. The next thing I know, we get the call to infiltrate Leo's mansion and hold him captive. Before I could even ask what was happening, you were being put in my care with strict orders to keep you safe, even from yourself, if necessary."

"Does he really think I'd do something so foolish?"

"Desperate people do desperate things. He wants you to be happy here, Cassie. I hope for the same, but I will warn you now, do not cross him, and never let him catch you lying. He once murdered his best friend for telling him a lie. He'll be angry at the truth, sure, but the alternative's much worse."

Cassie finished off her coffee and placed the mug back on the tray. "Am I safe with him, GG? I want to be protected. I deserve it after giving up everything to come here. I want to be happy and loved, is it so much to ask?" she blurted out, desperate for more answers.

"Yes, you'll be safe, happy, and loved, Cassie. But you must be everything you have promised him you will. Don't ever take his affection for granted." Grayson's intense stare made her know he told the truth. She wondered how many other women might've been delivered the same promises from the powerful man in the past. She imagined them trying in vain to please Victor, only to get sloppy and lose it just as quickly. Cassie promised herself she would not let the same happen to her.

By the time Victor returned, she and Grayson had finished their conversations and moved on to some basic Spanish lessons. It had been Cassie's idea. She wanted to be able to converse with Victor in his native language, rather than expect him to always speak English for her. He seemed impressed at the sentiment, which was exactly what she'd been hoping for.

She squealed excitedly and wrapped her arms around him when Victor unlocked the door and came inside, playing her role perfectly again, and he seemed positively taken with her.

"How's your day been, baby?" she asked, helping him out of his suit jacket and nodding to Grayson so he left them alone. She placed the jacket on the back of her dressing table's chair to keep it nice, while Victor slid into a leather chair that sat beneath the window. She'd thought earlier how it was the perfect reading spot, if only she could convince him to buy her books.

Victor looked tired, drained, and she climbed onto his lap. Cassie ran her hands over his face and into his dark hair, massaging his scalp gently while he closed his eyes and almost seemed to purr.

"It's been a long and hard day. I've had a lot of questions to answer about my brother, but at last the matter has been laid to rest. We will have a funeral for him tomorrow, just a small affair. We have no family close by, so it'll just be me and our most trusted people," Victor said, his hands sliding up her bare legs toward Cassie's warm mound.

"Would you like me to come with you?" she whispered as he slipped his fingers inside her panties and stroked her nether lips. Cassie found herself trembling uncontrollably. She desperately wanted him to stop. She'd barely felt comfortable with Leo touching her scars, and had forced herself to let Victor see and touch them the night before. Now, though, she just wanted him to get on with it, to slide his fingers inside, or stop altogether.

"Why are you so scared?" Victor asked, ignoring her question.

She closed her eyes and took a deep breath, mentally kicking herself for being such a weak and feeble girl. She hated how the past still had so much power over her, and promised herself she would stop doing this every time Victor touched her. Cassie knew he would soon grow tired of her hang-ups, and forced her mind to switch off its frenzied remembrance, willing her trauma away like a forbidden repulsion to Victor's touch.

"I'm sorry, baby. It's just still so new, you and

me. After everything that's happened, I need some time to forget about New York, and my life there," she replied, her body stopping its shudders only when he brought his hand away.

"You miss him, don't you?" he spat, his voice turning harsh and cruel in an instant. Cassie remembered the words Grayson had said to her about lying to him, and decided to be at least a little honest.

"Yes, but I miss my life more. I miss my friends, my jobs. I miss the person I was up there. Please don't be angry, Victor. I'm doing everything you asked of me, and more. I want to be perfect for you, I want you to be proud of me," she said, meaning it. Cassie really did want her life in Mexico to be the best version she could make it. She was well aware how awful her stay could be if she lost Victor's affection. She knew she had to try and make him understand she could be more than just a girl locked upstairs for him to fuck. As she peered down at him, silently commanding her body to yearn for his touch, she used her feminine wiles to her advantage in every way she knew how. As she took a deep breath, the movement lifted her breasts and accentuated her cleavage, which immediately caught his attention. Victor stared at Cassie's chest and bit his bottom lip.

"I guess it has only been one day. It feels like so much longer," Victor replied, visibly softening. "You're perfect already, Cassie, don't you see what you do to me? I never thought I would want a girl my own age, especially one who has such a feisty temper." He laughed, making her smile.

Victor trailed his hand across her thigh, showing her the contrast in their skin tones. "I never wanted something this pale against my body. I didn't think I would love the way you speak a language that is so foreign, yet so familiar to me. Every sound you make is music to my ears, and when you laugh, I feel as though every one of my sins has been forgiven," he said.

Cassie held her breath, suddenly feeling as though she might cry. She peered into his deep brown eyes, feeling a tiny flicker of unexpected affection. She knew she was still very far from feeling the same way about him as she did Leo, but Victor was starting to make this whole thing a lot easier on her with these tender moments of loving words and gentle touches.

They made love for hours again that night, Victor's body commanding hers entirely as he caressed her and held her close. Cassie hated this man for all the things he had done, but he was honest, and he was real. She was beginning to feel guilty for playing her role, wishing he were falling for the real her.

Victor never once apologized for his actions, and in a strange way, she respected him for it. At the same time, she wished he would show a little compassion for her losses. She hoped in time he would, but she was no fool, and vowed never to live in hope of him suddenly breaking down and begging her forgiveness. One of them would have to let go in order for this to work, and Cassie knew it was her. She decided she would earn her place in his heart, regardless of what she had to let him take from her in the process.

***

The next day Victor left to go and work, much like he had the day before. This time he pulled a black dress from her new closet on his way, laying it out on the bed.

"Be ready for noon," he told her, and Cassie nodded. She knew he was taking her with him to his brother's funeral, and despite the somber reasons, she was glad to be allowed out of this bedroom at last. Grayson helped get her ready, waxing her body and styling her in a way that sealed her assumptions on his sexual preferences. He touched her without any sexual agenda. He simply got on with it without taking sneaky looks, or putting his hands where they shouldn't be. Cassie felt safer in his company than ever before, chatting with him as they got her ready, and she was glad she had someone here with whom she could feel comfortable.

Preparations complete, she took a long look in the mirror, seeing herself, but also the mask she now permanently wore, reflected back at her.

"Damn, I look good," she said with a smile, swishing her skirt and giggling. Grayson had given her a classic, elegant look that suited her pale face and body perfectly. He kept her large breasts covered with the aid of a dark brooch he'd found in one of her many jewelry boxes, and he straightened it for her.

"We don't want to draw too much attention to you, and this dress shows quite a bit of leg," he told her, making it clear that while Victor's men were not a threat, they might still have ideas about her if she weren't careful. "Men can do desperate things if a woman gets inside his head too much," he said, Victor being a very recent example.

When he came to collect her just before noon, she felt her cheeks burn as his eyes roamed over her admiringly. Victor offered Cassie his arm, reminding her of the day they'd first met. Just like that day, she took it without hesitation. She was grateful for the freedom his hold would bring her, and followed his lead out of her bedroom. They made their way down the long hallway toward the stairs. Grayson followed a few feet behind, his eyes sweeping the rooms as they went.

Once through the large house and in the vast hallway, Victor stopped. There were people all around, talking in Spanish, and some seemed to be arguing loudly without a care for who might be listening. No one approached them or tried to catch Victor's eye. They all seemed to know he would speak to them when he wanted, but they should otherwise stay away. Cassie began to notice the power he had over them all. It reminded her of the times she had attended parties on Leo's arm, his commanding presence parting the sea of people before them as they walked, and his chosen guests staring up at him in admiration when he passed. Victor was exactly the same. He'd taken his brother's place atop their business, and was surrounded by men and women who both loved and feared him. They seemed to hang on his every word and did everything he asked of them without question.

Cassie thought she'd enjoy having the freedom from her room, but she found herself frightened of everyone she came across. She had no idea how to act, sensing many eyes on her, and she cowered under their scrutinizing gazes. The women were especially harsh. Their overly made-up faces contorted into vicious, evil looks full of envy and disgust when they watched her. She finally understood what Victor had meant about keeping her away from them. Cassie had absolutely no doubt they would be viciously aggressive to her given the opportunity, and hoped she would never end up alone with any of them.

"Don't speak to anyone but me or Grayson, and stay by my side unless I tell you otherwise," Victor whispered to her, but she was already planning those things anyway.

They came to a stop by a doorway that led out onto a huge terrace and swimming pool, and he addressed the crowd in Spanish. Cassie could pick out a few simple words, but not enough to properly understand his speech. She could decipher the meaning, though. His words were slow and his tone of voice soft, while everyone looked on in quiet mourning. This was the so called 'small affair' Victor had told her about. She realized either something had been lost in translation, or his meaning of the word was very different.

Victor turned and led the way, his arm still locked around Cassie's tightly, but he didn't show her any affection, nor did he seem to expect any from her. She got the impression he just wanted her close, and went along with it, as was expected of her now.

Once the funeral was over, Victor led the party back inside, where he toasted his brother. He handed Cassie a small flute of champagne, which she graciously accepted. She joined in with the rest of the group, raising a glass to the man she knew had died because she had chosen his death over Leo's. There was no victory in this moment, but she would've done the same again if she had to.

A woman to Cassie's left was in hysterics, screaming and praying loudly, until she was finally dragged away by some of her friends. Cassie wondered if she might have been Luis's wife, her reaction to his passing surprising her. In this sea of whores and henchmen, she assumed Luis, like Victor, had never allowed anyone close, but after watching that poor woman she realized how wrong she was.

"You're red," Victor whispered in her ear, stroking Cassie's arm, and breaking her reverie. He held his cool glass to her skin, and she groaned. She hadn't even noticed her pale skin burning in the strong Mexican sunshine, and cringed at her stereotypical British pallor. He fussed over her, but she insisted it was fine, looking at him with a grateful smile.

Cassie then caught a beautiful, yet vindictive stare watching her from a few feet away. The woman it belonged to was tall, skinny, and had long black hair that flowed almost to her waist. She watched Victor like she wanted to devour him, or be devoured, Cassie couldn't be sure. When the woman's gaze was on Cassie, she felt as though there were a thousand tiny daggers flying her way.

The woman approached, talking in Spanish with Victor while Cassie tried her best not to look completely lost. Her voice soon started getting louder and louder, and she thrust her finger right in Cassie's face. She needed no translation as the girl spat harsh words regarding his new arm candy. Without any hesitation, he struck the woman. The blow sent her flying onto the ground, and she clambered to her knees, peering up at him and begging without a care for who might be listening. She must've only been eighteen or nineteen years old, and Cassie's heart broke for her despite her rude words and evil glances.

Although, once again, Cassie could not understand her words, she could sense this young woman's pain, and quickly figured it out. Victor had dismissed her as his lover in preference of Cassie, and this girl had been left heartbroken. He didn't seem to care one little bit, his eyes darting up to a man whose face Cassie recognized from the plane. He approached and dragged the girl away.

Cassie didn't ask Victor to explain, nor did she show any reaction to the girl's dismissal. She stood still, remaining calm and collected beside him. When a second young girl sauntered up and kissed Victor's cheek seductively, Cassie readied herself for more shouting, but this woman was quite the opposite. She spoke to Victor in soft, hushed tones, and while he seemed more agreeable to her at first, he quickly grew bored and shooed her away with his hand. The girl shrugged and wandered off, trying her luck with another man, but she looked back at Victor every once in a while as though checking to see if he might be watching. Cassie made sure he never was.

The wake lasted well into the evening. She stayed silently by Victor's side the whole time, and after dark he finally took her for a walk around the grounds. He seemed to enjoy showing off his impressive complex, and stopped every now and then to kiss her or stroke her skin.

"You made this whole thing easier today. Having you beside me gave me strength," he told her, pressing Cassie into one of the huge trees that grew around the edges of his home.

"I'm glad. Thank you for doing as you promised. I realized today how many people loved your brother, and how hard this must've been on you. I know I'm the reason he's dead, and I'm sorry." She stroked his face in the moonlight, and she noticed his face fall a little.

"I wanted my brother dead for a long time, Cassie. You were the last of many reasons I had to kill him, so don't feel guilty," he replied, lifting her skirt so he could pull her thighs up around his waist. Cassie locked her feet behind him, not trembling at all as her slid his finger inside the hem of her panties and pulled them to one side, clearing the way for his erection.

Victor grinned, appearing to have picked up on the changes in her reaction to his touch. Her hands found his belt buckle, freeing his hardness before guiding him inside. He thrust into her, deep and powerful, while his lips silenced her delighted moans and his hands gripped her ass from beneath. When she came, her senses were overwhelmed, and Cassie saw stars for a moment before calming down. She rested her head on Victor's shoulder, kissing his neck softly as he continued to thrust into her.

It was then she sensed jealous and vindictive eyes on them. She looked up and saw the young woman who'd taken a slap from Victor earlier watching them from a nearby window. She wondered if he had taken her here on purpose, knowing they were beneath her room, showing the young woman she had been dismissed. Cassie couldn't be sure. She focused her eyes on Victor's again, kissing him deeply as he came, and ignoring their watcher above.

Chapter 25

Despite her fear and deep-seated hatred for the gangster who'd ripped her away from her home and the man she still loved, Cassie soon settled into her new life beside the Mexican drug-lord. Victor continued to be kind and genuinely affectionate with her, and she carried on playing her part as best she could. She was the dutiful lover, the trophy on his arm, and the submissive partner at all times. Cassie bit her tongue and forced her arguments aside no matter what, and Victor soon began showering her with expensive gifts and attention.

One night, he announced they were going to the nearby city and a nightclub he owned. He told Cassie to dress in her skimpiest outfit and highest heels, and seemed pleased with her choice. He asked her to walk up and down the bedroom for him, demanding she bend over to fasten the buckle on her shoes, and giving him full view of her scantily clad behind.

"Don't you dare bend over like that while we're out, otherwise you'll find yourself over my knee," he told her, grabbing her by the waist and leading her downstairs to their awaiting limo. She giggled but shook her head, leaning closer to him, and began nibbling at his ear.

"It's all for you, baby, every inch of me," she whispered. She squealed when he grabbed her by the waist and pulled her onto his lap. Victor kissed and fondled his lover while the car made its way into the city. He slipped his hand between her thighs and teased her clit with gentle strokes that had her writhing on his lap. It wasn't long until she bucked and shuddered with her release, moaning loudly for him.

"Fuck, you make me so hard," Victor told her. She knew exactly what he needed and gripped his hard cock as she released it. Cassie dropped to the floor, sinking it inside her lips, and sliding up and down his thick length until he came. She cleaned herself up and was back in her seat just in time for the car to come to a stop outside the busy nightclub. The queue was huge, but Victor led her right through the front doors. No one needed to ask his name, and as the powerful man's date she was greeted like royalty by the staff.

"My eyes will be on you at all times, Cassie. Stay close, and do not disappoint me," Victor warned, his tone warm, but his expression fierce. She looked across at him with a delicate smile as they made their way to the VIP area, and the hostess showed Victor to his table.

"I'm not going anywhere, not even to the dance floor. I'm afraid to say I can't dance for shit, baby," she told him. She shrugged when he laughed, and followed Grayson's lead over to a group of other women. They were chatting to each other in Spanish, and because of her limited grasp on the language, she said nothing as she hovered close by.

Cassie stood by a balcony overlooking the main dance floor. She watched the dancers below strut their stuff in a way she had never been able to. Grayson stood close by and kept watch while she waited patiently for Victor's meeting to be over.

***

Victor couldn't take his eyes off Cassie as she walked away, his gaze on her incredible legs. He took his seat at the table with the men he'd called to meet with him tonight, and caught their eyes on her too. They clearly approved of his new companion, but their gazes didn't linger long. He enjoyed the respect he commanded, and snapped his fingers, demanding their attention. Although Victor wanted to show Cassie off, he didn't like to share, at least until he was well and truly finished enjoying her.

The men talked for a while, deliberating over which one was worthy of becoming Victor's second in command. Now that he'd risen to the top, he needed to decide, and settled on one of his oldest and most trusted men, Eduardo. The group toasted his choice, and soon lined up shots of tequila to celebrate. They had far too many, and soon they were shouting loudly for the waitress to bring them more.

Victor ushered Cassie back over, and she did as he asked, hovering awkwardly when she arrived at the table. She smiled, waiting patiently for her orders, arranged in her submissive pose.

"Cassie, I have promoted Eduardo to be my second in command. I'd like to give him a present," Victor told her, eyeing her up and down. He wanted to show everyone he owned her, not caring that he was very drunk, so shouldn't really be making decisions.

"Congratulations, Eduardo. Would you like me to ask the waitress for another bottle of tequila and some cigars?" Cassie offered, looking over at Victor timidly.

"No, baby. I'd like you to give him your panties," he replied with a challenging stare, daring her to say no. He knew her ass was barely covered by the dress as it was, and by removing her panties she would feel exposed and vulnerable, but he wanted to test her. Cassie did as she was ordered, slipping them off, and tucking her tiny thong into the breast pocket of Eduardo's suit jacket. He blushed but grinned broadly, thanking her in Spanish before Victor shooed her away again without a word. He enjoyed watching her walk away, tugging at the hem of her dress in an attempt to pull it down, and preserve what little dignity he'd left her with.

Victor's eyes settled on his trusty guard, Grayson. He'd been his first, and only, choice for the protector of his prize. He kept everyone away from her when Cassie resumed her position overlooking the balcony, protecting her from drunken propositions of men and women alike. This pale beauty, with her combination of long, skinny legs and in that tight, skimpy dress, was a vision of loveliness. Cassie was a stunning contrast to the dark-skinned, curvier women who frequented the club, and Victor could tell she wasn't enjoying the attention.

Victor noticed how she kept one eye on Grayson the entire time, seeming grateful for his protection, but he wasn't jealous of their blossoming closeness. He was pleased with her in so many ways, and knew Grayson was a big factor in why she seemed so happy here.

When it was time to go, Cassie appeared glad. She had to climb carefully into the limousine, holding her dress down to cover her ass, and she crossed her legs tightly when Victor invited his men to ride back to the complex with them. Eduardo didn't take his eyes off her, and Cassie seemed relaxed, but held onto Victor tightly the entire time.

***

When they reached the complex, Cassie set off toward her bedroom, but Victor stopped her. He put an arm around her waist tightly and led her into the house through the large hallway with his men. They came upon a room filled with scantily clad women dressed in even less than Cassie, who were ready to provide Victor's guests with whatever they needed. He saw to it that his men were comfortable before taking a seat and lighting a cigar.

When Victor patted his knee, Cassie climbed into his lap, groaning uncontrollably when he forbade her from crossing her legs, and his hands stroked her inner thighs. She was grateful the other men were now occupied, and their gazes were off her, but she still felt uncomfortable. When most of the men disappeared off to the guest rooms with their chosen partners, she expected Victor to take her upstairs out of sight, but instead he unzipped his fly.

"I want you." He pulled her around so she straddled his lap. In his drunken haze, he didn't seem to care who was left behind with them, and pulled her dress over her head as Cassie began riding him. Victor threw it to the floor and cupped her large breasts before sliding them free of their satin cups. His mouth covered each nipple in turn, sucking on them hard. She cried out, but didn't stop him.

Cassie felt eyes on her, but desperately tried to ignore them. Eventually she could not stop herself from opening her own eyes, and she caught Eduardo watching her from just a few feet away. His sinister grin gave her the creeps, while a woman rode him in the exact same way she was doing with Victor. She focused her attention back on her lover, laying her head on his shoulder until he finally came. She hastily grabbed her dress and pulled it on, then cleaned them both up.

Victor's slow-moving body took her lead, climbing up off of the chair after her with a groan, and he followed her upstairs to her room. Once inside, Cassie stripped him off and they climbed under the sheets without another word. Victor fell asleep, snoring within seconds, but Cassie barely slept that night. Her mind kept going back to the eyes she'd felt on her so many times over the night. The horrible knowledge that she'd caught Eduardo's attention gave her chills. She knew she would have to be very careful with Victor's second in command now, and decided she would find a way to take him down if she had to. Cassie knew she couldn't ever let Eduardo have his way with her. Doing so would forever taint her in Victor's eyes. For sheer self-preservation, she could never allow that.

Thankfully, Cassie didn't see Eduardo for weeks following that night, and wondered if his boss might've warned him off. Victor hadn't said anything to her about what had happened, and it wasn't his nature to apologize, but he'd been very quiet the morning after their evening at the club, and had been extra vigilant with Cassie's seclusion ever since. She also found those same panties she'd been ordered to give Eduardo washed and put back in her drawer the week after, a clear signal he'd been ordered to return them. Victor never spoke of it again, so didn't say a word to confirm or deny her suspicions, but he also made a point of never again taking her to the nightclub on his arm.

Chapter 26

After a few more weeks of welcome captivity, Grayson came to wake Cassie with his usual breakfast of coffee and a homemade muffin, informing her that Victor had instructed him to take her into the nearby town so she could choose a dress to wear for a party that night.

"He's not got time to choose one for you, so I've been told to take you to a small boutique and help you choose something," he told her, grinning broadly.

Cassie jumped out of bed and squealed in delight. It had been so long since she'd been allowed to wander around free from envious stares and hard-nosed criminal glances. She couldn't wait, and knew it would be lovely going out into the world outside these walls, and without Victor's hand holding her tightly, even if it was only for a short while.

"Oh my gosh! I'm so excited, GG," she told him. Grayson rolled his eyes, but continued to smile. Cassie had grown close with him during her time here, and despite her constant smile, she got the impression Grayson could see through it. Right now, she knew her eyes were alight. Her happiness was rolling off her like a wave of pent up emotion she'd hidden away for so long, but now Cassie felt truly delighted.

Grayson helped her get ready, and together they made their way out of the complex onto the dirt roads. Cassie sat in the back while Grayson drove, her happiness still buzzing in her veins, and she watched with a wide smile as the dirty, barren world beyond Victor's walls whizzed by.

"We need to buy something that fits the theme, which is black and white. You're wearing white, as per Victor's orders. It's a fancy ball, but he wants nothing extravagant," Grayson informed her, his eyes flicking up at her as he drove. "I hope I don't need to remind you how much he's trusting you with this? I'll be expected to give him a full report of your behavior, Cassie, and you know I won't lie for you." He turned onto a main highway, and she saw a sign signifying they were heading west, but didn't concern herself with reading the others as they sped along.

"You gonna write him a step-by-step report? Or does Victor prefer essays?" she teased.

"I'm not kidding. I want you to stay with me the entire time. Don't ever wander off, and you certainly don't try and run away. You know the punishment would be severe if you did," he added, his concern for her safety written on his face. He maintained his businesslike tone as he went over the rules, but he really didn't need to.

Laura Morgan

Cassie was no fool. She knew the risks far outweighed any chances she had of actually getting away, and she also presumed Victor's ultimatum still applied. If she ran, he would no doubt be on his plane headed for New York within hours, and her friends would be punished for her foolishness. They were forever on her mind, even now. Cassie kept going for them and their safety. She would keep on going as long as she had to, because no matter the life she might have with Victor, her heart belonged there. A huge part of her was still with Hanna, Jamie, Mrs. Brown, and especially Leo. Cassie knew she would die if she ever let them come to harm.

"Save me the lecture, GG. Today is the best day of my life, and I'm sure as hell not going to ruin it by being a dumbass," she retorted, making him smile.

It wasn't long until they reached a small town, which was definitely not one of the big cities Grayson had told her about. It was a single street lined with shops, salons, and an ice-cream parlor. Grayson took Cassie's arm, holding her close, and she didn't fight it.

"Can I have *anything* I want?" she asked him, and Grayson nodded. "From any shop, or just the dress store?" Cassie added, knowing she was being cheeky, but it couldn't hurt to ask.

"He told me to bring you into town, and you could buy whatever you wanted. He specified that you had to come back with a dress, but other than that there were no limitations. If you wanna visit the other stores, I don't mind. Just as long as you're being a good girl," Grayson replied, raising one eyebrow.

"Calm down, GG. There's only one place I want to go after the dress store, I promise. And I'll be a good girl, pinkie swear." She lifted her little finger in the air, and he shook his head.

Grayson led the way to a boutique a short walk up the quiet street. He walked fast, too fast for Cassie's liking, as she was trying to take it all in. She wanted to savor her tiny dose of freedom, but followed his lead and didn't argue once. That was her way of life nowadays, and she wasn't intending to ruin her morning of relative freedom.

When they were inside the store, Cassie's mouth dropped open. The place went really far back, so was deceptively large. Inside were rows and rows of stunning dresses in every color imaginable. The young woman behind the counter greeted them warmly. Cassie understood most of what she was saying, thanks to her daily teachings from Grayson, but he was the one who did the talking. He described her needs to the tall, slender woman, who nodded and led them toward the rail of light colored dresses. She held out a few to Cassie, who eyed them with a smile. Grayson finally let go of her arm, and she followed the woman into the changing rooms to try a few on.

"Leave the door open, please," Grayson called to Cassie. She could tell he needed her in his sight at all times, and pulled a face, but did as he asked. Grayson had seen her naked many times by now, and she wasn't shy about stripping in front of the saleswoman. In an odd way, she was grateful for

Victor's dismissiveness of her body consciousness because it had helped her finally get over her issues, albeit forcefully.

"You are English?" the lady asked, helping Cassie out of her dress, and she nodded.

"Yes, do you speak any?" She was glad when the woman nodded.

"A little. This is good for your skin," she told her, rolling her r's softly. She laid a soft white satin dress against Cassie's pale arm before replacing it with a piece of lace. The contrast was very different against her pink skin tone. The satin looked amazing, the two light colors complimenting one another, whereas the lace made her look even paler. The see-through fabric drained her of what little color she had, and Cassie could tell right away the satin would be the better choice.

"Thank you, can I try some in this material please?" Cassie replied. She smiled, and the woman quickly began lining up gowns for her to try.

After over an hour of trying on dress after dress, she finally found the perfect one. It was sophisticated, covering her cleavage, and flowing all the way down to the floor, with a split up one side. Even Grayson's eyes lit up when he saw her in this dress. The woman gasped when she saw Cassie, so she knew right away she had to get this one.

"Perfect, and these," the woman said, handing her a set of matching shoes and a clutch. "For lipstick." She patted the small purse with a wink.

The dress was soon packed up, along with the shoes and purse. Grayson paid the bill while Cassie fiddled with some jewelry to the side of the register, trying on rings and bangles.

She'd adored being here, and even loved how long it had all taken. If she could've dragged out their shopping trip a little longer, she would have. Soon she would be back home, confined to her room.

Despite still feeling as though Victor had her in his own little prison, that room had also become her safe place. In there she was away from all the criminals and whores who lived in the complex with them. She understood he needed them all close. It was an unfortunate necessity, but she wished she had some freedom inside their walls. To be able to wander down to the pool and take a swim, or rest on a lounger whenever she wanted, was nothing more than a fantasy. Instead she stayed upstairs with her bodyguard, and the door forever locked.

When they left the store, Cassie having said a cheerful farewell to the kind owner, Grayson took her arm again and led her toward the car.

"You promised. Just one quick stop, I won't be long." She smiled up at him while batting her lashes, and he groaned, checking his watch.

"You've got ten minutes," he replied, stowing the dress and the other boxes in the trunk. Cassie noticed there seemed to be one more than before. She only needed one for the dress, and a couple for the accessories. She wasn't sure what else he might've bought, but didn't say anything. Cassie had seen the woman delicately folding her new dress, and carefully wrapping her shoes and bag in tissue paper before boxing them, but nothing else. She wondered if perhaps she hadn't noticed a jacket or sash being added while she was trying on the jewelry.

"Ten is all I need, GG," Cassie replied, pulling him over the road toward a small art supply store. He hesitated, pulling her back, but she pressed on. "You promised," Cassie reminded him before yanking him inside.

She picked out a few blank sketchpads in various sizes, a pack of pencils, and some pastel crayons. It was a tiny dent compared to what she would've bought if given the chance, but Cassie didn't want to push her luck. She handed her small stack of things to the owner, who smiled kindly and began bagging them up. Grayson paid the man and then led her away, checking his watch again, and then depositing Cassie in the back of the car. He kept the bag of art supplies in the front with him, and gave Cassie a warning look when she leaned forward to grab them.

"I need to ask first," he told her as he started the car and headed back in the direction of the complex.

"It's not like I tried to buy a phone, or a computer, or something stupid. I just want to draw. I need something to occupy my time," Cassie replied, pouting.

"I know, but I still gotta okay it," Grayson said. He was then quiet for the rest of the journey. Cassie watched out the window as the small town faded away, and the barren land came back again.

When they reached the complex, Grayson led her upstairs with the boxes in his hands and the bag of art supplies hanging from his wrist. She longed to grab them, to put her fraught feelings onto the paper, and express herself the only way she truly knew how. Cassie had been creative her whole life. She'd studied art in college, and had loved her job painting and decorating sets on the West End and Broadway. Hopes of becoming an actress had never been a factor in any of it. Her passion had always been for the design and the artistic elements of the storytelling. She had helped with costume design and painted the actors' faces, relishing anything creative she could get her hands on, and now she was itching to draw something, anything.

"Go take a shower," Grayson told her once they were in her room, laughing when she pouted again and crossed her arms in a blatant huff. Cassie soon did as she was told, though. She sauntered off for a welcome blast of cool water against her sweat-dusted skin, and pulled her hair from its tight ponytail. After stripping and climbing in, Cassie rubbed the shower gel Victor had chosen for her all over her body. After a quick towel dry, she pulled on a robe and wandered back into the bedroom. The bag with the pads and pencils was placed casually on the table under the window, and Cassie longed to touch them, but didn't dare.

Grayson had left her alone for now, no doubt giving Victor his report on their outing. Leaving the supplies where they were, she moved to the closet. Her lovely new dress hung there already, the shoes and bag not far away. Cassie ran her hands over the delicate satin of her new purchase, smiling to herself, and she hoped Victor would be pleased with her choice.

This one item was all hers. Cassie knew this

dress would always signify her wonderful morning of freedom and Victor's trust in her, and hoped she would always have it hanging in her closet to remind her of this lovely feeling. She soon began humming as she pulled on some panties and a bra, one of the Broadway show tunes she knew all too well from her days working behind the scenes. Before long, she was singing at the top of her lungs in a vibrant, operatic tone, a talent she rarely showed off. She picked a bright pink dress to wear, the color matching her bright mood, and she stepped out to find Victor standing inside the doorway waiting for her, his face like thunder.

"Victor, baby. I didn't hear you come in. I'm sorry, I would've greeted you sooner," she said, feeling nervous under his dark gaze. She stepped closer, trying to read him.

"Why do you want those things?" he asked, looking over her shoulder at the bag of supplies, and she cringed. Cassie knew she should've asked him first, but when she'd seen that store, she hadn't been able to help herself.

"You know I draw and paint pictures. I just want to be able to let out some of my creativity, and you were so generous letting me go and buy that dress today, I wanted to give you a present in return. I want to draw for you." She closed the gap and wrapped her arms around his shoulders.

"You just want to draw?" he asked, looking slightly confused.

"Yes, that's all. You can look at every single thing I do. I won't tear out any pages to put in the bin. You can check everything," she told him, laying a soft kiss on his lips, and Cassie felt Victor begin to relax. "You can trust me, baby. I'm all yours."

"Yes, you're mine." He grabbed Cassie by the waist and pulled her against his powerful body. The breath rushed out of her, but he held her tight, seeming unwilling to let her go. Cassie let him, hoping he was enjoying her touch and the feel of her lips against his.

"Let me show you." Her voice was quiet, full of need, and he thrust his hands into her hair. He yanked her head back and devoured her, sliding his tongue inside and commanding every one of her senses.

"Get on the bed," he murmured into her parted lips, grinning darkly. "And I want that dress gone," Victor added, following her over to her huge bed. Cassie did as he asked, pulling off the dress. Just as she was about to climb up onto the silk sheets, Victor's hand grabbed her neck from behind. The other came around in front, and held his thick, curved knife to her throat. She hadn't even heard him remove it from the sheath, but she stayed perfectly still while she waited for his next move. Fear rose up, creating that strange numbness again, and Cassie could tell he was surprised to find her taking slow, calm breaths.

"To be a true submissive is to be both rewarded and punished by your master," Victor whispered in her ear. "But the dominator needs to own every inch of their sub's body. Every thought and feeling you have belongs to me. I thought we'd gotten rid of your demons, Cassie. If we had, you wouldn't have these urges to disobey me. You made the decision to buy those things without asking me first, which is a clear sign you're still resisting my ownership of you. It's time you were punished."

"No, baby. Please," Cassie whimpered, her body starting to tremble. Victor silenced her pleas when he dug the knife into her neck. She could tell it was only the blunt edge against her skin, but still Victor was deadly with it. She didn't dare underestimate him, or his ability to cut her in whatever way he pleased, knowing she'd never be able to fight back.

"My brother gave me this knife. He trained me to use it, and since that day I've been a killer, a drug-dealer, and a cold-hearted gangster. But since you came into my life, this knife has become something more. It is a constant reminder of who I am now, rather than who I used to be." He ground his hips into hers, pushing his hard-on against her ass, and Cassie groaned. Her hands reached back and found his hips, gripping them hard.

"I used the same knife Luis gave me to murder him in cold blood, and I did it for you." Victor pulled the knife away and pushed her down on the bed. He flipped her over and slid the knife over her trembling face and torso. Victor didn't cut her, but she held still and panted, satisfying his dominant urges. He couldn't seem to resist pushing her harder, and continued down to her panties. Victor sliced right through the sides of the material and pushed Cassie's thighs open. He lowered the material covering her mound, leaving her completely on show to him, but she didn't dare shy away.

She cried out and tears fell down her temples

when Victor slid the knife over her opening. He delicately traced the lines of her scars with the blade while she completely fell apart. The frenzy of fear, anger, and the traumatic auto-response to the blade's touch overwhelmed her. All Cassie could think about was Jonah. The memory of the blinding pain when he'd cut into her body, and the vision of blood as it had pooled between her thighs made her scream.

"Your past suffering is mine now, Cassie. Let it go, and don't ever let it hurt you again. I own that memory, along with all your past, present, and future. Trust me to take care of everything." Victor pressed one of the flat sides of the cold metal against her core, and she cried out in shock.

Cassie's tears quickly ceased, her mind stopped racing, and her body finished its trembling. She suddenly felt calm. The knife was still there, the pressure on her clit was undeniable. She hated knowing a blade was against her intimate area again, but at the same time, she trusted Victor was not going to hurt her with it. She leaned up onto her elbows and peered down at him, her face puffy from the tears, but she was now strangely calm. It was though a huge weight had been lifted from her shoulders.

"You won't hurt me, will you, baby?" she said, more of a statement than a question. "I can trust you." Cassie stared into Victor's deep brown eyes, and he nodded. He pulled the knife away from her and slipped it back into its sheath on his hip.

Victor climbed over her on the bed, unbuttoning his pants as he went, and pressed his rock-hard length into her now very wet opening. They both came quickly, Cassie shocking herself after already unraveling in other ways thanks to his forceful tactics. Victor then held her for a while afterward, soothing his lover as she held onto him tight, feeling raw and desperate for his loving embrace.

Chapter 27

"I cannot stay, my love. I'll see you later for the party. Wear your new dress, and do everything Grayson asks of you. Never forget your promises to me," Victor told her, climbing out of bed.

"Never," Cassie whispered, kissing him again. He pushed her away gently, as though having to force himself to step away, and he left, locking the door behind him. She still felt very strange at having taken a huge step in her submission, but was glad she'd trusted him. Despite his severe tactics, she felt happy and free.

She was glad she was able to calm Victor down and appease his paranoia regarding her purchases. Cassie wondered what he presumed she was planning on doing with them. Surely he couldn't think she would be sending letters to Leo somehow? Or perhaps he had convinced himself she would pass notes with cries for help written inside to shop keepers and maids? Either way, she wasn't that stupid. Cassie knew she was playing the long game here, her time as Victor's lover locked up in her tower was frighteningly infinite. If she ever left the confines of this place, it would only be after countless hours of planning, or perhaps if Leo ever attempted a rescue.

Despite their recent progression, Cassie was sure if she ever managed to pull the wool over Victor's eyes and carry out a cunning escape, it would only be after years of perfecting her role, and having gained his trust. The element of surprise would be the only thing she would ever have going for her.

Cassie spent the rest of the early afternoon drawing in her new sketchpad. She felt wonderful, enjoying as she let her mind wander, and the pictures soon came into fruition on the page. She was careful not to draw Leo, even though his face was still constantly on her mind. She drew Hanna and Jamie as two star-crossed lovers, finding their way to each other through a dark and dismal village. On the very first page, though, sat Victor's portrait. She drew every contour of his face perfectly, every line of his smile, and the glint he had in his eye when he looked at her. This was her favorite look of his by far, the gaze she was rewarded with when her domineering lover was pleased with her. She took more time on his drawing than any of the others. This one needed to be perfect.

"That's amazing," Grayson said from behind her, making Cassie jump. She blinked up at him, having to focus her eyes after working so closely for hours. The time had whizzed by at super-speed, something she was grateful for, because it let her know she needn't be bored during her long days of solitude in the future. Victor had given her this, and she endeavored to never give him a reason to take it away again.

"Thanks, GG. Is it time to get changed already?" She checked the clock on the wall, and he nodded.

"Clean your hands first," he joked, pointing at her pastel-covered hands, with smudges that went all the way up to her elbow on her left arm. Cassie laughed and stood, heading off to the bathroom to get cleaned up. While in there, she also washed her face, reviving her tired mind, and stared into the mirror. Her real self was reflected back at her. Cassie was shocked, and tried desperately to get back into the character she'd created for herself, but the realization dawned on her, she no longer had a role to play. This was her now. She had become Victor's submissive lover for real. Cassie had crossed over from acting, to it becoming real without realizing it, and it scared the hell out of her.

In that moment, she knew she'd lost herself to him, and didn't know if she would ever find her old self again. There was a part of her that liked this new safe numbness, though. Leo had never taken her fears away, like Victor had today. As hard as it was to admit to herself, Leo had only seemed to add to her burdens, and the part of herself that missed him diminished a tad as resentment took its place.

Cassie realized she'd been staring into the mirror for a long while, and shook it off. She finished up, spraying herself with a fresh layer of deodorant, and putting on a generous layer of body lotion before heading back into the bedroom. Grayson was waiting for her, the new dress at the ready, and she stepped into it. He zipped up the back and ran his fingers through her long hair, teasing the waves gently to check they looked good against the white satin.

"Hmm, up or down?" he mumbled, looking over Cassie's shoulder into the mirror, and she turned her head from side to side.

"I think it looks nice down. What do you think Victor will like?"

"I very much doubt he'll even notice," Grayson replied, making Cassie blush. He touched up her makeup and pinned the front of her hair back in some bejeweled clips. He pulled it away from her face slightly, rather than tie it up, and seemed pleased with the results.

Before long, she was sliding into her new shoes and holding her clutch at the ready. Grayson stood beside her, offering Cassie his arm. She was surprised Victor had not come for her himself, but she took his elbow without question. The two of them strolled down the empty hallway and through the eerily quiet foyer, heading toward the front of the mansion where Grayson helped her into the waiting car.

"Victor's meeting us there," he told her, smiling as he took the driver's seat and drove them out of the complex. They headed back in the direction they'd driven toward the small town, but carried on past it for a long while. Cassie wasn't sure where they were going, or what to expect when she got there, but hoped their evening out would be fun. She envisioned lots of beautiful gowns, posh Mexican men wearing tuxedos and smoking cigars, but soon realized she had no idea of the kinds of parties Victor attended outside the complex. Other much more sordid ideas soon filled her mind. Cassie imagined masquerade balls where the attendees swapped partners, one of the few types of parties she'd refused in Manhattan. She imagined rooms full of sweaty men all pawing at their dates, the very idea making her skin crawl.

Cassie was still lost in thought even as they began slowing down. They eventually came to a stop outside a huge building that looked almost like a library, except for the huge cross that towered at the top of the steeple overhead, and Cassie immediately froze.

"GG, what are we doing here?" she asked, but he didn't answer. After climbing out, he simply opened the door, took her arm, and led Cassie to the base of the steps that went up to the huge wooden door. She was panting for breath, her eyes wide with fear as they stood there, and her mind raced as she wondered was going to happen inside.

Chapter 28

Leo snorted another line of cocaine, and downed the rest of his vodka, sending the empty bottle hurtling toward the wall with a roar. He hadn't heard anything from Victor since he'd taken Cassie away, and it was killing him. He couldn't stand that she had sacrificed herself for him. He was here, free and alone, while she was down in Mexico at Victor's command. He knew without any doubt that Victor would've expected her to fuck him. Leo imagined her being tortured, beaten, and emotionally manipulated. Visions of her locked up somewhere in his compound, scared to death and alone, haunted him.

Leo was furious he'd been so foolish. He never should've allowed himself to get close to her, and especially not let Cassie sacrifice her freedom for him. He'd known from the moment he chose his criminal existence that he would most likely die young. It was the exact reason he'd never sat on his money all these years. If he wanted to do something, he would. If he wanted to buy something, he did. But now there was only one thing on his mind, and Leo hated knowing there was nothing he could do to stop the awful things he was imagining Victor doing to that beautiful body and spirit.

Tina hobbled into his office, still relying on a walking stick. Her face was pale and her expression pained. In fact, her entire demeanor had changed since those terrible few days in his home. Victor had beaten and shot her during his interrogation. Leo had watched the entire thing, even as Victor's men laughed at her pleas for mercy, before some had raped her. She was alive, and that was all that mattered, but he wondered what sort of life it now was. He no longer dominated his assistant the way he had before. In fact he pitied her, and had done everything he could to keep her safe since. Tina placed a fresh bottle of vodka on the desk and sat down opposite him, glancing at her boss timidly.

"So, what are we going to do?" she asked. "You can't go on like this. You need to reach out to him."

"I know. I'm gonna go down there, see him face to face. I need to know if she's okay," Leo replied, running his hands over his face and then up into his messy hair in angst. "Then I'm going to kill the bastard."

***

Grayson half led, half dragged Cassie up the steps and into the church. Her hands gripped his forearm tightly. She didn't dare say a word, and Grayson thankfully paid no attention to her unmasked fear. When they were inside, the congregation stood and looked back at her. Their faces seemed pulled into fake smiles, and she barely recognized a single face there. She looked down the incredible length of aisle before them, her eyes settling on the massive grin she found at the end of it—Victor's. Cassie forced herself to smile back, only managing what she assumed must be more of a petrified smirk, but hoped she looked convincing enough.

"Don't you dare let me walk up there alone, GG," she mumbled, sensing Grayson was trying to pull away so she could walk toward Victor alone. She needed him to keep her steady, but it was no use. He thrust a bouquet into her hands and slid a diamond band into her hair that pinched behind her ear. In one fluid move, he pulled forward a veil attached to the band that covered her face, and went right down to her stomach. The back of the veil was even longer, and trailed down almost to the floor.

The organist began to play, and Grayson laid a hand at the small of Cassie's back, pushing her off for her lonely walk to Victor's side. She stared down the long walkway, taking deep breaths, and desperately tried to stop herself from running or fainting. Cassie hated this, hated him, and everything about what he'd done.

She mentally kicked herself for not realizing sooner. Nobody wore white dresses to a ball, why hadn't she picked up on the obvious hint that morning? Cassie knew she'd been so excited about being let out for a shopping trip, and hadn't thought about it all properly. There would've been nothing she could do about it anyway, but at least she would've had time to mentally prepare herself. Now, she felt like a cornered animal, afraid and ready to strike, should anything push her further over the edge.

When Cassie finally reached the altar, Victor stepped forward and took her hand in his. The affectionate gaze and loving smile he gave her made this a little easier, but she was still scared. She wished she felt the same way about him, but she didn't. There was no doubt about it, regardless of her role-playing having apparently ended, she knew she didn't love him. Unfortunately there was also no going back, no getting out of this. Cassie took a deep breath and followed Victor's lead, moving in whatever way he ushered her, and saying the words as he indicated. Before she knew it, the rings were on their fingers, and they were pronounced husband and wife.

Victor pulled back the veil and kissed Cassie. He kept from performing anything too elaborate in front of the priest, but his show was more than enough to incur a few cheers from the men in the front rows. He chuckled as he pulled away, giving Cassie the happiest look she had ever seen, and she couldn't help but soften. She hoped this meant his infatuation had turned into something stronger. She was convinced she sensed his love and respect for her, and hoped she might have a little more freedom as his wife, but didn't get her hopes up.

The pair of them linked hands and walked back down the aisle together, grinning as cheers and calls of encouragement followed. Outside, they posed for photographs while their guests threw rice and cheered for the happy couple. They all seemed overjoyed by their union, and Cassie carried on following Victor's lead, still in shock. Before climbing into the back of a white limo, Cassie tossed her bouquet into the hands of her eager female guests, none of whom she recognized, but she smiled and waved at the young girl who'd caught it.

Once inside the car, Victor seemed unable to hold himself back and pounced on his new wife. He kissed every inch of skin he could reach in the short time they had.

"Why did you keep it a secret, baby?" Cassie asked. Her hands stroked his cheek, and she looked at him with the most affectionate gaze she could manage.

"I wanted it to be a surprise. I knew you'd be scared, so I put it all together as a gift," Victor replied, sliding his hand up the slit of her dress. "You've been such a good girl, especially this morning when you surrendered to me so entirely. I promised your rewards would be everything you'd ever dreamed of. Now you are married to one of the richest men in the country, Cassie. I belong to you now, just as you belong to me. I want to make you happy."

"You already make me happy, Victor. You've been so wonderful, and you've done everything you promised. Now that I'm your wife, I won't stop being everything you want me to be. I will love you as much as I can, and I'll show you every day how grateful I am for your gifts," she replied, lying through her teeth. She purposely hadn't said she loved him, but that she would love him as much as she could, which for now was barely a tiny bit.

It wasn't long until their limo pulled up outside a posh looking restaurant, and the newlyweds climbed out. They were the first to arrive at what Cassie could only assume was their wedding reception. He led her around the back to a stunning garden. It was already set up with trellises and a white marquee, under which sat elegantly dressed tables and a small dance floor with a stage. It was truly beautiful, and she finally began to appreciate the effort he'd gone to. She leaned in close and kissed Victor's cheek, smiling across at him affectionately, and he grinned back at her.

"Who were all those people at the church, baby? I only recognized a few of them," she asked, wondering who had been part of their very personal day. None of them had been her guests. Cassie wondered if he'd even bothered looking into her family back home in England, but knew he couldn't have, otherwise they would've surely flown over. She was glad. Having to act out her happy role under their eyes would've been hard, and she would've spent the entire time hoping they were not about to catch her in the act, for their safety as well as her own.

"*Mi familia*," he told her in Spanish. "This is my home, Cassie. I brought you here to marry you in the church where I was baptized, and under the eyes of my people. That's how much you mean to me. I've been planning this for weeks," Victor told her, making Cassie's mouth drop open in shock. She quickly laughed it off, kissing her husband in a display worthy of applause.

"I truly am a very lucky lady. Thank you for doing all of this for me. Do they know I was married before? And that I'm not Catholic?" she asked, and Victor shook his head.

"Absolutely not, and you're never to tell. As far as they know, I'm just a businessman. They have no idea how I make my money, or how I live my life. Luis's death was put down to a motorcycle accident, in case anyone says anything. They barely speak a word of English, so I'm sure the conversation won't be plentiful." He laughed, pulling her closer for another kiss.

"Not like you, your English is perfect," she replied, and he seemed to enjoy the compliment.

"Luis taught me well." Victor tailed off, obviously not wanting to talk about him, and his face turned serious. "I expect you to stay on my arm. Do not ever leave my sight, Cassie. Rest assured, I have not dropped my guard where you're concerned. Grayson will not hesitate to slip you a sleeping pill and stuff you in the back of the car if you try anything silly. I'll just tell everybody you've gone to prepare for our wedding night." He held Cassie's arm a little too tightly for her liking, and she peered up into his eyes.

"You don't need to threaten me, Victor. I'm here aren't I? I just became your wife, surely you don't think I was lying up there in the eyes of God?" She felt sure she was going to Hell for having done just that. "There's no need to worry about anything other than having fun, and giving your wife the perfect wedding day. Did you at least buy me some sexy lingerie to wear for you later?" Cassie added, turning his attention away from the threats, and it seemed to work. Victor's features softened, and he released his hold. He leaned in, kissing her cheek and neck softly.

"You don't need any. With or without clothes, you're the most stunning woman I've ever seen. This dress is the most sublime thing you've ever worn, and I can't wait to rip it off you when we're alone tonight," Victor whispered, his voice a haughty groan, and she grinned. Deep down she sensed something change between them. It was a sudden awareness that he might finally have given her some power over him, and Cassie wondered to herself if Victor even realized how much.

Chapter 29

Victor wrapped one arm around Cassie's back, holding onto her tightly, and she immediately snuggled into him in an attempt to show her husband he needn't worry. She didn't know how many times he needed her to declare her promises, but wondered if he could tell she wasn't being sincere. Cassie almost felt a little guilty, but couldn't change the way she felt, no matter how hard she tried.

He pulled them back slightly to the entryway, ready to greet the guests. Before Cassie knew it, she was shaking hands and receiving hugs from various men and women. They all fussed over her affectionately, commented on her beauty, and complimented her pale skin. She'd learned enough Spanish to understand that much, but still had no eloquence when it came to speaking the language, so just smiled politely and let Victor speak for them both.

He explained how she spoke no Spanish, but was learning, and they all seemed pleased. They were clearly impressed when she showed understanding. Victor's mother, a chubby, dark haired woman, hugged her so tightly Cassie thought she might pop. She laughed when Mrs. Sanchez dropped her and nodded in appreciation.

"Good bones, many babies," she told her in pidgin English, making Cassie's cheeks burn, and Victor grinned. He spoke to his mother softly, and Cassie saw his even gentler side as he regarded her, seemingly pleased she'd given Cassie her approval.

"*Gracias Señora,*" Cassie replied, sliding back into her spot beside Victor, and he placed his protective hand at the small of her back again.

"Mama," Victor's mother corrected her, the sentiment in her tone making Cassie's eyes fill with tears. She gulped, desperately trying to fight them. The old woman noticed and immediately pulled her into a proper hug, running her hands over her back affectionately, and she wrapped her hands around the rotund woman. When they pulled back, Mama Sanchez kissed Cassie's cheek and placed her back in Victor's arms with a warm smile. She then spoke to her son, and Cassie understood every word. They made her smile so wide her tears were soon forgotten.

Mrs. Sanchez had, in no uncertain terms, told her son to take care of his lovely wife, and he'd better make her the happiest woman alive, or else she would take him across her knee.

Victor laughed at her threat, politely reminding his mother he was no longer a boy. He did promise not to disappoint her, planting a passionate kiss on Cassie's lips that earned them a loud cheer from the other waiting guests.

The party that soon ensued was wonderful. They cut the huge cake, had their first dance, and there were many speeches from Victor's family. Everyone wished them well and instructed Victor to take good care of her, and bring Cassie home more regularly so they might get to know his new bride better. When it was Victor's turn, he stood and raised a glass. He asked the crowd to toast his new wife, and they all did, while Cassie felt herself blush, but smiled up at him affectionately.

"This woman has stolen my heart and soul for all eternity. Forever mine, as I am hers. I will love her for as long as she will allow, and then longer," he said, surprising Cassie by talking in English first, and then repeating the speech in Spanish. The crowd before them cheered loudly and toasted the happy couple one last time. Mama Sanchez started crying, as did Luis's widow, and Victor held his hand out to Cassie, ushering for her to stand beside him. She smiled while Victor showed off his prize with a clear sense of pride.

At the end of their wonderful wedding reception, Victor led Cassie out to the waiting limo, and they said their goodbyes. Cassie already felt like part of his family in some strange way, even though this entire thing still felt so surreal. She hoped in time she would come to love Victor, but for now she would settle for knowing he loved her, and would do anything to make her happy. This was a far better position than Cassie had thought she'd find herself in down here, and she was determined to keep things this way.

She followed his lead, climbing into the limo and sliding over to let him join her, and the driver whisked them away. Cassie assumed they would return to the complex, but instead the car pulled into a private driveway just a few minutes down the road, and large iron gates opened to let them pass.

A stunning house sat before them. It was quaint, yet beautiful in terracotta brick, and most importantly, it was all theirs. Victor led Cassie inside, his men having prepared and secured the place before disappearing again. Cassie knew they wouldn't be far and would keep watch, but no one would be permitted inside the house now that the newlyweds had arrived.

Cassie giggled loudly as Victor swept her into his arms and carried her across the threshold. He kissed her lips before settling his wife back on the ground. She took it all in. The house was lovely and homely, the size far from that of his huge mansion, and she liked the feel of it. Floor-to-ceiling windows looked out onto the garden, showing a pool and terrace outside. Cassie desperately wanted to take a dip, and realized it would be the first swim she'd had since arriving in Mexico.

Victor stepped close behind her, looking out at the night's sky over his wife's shoulder. He moved her long hair to one side so he could kiss her neck, while his hands pulled at the zipper on her dress. When the gown was off, he placed it carefully to one side, apparently having decided against ripping it off her, and Cassie grinned. She watched as he eyed her white satin bra and panties with an appreciative stare. They matched the material of her dress perfectly, and she felt amazing.

After kicking off her shoes, she wandered over to him, climbing up into his arms. She wrapped her legs around his waist while he carried his bride up to the bedroom.

"You make me so happy, Cassie. How can I make you happy tonight?" he asked, setting her down on the bed and slipping off her underwear. She sensed his desperate need to touch and taste her, and cried out as he stroked her folds. Victor slid his tongue inside her aching cleft, his thumb rubbing her clit with just the right amount of pressure. It was just a few seconds before a wave of pure ecstasy washed over her, gushing her juices into his mouth, and he groaned appreciatively. "Yes, baby," he whispered, his tongue sliding up over Cassie's stomach as he placed his wet kisses all over her torso.

"I want you hard and deep, Victor. Don't stop, even if I ask you to," she said, looking down at him with a cheeky smile. Cassie's core tensed as she remembered saying the same words the morning she'd spent with Leo, but of course, Victor had no idea. He stood and slowly removed his suit, placing it neatly over a chair, all the while watching her with a dark and brooding look. She loved it, especially the sly smile curling at his lips as he seemed to be thinking it over.

"I don't think you realize what you are asking of me. I'm very much used to fucking girls hard and deep. Saying no was never an option for any of them, but I never wanted that for you. I want to make love to you, but never force you. I want you to scream yes, but never tell me no. I want you to come for me over and over again, while I worship your body with mine," he said, staring at her intently. "Do you think you could do that?"

Cassie was on fire. She climbed up on the bed, her body going into overdrive at his powerful words. She raised her index finger, curling it so Victor came closer. When he reached her, she ran her fingertips over every inch of his brown skin she could reach. Her hand soon curled around his hard length, and she pulled him toward her, guiding him inside her already very wet cleft.

"Yes, Victor. Yes." Her voice was soft and quiet, and her lips trembled as she spoke the words. Cassie realized the place inside of her that had feelings for him was starting to expand, but she no longer cared. This was her life now, no matter what Leo had wanted for her, and for some reason this man adored her. In the time they'd been together he'd kept his word, and if this was second best, it was pretty damn good.

***

Victor's body was dripping with sweat, soaking Cassie as he leaned over her, but she didn't seem to care. Sweat was pouring from her naked body, too, and the bed beneath them was drenched. The sun was rising in the sky outside, and they'd not stopped making love since they'd arrived at the house the night before. He came again, pressing himself into her still clenching body, and finally climbed off. Victor lay beside his panting wife, taking her hand in his as he started to doze, but she roused him when she climbed up to go to the bathroom.

"I won't be long, baby." She ducked inside, but she left the door open, as though knowing he wanted to keep an eye on her.

Part of him wanted to follow her, but he knew it was too much. She had nowhere to go, and he knew he had to learn to trust her. Cassie had done everything he'd ever asked, even though she hadn't always wanted to. She'd thought she was fooling him with her fake affections, but he'd noticed the difference early on between the times she was genuinely responsive to his touch, and when she had forced herself to go along with it.

He'd seen the terrified look that had swept across her face the day before as she entered the church. She had managed to hide it from everyone except him, but he'd understood her reasons, and hoped he would never see that look on her face again. He thought back to the last few months with a smile. Cassie truly had been everything he'd bargained for in New York. It still shocked him how addicted he was to her. Victor knew their marriage had been rushed, but he didn't care. He wanted the security that having Cassie as his wife afforded him, and would never let her go.

"Hurry up, I'm getting cold!" he called.

"Yeah, yeah." Cassie's soft voice filtered in from the en-suite, and he grinned. Victor tried his best to be patient, imagining what she might be doing, while he listened to the running water and pulled the duvet up over his chilling flesh.

While lying there, he thought back to the person

he used to be before Luis gave him his knife and trained him to be a cold-hearted killer. Back when he was a boy, Victor had been a sensitive, loving soul. He'd been a mama's boy in his childhood and respected women. He would never have believed back then he would've turned into a man who took young girls into sexual slavery, sold their virginities to the highest bidders, and delivered beatings to anyone who tried to defy him.

He knew his men feared him, and he enjoyed it. After his initiations were over, Victor had gone on to kill his oldest friend, Carlos, because he had fallen in love with one of their girls. He'd hidden her from the other men to keep for himself. The fool had lost them countless hours of her service, so Luis had ordered Victor to torture him. When he'd confronted Carlos, he lied about the entire thing, trying in vain to cover up his wrongdoings, which only served to enrage Victor. In his anger, he'd killed him, and used it to send a warning to his other men. By that point in his life, Victor was far from the boy he'd once been, and he appreciated having the opportunity to offer his men a very poignant message, a message that was still whispered about to this day.

"I nearly sent you a search party," he teased when Cassie returned, and she rolled her eyes playfully. She smelled far better than he did, yet slid straight into his arms without hesitation and dirtied herself in his scent again without complaining. She snuggled into his hold, and he held her, the pair of them soon drifting off to a deep sleep.

***

When Cassie awoke a few hours later, Victor was still fast asleep beside her, and all she could think about was that swimming pool down in the garden. She climbed out of bed, surprised she hadn't woken him, and brushed her teeth before getting ready. After standing beside her sleeping husband for a moment, she gently shook him awake. Victor roused with a moan, and she quickly asked for his permission to go and use the pool.

"*Si, si,*" he mumbled, before turning over and going back to sleep. Cassie thanked him and practically skipped down the stairs in the new bikini she'd found in a suitcase at the end of the bed, with a towel tucked under her arm.

Thankfully, the pool was partially covered. Cassie dove straight in the deep end, grinning as she came up for air, and she then swam as many lengths as she possibly could. She enjoyed the workout, and feel of the cool water as it enveloped her otherwise hot body. She felt peaceful and carefree for the first time since she could remember.

She had no idea how long she had been in the water, but when she eventually stopped her lengths, she floated on her back for a while, staring up at the clear blue sky through the netted roof, awash in contentment. Cassie loved this more than she would ever admit, and she basked in the blissful glow she felt resonating from deep within.

A whiff of smoke disturbed her almost meditative session, and she pulled up to look around. Victor sat on one of the loungers, smoking a large cigar and watching her with a hard scowl.

"Hey, baby," she said, trying to sound calm, but she sensed he was angry. "You going to join me?" She swam over to the edge and peered up at her husband as best she could in the bright sunlight. He was wearing nothing but a robe, and he watched her for a few seconds with that same hard stare before finally answering.

"No. But I would like you to explain why I woke up alone on the first day of our married life." He calmly patted the lounger in front of him, indicating for her to come and sit with him. Cassie swallowed the lump in her throat and climbed up out of the water, trembling as she slowly stepped toward her husband, but it was not from the cold. If anything, the hot air dried her body within seconds of emerging from the cool water rather than give her a chill.

"I woke you. I asked if I was allowed to come for a swim, and you said yes," She mumbled her words, but she knew he could hear her clearly enough. Victor opened his legs and motioned for Cassie to sit between them, and she perched on the wooden chair's edge. "Please believe me, baby. You said yes." She knew she was pleading with him now, but his forced calm was making her feel uncomfortable, and she was desperate to make him see she hadn't sneaked out.

"Hmm. Now that you mention it, I *do* seem to remember telling you yes. Come here," he replied, his voice slightly softer, and she climbed onto her knees between his open thighs. Cassie placed her hands on his cheeks and leaned in for a kiss, tasting the cigar on his lips, but she didn't care. All she cared about was obtaining his forgiveness. She was telling the truth, he'd given her permission, but she also realized he'd been half asleep at the time, and hadn't necessarily known what he'd said. She'd been so excited to have her swim and had rushed it, rather than stay and wait for him to wake up properly. Cassie let out a yelp as Victor wrapped his arms around her tightly, catching her by surprise, but she let herself fall onto his lap while their lips remained locked.

"I'm not going anywhere, Victor. I promised. Did you worry?" she asked when she could finally pull away, realizing how he must've panicked at finding her gone, and he didn't reply. His expression told her she'd assumed correctly, though. Cassie knew she needed to make it up to him, so untied his robe and slid down to take his hard length in her mouth. Just like she had when she'd indulged in that threesome with Hanna and Jamie, she bent her body so her hips went as high as she could get them, while arching her back seductively to give her husband a good show.

She slid her mouth up and down his hard-on, taking him as far as she could, and Victor groaned in appreciation. His hands ran over her back and hips as she moved, and when he came he pressed the back of her head into him. The move deepened the connection, and before he let go, he leaned forward and brought one hand down on her ass cheek in a slap so hard she would've cried out if she weren't effectively gagged.

Cassie threw herself back and stared at him

angrily. She didn't dare say a word, but a single tear betrayed her resolve and slipped down onto her cheek. That had hurt, badly, and she wanted nothing more than to lash out at Victor in retaliation. She knew better than that, so seethed inside, rubbing at her backside to soothe it. Victor just smiled triumphantly and sat back in his seat, covering himself and taking a long draw of his cigar.

"You'll burn in this sun. You should go and wait in the bedroom for me," he told her, and Cassie shook her head, finally standing up to him just a little.

"I didn't do anything wrong!" she cried as another tear fell down her cheek. She stormed back in the house, grabbing a muffin and a coffee on her way upstairs in search of a shower. She most certainly was not going to the bedroom to wait for him.

When she emerged from the shower, Cassie slipped into one of the stunning dresses Victor had packed for her and applied some makeup. She spent the entire time trembling in anticipation of Victor's return, but he didn't come upstairs. Instead he stayed in the sun by the pool, seemingly waiting for something, and she eventually went back out to his side. She sat on the lounger beside him, opening the umbrella to provide her with some shade, and sat back silently. Her whole body was stiff as she awaited his response to her outburst.

"How's your ass?" Victor eventually asked, turning to face Cassie with a sly grin. "When I get cheek from you, your cheek gets the punishment, simple. Be a good girl from now on and you won't have to worry about it. But right now, I believe you owe me one more slap for the way you spoke to me." He appeared to enjoy reminding her outbursts were not acceptable.

Cassie hated the thought of him delivering another blow, but sensed he wanted her to go to him willingly. Victor clearly relished her timid submission. He watched with a satisfied smile as she stood and stepped over to him. She bent down so she was laid over his knee, and he lifted the dress up over her hips. Cassie's face was close to the floor on the other side of the lounger, and she braced herself with her palms on the warm ground. She had no idea when he would strike, but knew it would be painful, and closed her eyes tightly in anticipation.

When Victor's hand came down, her nose almost hit the ground, having been forced downward with the blow. She screamed in agony, writhing against his hold, but he pinned her down. The hand he'd used to spank her rubbed the sore spot to soothe it, before he stuck two fingers inside her cleft. He was drawing on pleasure to accompany the pain he'd delivered, and it worked. Cassie stopped squirming, her body focusing instead on the activity between her thighs, and she soon came for him.

When she sat back up, Cassie was in a whirlwind of emotion. She felt angry, yet afraid to infuriate her husband any further. She perched quietly, unable to sit on the lounger properly due to her stinging cheek, and Victor watched as tears she could not control slid down her face. Without a word, he pulled Cassie to her feet and up into his arms, kissing her before stepping forward. He jumped, sending them both straight into the deep end of the pool with a splash, rendering Cassie's efforts to get ready for the day useless.

"You're such an arse," Cassie said as she treaded water beside him, and Victor just shrugged and grinned. He pulled her over to him for another kiss, and she didn't fight him.

"I can't bear to see you cry, so I threw you in the pool," he said, stroking her face tenderly. "I have to own your tears as well as your smiles, you know?"

Chapter 30

Their one night turned into three when Victor informed his new wife he could spare a couple more. He seemed to enjoy having Cassie to himself away from the confines of the complex, and she had to admit she felt the same. In this tiny village, holed up in their home-away-from-home. Cassie loved it, even with his intrusive family stopping by unannounced more than once.

She continued to be the perfect lover, acquiescent to his every desire, and knew it wasn't an act. Cassie loved having freedom from her locked bedroom and wasn't looking forward to heading back into captivity again.

On their final night in the small town, Victor arranged to take his family out for dinner, all thirty of them. He booked the entire restaurant where they'd had their wedding reception. She'd overhead him on the phone earlier that afternoon, instructing the chef to give his guests whatever they wanted. He would cover the bill.

"You're very generous, baby." She stroked his

cheeks, running up through his dark brown hair while she kissed him, and he leaned into her touch as though savoring her compliment.

The pair joined his family, and they all settled down to a delicious feast. Everyone chatted loudly and spoke with their mouths full. The women criticized each other's dress sense and choice of hairstyle, and the men talked sports and cars. The din of conversation and laughter was intense, all of them so incredibly loud, but Cassie felt at ease and happy in their company. She was just about managing to follow the discussions, but was still unable to talk back much. Victor's mother and cousins tried to ask her where she was from, and how she and Victor had met. Despite their best efforts, hardly any back and forth happened between the women, but she wondered if part of him liked it that she couldn't talk with them too openly.

"Meet at England?" one girl asked. She'd been introduced to her at the wedding as Victor's youngest cousin, Gabriela. He'd told Cassie she'd never left his village, but had done well at school, and knew her geography well.

"No," Cassie replied, smiling at her kindly. "New York, America."

"Wow, good?" Gabriela asked, and Cassie couldn't be sure what she was asking, so she just nodded and told her yes. Gabriela then stood and tried to get Cassie to join her, making wild hand gestures toward a small area where she seemed intent on dancing in. Cassie looked back at Victor, silently asking his permission, and he nodded but leaned in close to whisper into her ear.

"I'll have my eyes on you at all times. You stay where I can see you," he instructed, and she nodded in understanding. Cassie jumped up and joined the excited young woman on the floor, where she tried in vain to learn some salsa dancing techniques.

Mama Sanchez had seemingly caught their moment of interaction, and Cassie saw as she asked her son why his wife needed permission to dance, but he shooed his mother away. She presumed he was telling his mother it was none of her business, but even Cassie could see the tension in him.

She ignored it, though, leaving his family issues for Victor to sort out, and tried desperately to pick up the moves Gabriela was teaching her. Instead, her ineptitude on the dance floor shone bright and she guessed she must look awkward and tense. Some other girls joined them and assisted in her teachings, all of whom couldn't help but laugh along with Cassie when she laughed at her lack of skill. They weren't mean about it. They were kind and fussed over their new family member affectionately. When she finally started to get some of the hip swings right, Gabriela clapped, making Cassie smile, and she carried on, pleased with herself for having mastered at least one of the moves. When she flopped back down in her seat beside Victor, he pulled his panting wife close, leaning in to whisper in her ear again.

"I'm the envy of every man here," he said, running his lips across her jaw. "Even when you were dancing like a crazy person they couldn't help but watch." He laughed, and Cassie jabbed him in the ribs with her elbow in protest. "When you learned to swing your hips, the world fell away and we were all captivated by you. I want to see you dance like that again soon, but next time just for me," he told her, grinning sexily.

Cassie bit down on her bottom lip, feeling hot and bothered by his sensual words, and Victor knew it. He soon made their excuses and the pair left, eager to get back to their honeymoon home.

***

The next morning Victor sat at his laptop, sending a few emails, while Cassie lay asleep in the bed. Her naked body lay sprawled across the sheets, on full show, her body issues now thankfully long forgotten. He opened up a new email, unable to control himself, and added Leo's address to the top bar. He couldn't resist including a few photographs from his and Cassie's wedding day to the mail. Victor chose the most stunning shots in which she was peering up at him lovingly, and then attached them with a smirk. He hovered over the message box before writing:

Dear Leo,

I hope you are keeping well, old friend? As you will see by the attached pictures, I am very well, and have been taking excellent care of my new acquaintance. I look forward to seeing you again, and am sure the whole unfortunate incident will be put behind us by the time of our next meeting.

Kind regards,
Victor

With a satisfied smile he hit send and locked down the laptop. He stashed it out of sight, just in case Cassie ever grew curious, and joined her on the bed. Victor roused his wife by laying kisses across her back and pressing his body into hers. She sighed and stretched, pushing back into him, spurring his hard-on to grow heavier.

"Oops," she mumbled, giving a fake apologetic smile, and Victor groaned in her ear. He pinned her to the bed and pulled down his pants in just a few seconds, his body silently commanding hers, and she lifted her hips up invitingly. Victor quickly accepted her enticing offer and slid inside, holding Cassie's hips tightly while she pressed her hands against the headboard beneath the pillow, and Victor delivered powerful thrusts to her ready cleft.

"Time to go home," he told her when they were finally spent. She groaned and snuggled into him, seemingly not wanting to go back to her imprisonment back in the complex. "I'll have the swimming pool cleared for you, if you're a good girl." He knew how much she'd enjoyed her times in the pool these last few days, and Cassie smiled up at him. "In fact, I might make it so from now on only essential personnel have access to the main house. All of the girls, and my men, will not be allowed inside unless invited. You'll have complete privacy, and you'll be free to roam where you please, with Grayson in tow, of course, but otherwise unbound. Do you like the sound of that, baby?" He got his answer right away with the bright smile that took over Cassie's entire face and lit up her eyes.

"Would I have free rein of the house at all times, not just here and there?" she asked, and Victor nodded.

"Anything to keep you happy, my love. You know that." He kissed her deeply, delighting in her happy vibe. After that, Cassie took no time at all in getting showered and changed to go home. Grayson came in once she was decent and helped her pack up the things before leading her out to the car.

Victor climbed in the back of the limo, traveling separately, and waved her goodbye. He blew Cassie a kiss, which she returned, and then slid behind Grayson in the less conspicuous second car.

***

"Just you and me again, GG?" she said, delighting in the smile he gave her over the rear view mirror.

"Yes, Mrs. Sanchez. Your husband is very particular about your security, and would prefer you to travel separately on long journeys where possible. Plus, this car has bulletproof windows and panels, so it's very safe. Nothing can get in…or out," he replied, answering her unspoken question.

"My darling husband really does think of

everything," she muttered, but she settled back in her seat and hummed quietly for some of the journey. They chatted a little here and there, but she was surprisingly relaxed, and even found herself dozing toward the end of the long car ride.

When they came to a stop outside the mansion, Grayson's cell phone rang in his pocket. He was quiet with his responses, answering with nothing but yes and no, before he climbed out and practically frog-marched Cassie up to her room and locked the door behind them.

"We need to stay in here," he told her, gesturing for Cassie to take a seat on the bed.

She slumped down, crossing her arms in a huff. "He promised me this would change. Have I done something wrong, GG?"

"Mrs. Sanchez, please. Not everything's about you," he chastised, and Cassie had to resist the urge to send back a snide retort. "Just do as you're told. Victor will allow you freedom to roam the house when he decides the time is right. In the meantime, sit tight and he'll let us know his plans when he's ready."

"Yeah, yeah. I'm going for a bath," she replied, heading for the bathroom to freshen up.

Chapter 31

Down in Victor's office, Leonardo Solomon sat across from his Mexican associate. He watched him with a forced smile, faking gratitude as he accepted a glass of vodka on the rocks. The two men had barely spoken to one another yet, but the air was thick with the many things Leo wanted to say, and do. He could barely contain his anger, feeling it bubbling beneath the surface with every smug smile Victor shot his way, but he forced himself to stay calm.

Leo knew he was pushing his luck turning up unannounced. But, after all, Victor had done the same to him, so he'd had no qualms about returning the gesture. He had been disappointed, however, to find Victor alone in his limo when he returned to the complex. He'd spent the entire buildup to his visit hoping for at least a glimpse of Cassie, but Victor had somehow been one step ahead.

He'd invited Leo inside with a warm smile and a friendly pat on the back, but had offered no information on the whereabouts of his prisoner.

Victor had even enquired after his and Tina's health, acting as though he was not the reason for their wounds, and Leo just sneered and replied nonchalantly.

He maintained that he was here solely to rekindle their business relationship, and nothing more. Leo had seen his email that morning when his private jet came in to land. He had been so enraged he'd trashed the bedroom suite of his plane before downing a stiff drink and smoking a joint to help calm him down. Leo never used to partake in his merchandise, not until Cassie tore his world apart, but now he regularly used both cocaine and weed.

He knew she would be disappointed in him for using, but highly doubted she'd ever know. Leo got the sense Victor would keep her well hidden, so he wouldn't have to answer for his substance abuse anytime soon. He hoped in time he could move on and let Cassie go, but forgetting all about the woman he'd failed so miserably was proving to be far from easy.

Part of him wanted nothing more than to carry on like he had before, cold and heartless, without a care in the world, but he was still struggling to find his way back to that man he used to be. He knew it was the guilt of Cassie's decision weighing him down, and that was exactly why he had come here. If he could see that she was truly happy with Victor, Leo told himself he would walk away and never bother with her again. Or, that was the plan, at least. So far, he'd yet to lay eyes on Victor's new wife, and something told him she was being kept away on purpose.

***

"So, how are you, Leo? I must admit, you look like shit." Victor eyed the bags under his visitor's eyes with a feigned look of compassion. He noticed right away that Leo couldn't quite focus his eyes on anything too long, seeming jittery and distant, and Victor knew he was using. He watched him for a while, noticing how Leo had tried his very best not to stare at the wedding photographs Victor had already had printed and encased in stunning silver frames. His men had dotted them around their home, and what had started as a surprise for Cassie was now acting as a constant kick in Leo's metaphorical teeth.

Victor very much enjoyed the effect they were having on him. Having Cassie's happiness shoved down his throat at every turn was clearly antagonizing Leo's demons, and he couldn't seem to drown them in vodka quickly enough, or mollify them with the many drugs in which he was obviously indulging.

"I'm getting there. It's been a hard couple of months, you know, with getting shot and all," he retorted angrily. Victor shrugged, watching as Leo forced his calm manner to return. "Let's make sure things never get so far out of hand again, Victor," he added, his tone indicating admitted defeat, and the Mexican grinned.

"Of course not. I got what I wanted, and as long as you are not planning to try and steal what belongs to me, there's no reason for us to have a problem continuing our business partnership." He fixed him with a hard, ferocious look. "So, I have just one question, Leonardo Solomon. I know you are a man of your word, so can I trust you not to try and run off with my wife?" Victor sat forward with a stare he bore right into Leo's skull.

Without hesitation Leo climbed forward in his seat, eyeing Victor like a tiger ready to pounce, and he reached out his hand for him to take.

"I promise. I have no designs to try and win Cassie back. She's yours. She made her choice and has become your wife, rather than harbor any old feelings toward me. Any part of me that once yearned for her has gone, and you can trust me never to try and take her away." He spoke eloquently, and with a determined tone.

Victor reached forward and shook Leo's hand with a firm grip, having been ready to fight for her if necessary. He'd been like a coiled viper, poised for attack, but in an instant both predators sedated their vicious sides and snapped back to the friendly way they'd always had with one another.

"In that case, allow me to introduce you to some of my girls. You're a free man, after all, and I would hate for you to go away unsatisfied." Victor grabbed two cigars from the box on his desk and stood, indicating for Leo to join him. "They are no longer permitted in the house, I'm afraid. Wife's orders," he added with a smirk. He led Leo out of his office and through the quiet house, before heading out toward the dorm rooms that housed his best whores.

The men walked through the bustling grounds, smoking their cigars and talking quietly. The conversation felt forced, but their business-heads were back on, and soon Victor began negotiating a deal he had in place for a new, purer line of crack cocaine.

They eventually stopped at the smaller of the complex's two pools, the larger one to the back of the main house now out of bounds to the whores. An array of women sat lounging around and sunbathing, while their guards kept watch nearby. Each of the girls grinned broadly as their employer approached, and he knew they were hoping he'd discarded his lover in preference for his old ways. He hated to disappoint them, and relished the girls' pouts as he turned them away. He was only here to keep his guest occupied, and to see for himself that he was over his former flame.

Victor walked Leo around the pool, giving him the girls' names and describing their best talents, before he insisted his visitor take his pick. Appearing as though he didn't want to be rude this time around, Leo made his decision and led a tall blonde away. He followed her to her room while Victor stayed behind, lapping up the attention from the women who worked for him. He didn't take any of them away, though. He finally understood why Leo had said no during his last visit. After being with Cassie, these girls were nothing. Much to his surprise, he wasn't interested in any of them anymore.

Victor contemplated sneaking up to see his wife while Leo was being kept busy, but thought better of it. She was best kept completely out of sight and mind right now, even though he'd made her promises to the contrary. He knew she might not be impressed when he finally went to her.

Chapter 32

Cassie worked on her drawings all day, quietly sketching the lovely town where she and Victor spent their honeymoon. She carved out the faces of the people she'd met there in pencil, adding every small detail she could while it was all fresh in her mind. She drew elaborate scenes depicting their wedding and the reception that had followed, and of her dancing with the other women at the restaurant. The swimming pool was next, the azure water overlooking the red desert, and her floating inside it, free. Cassie thought back over the last few days with a smile. The house they'd rented for their wonderful time away from her boxed-in home in the complex became her mind's retreat from its prison.

Cassie's hands moved effortlessly over the pages. This was her version of keeping a journal, never having been one for words. Her mind was alive with all the wonderful pictures, and she truly enjoyed capturing them on the page. She had to force herself to take breaks, resting her weary eyes, before eventually falling into an exhausted sleep once the light became too dim to keep working.

Grayson woke her the next morning with the usual coffee and cake. She tried to get him into conversation regarding her husband's whereabouts, but he wouldn't tell her what was going on, and she quickly grew frustrated again.

"Fine, be an arsehole," she spat with a pout. She then laughed at how posh her curse sounded in her accent, and Grayson joined in. "Ass," she tried in her best American inflection, grinning.

She let it go, not wanting to be too pushy, and drank her coffee. After devouring her banana muffin, she slid back under the covers in a huff and treated herself to a lie in. Cassie figured if her husband was going to keep her locked up here in her tower, she deserved an extra few hours' sleep, so she didn't care if he approved of her long snooze or not. After all, Victor hadn't been by to tell her otherwise.

It was almost noon when she woke again, finding Grayson by the door reading a newspaper, and he looked up with a cocky smile.

"Finished sulking yet?" He tucked the paper beside him and then he began talking to Cassie in Spanish, asking her how her wedding was, and if she'd enjoyed her banana muffin. They were basic sentences, and she knew he was trying to get her to respond in her struggling dialect.

"*Sí, muy bueno,*" was all she bothered with, and Grayson shot her a stern look. She rolled her eyes and worked at it again, managing to sound out the words in a simple vernacular at first, and he pressed her harder. He was a strict teacher, pushing Cassie to perfect her pronunciation, and she spent the next few hours lying in bed while practicing her Spanish speaking skills.

Only when he was satisfied did Grayson leave Cassie to get ready. He grabbed her an early dinner of chicken stuffed with feta cheese, and a huge salad, and she grinned at the sight of it, her stomach rumbling loudly. The food was delicious, but Cassie hated eating in her room alone. After their first few days together as husband and wife, she'd really begun to enjoy Victor's regular company and found herself missing him.

"What's going on, GG?" she asked her minder later that night. They'd been left up there all day again, but Grayson just shook his head, clearly unwilling to tell her. "At least tell me if he's okay. I don't understand why he's locked me in here without coming to see me." She looked down at the picture she had drawn of him before their wedding, and realized she was actually worried for him.

"He's fine, just got business to take care of. Then he'll come and see you," he replied, smiling across at her, his stern expression fading.

"Is he fucking someone else?" Cassie found herself asking. She felt paranoid and jealous, and she hated it. She wanted to kick herself for feeling this way, but it was the only reason she could think for him to stay away. Grayson's hand rested gently on her shoulder, the contact making her jump, and Cassie looked up into his warm brown eyes.

"Absolutely not, you're everything to him. That's exactly the reason why you're up here, he's keeping you safe." Grayson handed her the sketchpad and took his seat by the door again, leaving Cassie to her drawing.

***

Victor plied Leo with drugs, alcohol, and numerous women during the first twenty-four hours of his visit. Neither of them slept, and Victor enjoyed watching the broken man try to find himself at the bottom of a bottle, or in the bed of a whore.

By the second night, Leo lay exhausted on one of the poolside loungers. His mind and body seemed to have had enough, and Victor helped him inside the main house to sleep it off in one of the guest rooms. Once he left Leo, he monitored his guest via the hidden camera in his room. Leo undressed and slid under the covers, falling off to sleep quickly.

Victor called his right-hand man, Eduardo. "Lock the door and keep watch over my fragile minded friend, will you?" he asked, knowing his top man was aware he was being asked to stand guard, rather than simply keep watch.

Victor made his way upstairs to his own room. He tinkered with his laptop, his knowledge of both the computer systems and electronic circuitry marching through his mind. Within minutes he'd carried out his desired task, to send the live feed from Cassie's bedroom directly into Leo's.

He checked the monitor, watching as the television mounted on the wall beside Leo's sleeping form flickered to life and showed him his lost lover. Leo slept on for a while, missing nothing but Cassie climbing under her covers and turning out the light, the screen then changing to a green contrast that recorded through a night vision lens. She tossed and turned for a while, seemingly unable to settle, and then she startled and flicked on the light.

***

"Where've you been, baby?" Cassie asked Victor as he entered her room via their shared bathroom. He'd made her jump at first, but she quickly recovered when she realized it was him. "I've been going crazy up here." She climbed onto her knees on the bed and pouted at him.

"Oh, baby. Did you think I'd forgotten all about you and your sweet pussy?" Victor teased, stepping closer and trailing his hand up her thigh. "I'm sorry I neglected you. Let me make it up to you. I wanna make you scream and cry my name, baby, I need to hear you moan." A sly grin curled at his mouth.

She trembled at his words and the stroke of his hands against her body. Now, though, her shudders were not out of fear. They were in anticipation of his touch. She groaned and leaned into his hold when his fingers found her clit and began rubbing gently. Her kisses were vehement, full of need for her lover, and Cassie began stripping him of his jacket and shirt. Her nightdress went next, followed quickly by her panties, and Victor ordered her to lay back on the bed.

He moved her to the left, seeming to be positioning her in some way, but she had no idea why. Before she could ask, he leaned over her quivering thighs and sucked her swollen nub between his teeth. Victor teased her for what felt like forever, sucking and lapping at the tender spot, and she groaned loudly. Cassie ran her hands over her breasts, rolling her hard nipples between her thumb and forefingers to appease their need. She stroked her hands downward and ran them through his dark hair, crying his name as an epic orgasm had her seeing stars.

Victor more than made up for his absence that night, focusing all of his attention on his wife's pleasure. It was as though he was hell bent on orchestrating her most pleasurable night ever, and she didn't hold back when she cried out for him over and over.

When Victor had finished with his deep and wonderful thrusts inside of her, he still didn't stop. He pulled Cassie up onto his lap, where he kissed and stroked every inch of her body while she writhed on him, Victor's fingers inside her wet crevice. Cassie came again and called his name as she unraveled for him. She slept in Victor's tight grip afterward, and woke the next morning with a satisfied stretch, disappointed that her salacious husband was gone again.

***

Leo lay on the bed curled in a tight ball, his head buried in his hands. He'd fallen into a deep sleep the night before, but had been forced awake shortly afterward when a series of loud groans disturbed him. When his groggy vision came back into focus, he'd seen Cassie on the TV screen. She was screaming and crying out for Victor, who was nestled between her thighs and servicing her so skillfully that her groans and cries of delight were almost deafening. He'd tried to turn the screen off or turn the volume down, but it was no use. Leo was left with no choice but to let his eyes wander over the display and take in the sight of his former lover. Cassie looked wonderful, her inhibitions clearly long forgotten, and she seemed much happier than Leo had ever thought she would after having spent the last few months with Victor.

Leo could tell she'd been positioned so the hidden camera overhead would show her body perfectly to him. She was enjoying herself, and Victor was putting on one hell of a show. Leo knew he was doing all of this in the hope that her disgruntled ex was now watching them from a room on the other side of the large mansion, and Leo couldn't stop himself from falling into his host's trap.

He believed in that heart-wrenching moment that she was gone. She truly had chosen Victor over him, so Leo returned to the bed and pulled the covers over his head. He tried with all his might to block out the sound and resist the temptation to take his last looks at the woman who had stolen his heart, and then broken it into a million black pieces.

Whether she knew it or not, Cassie had forever changed him. Leo was sure of it, but he also knew there was no going back to the man he was before her. By the next morning, he had decided to clean himself up and get on with his life. This time he would stay away from women completely, or else find himself someone who might make him feel the way Cassie had. Leo would settle for just a little bit of love in this awful world, and before he was even washed and dressed, he'd already made the decision to head home again after breakfast.

Victor was a gracious host that morning, offering him coffee and cake, but he refused. Leo would never ask him about the live feed that had been pumped into his room the night before, and somehow knew Victor was not about to bring it up either. But each of them knew the matter had well and truly been laid to rest, and in a way Leo was glad. He gathered his things and called his driver, heading out, but he turned back to say a quick, forced farewell to Victor and thank him for the hospitality.

"You've won, Victor. It's time to call it even," he said, needing to end this feud once and for all, and Victor smiled up at his once formidable foe.

"Yes, you're right. I have won. You said you have no siblings, but you and I are like rivaling brothers, Leo. Don't you see?" Victor grinned, but Leo remained stoic. "Yes, we are even. And you're right, this matter is now settled. I look forward to seeing you again, brother. Perhaps next time you won't be using and will be sounder of mind so Cassie might consider joining us. I'm sorry she didn't want to see you this time, but you know she cannot be around addicts." He patted his arm gently, and Leo shook his head and climbed in the car. He waved to Victor before instructing his driver, Javier, to get him out of this hellhole.

Chapter 33

Victor waited until he had confirmation that Leo was airborne and bound for New York before he sent Grayson the message to bring Cassie down to him. He smiled at her from the dining table as she joined him. He could tell she was clearly still buzzing from the night before. Victor had made it his mission to pleasure her in every way he knew how, which happened to be many. He lowered his newspaper and motioned for her to join him in his seat rather than in one of her own, and his stunning wife climbed onto his lap without hesitation.

She kissed every inch of his face, and he lapped it up.

"I missed waking up to you this morning, baby," she whispered, kissing his lips tenderly. "What can I do for you?" she asked, looking down at him while straddling his lap. He said nothing, however he ran his thumb over her soft lips, a sly smile curling at his own. Cassie didn't need any other instructions. She slid down onto the floor and unzipped his chinos, before climbing between his legs and sliding his thick hardness into her mouth.

"No. I don't want to come in here," he groaned after a few minutes, sensing his impending release. He pushed Cassie backward and offered her his hand, pulling his wife back up onto his lap. Victor grabbed her ass cheek hard and caressed it. "I want to come in here," he told her, and Cassie shook her head.

He guessed she'd never done it before, and the look she gave him had him thinking she hated the very idea of anal sex. She seemed to have no desire to even try, so tried to climb back down to the floor, making him want it even more.

Cassie bent to take Victor's still rock-hard cock into her mouth, but he pulled her toward him again. "Do this and you'll be rewarded, Cassie. I promise I'll make it good," he told her, brushing her cheek affectionately. He pushed his chair back and reached out his hand, pulling her up to stand before him. Cassie nodded but whimpered when he stood and turned her around, pushing her forward so she pressed her torso down onto the table. She tilted her hips back, opening herself up to Victor in an obvious effort to please him, and it worked.

***

Victor surprised Cassie by sliding inside her wet cleft first, coating himself in her juices before pulling out and pushing inside the other opening with a satisfied growl before he began to move slowly.

She didn't hate it as much as she thought she

would, the sensation being almost enjoyable, but afterward it felt strange and sore, in a way she did hate. "You'll get used to it, baby." Victor clearly enjoyed teasing her. He grinned when she made her way back in from the bathroom and sat down opposite him with a wince.

"What's my reward?" she asked, desperate to find out, and also eager to take her mind off the strange soreness between her cheeks. Victor stared at her for a moment, softening only when she dropped her eyes from his hard stare. He leaned forward and placed a cell phone on the table between them.

Cassie peered down at it, unsure what to do at first. It had been so long since she had used one. Victor laughed, evidently sensing her hesitation, and he leaned forward, grabbing the cell back again. She went to protest, but he held up a hand to stop her. He unlocked the screen and dialed the New York international code, looking up at Cassie questioningly. She quickly gave him Hanna's number, trembling as he hit the call button and handed it over with a satisfied smile.

She realized then just how much control Victor had over her. Even with his permission, she was still terrified of talking to Hanna, especially with him watching over her like a hawk.

"Hello?" answered a voice on the other end, sounding confused by the unknown number and the silence that followed. "Hello? Is this some kinda stalker pervert? 'Cos I'm not interested." Hanna insisted, sounding angry.

"Hey, sweetie," Cassie whispered, holding the

handset up to her ear as a tear slid down her cheek. "You get properly engaged to that drug-dealer boyfriend of yours yet?"

"Fuck me! Cassie, where are you? Are you okay?" Hanna fired questions at her quickly. "Did you manage to sneak a phone away from that monster? I'll call in whoever I need to and get you outta there, sweetie. Please tell me you're still in one piece?"

"Han, calm down," she replied, looking across at Victor. She could tell he'd heard every word of her best friend's rant. "No need to call in the heavies, I'm fine. Victor gave me the phone. He's been taking wonderful care of me," she added, and he seemed placated, for now. Victor grabbed his paper and began perusing it again, his attention off Cassie for a short while. She was glad he wasn't staring at her anymore, willing to let her talk in relative privacy, but she knew he would be listening in.

"Are you serious? I've been so worried about you. What have you been doing?" Hanna asked, her tone softer now, and Cassie relaxed.

"Nothing too much really, just me and Victor being together and getting to know one another. He really is taking good care of me, Hanna." She took a deep breath and looked down at the wedding ring on her finger. "We got married."

"You what? Jesus, Cassie. What the fuck were you thinking? Don't you see he's controlling you? Even now I can tell you aren't yourself. You've probably got that Stockholm syndrome thing! Let me guess, he's being all nice and loving, just as long as you do everything he says?" Hanna huffed loudly.

"Don't be like that, Han. I may not be the same old me anymore, but I gave that person up willingly to keep you all safe. I'm happy, and Victor is the one making me that way, just like he promised. I don't wanna argue with you. Please, let's just move on from this and catch up like old times. I haven't got long," Cassie pleaded, catching Victor's gaze on her again from the corner of her eye, but she continued looking down at her hands.

"Okay, but you tell him if he hurts you, I'll be down there to talk to him with a brick, and then remind him of his promises to you with a swift kick in the balls," Hanna replied, making Cassie laugh.

"I will," she said. "So, come on. Tell me what I'm missing," she insisted, desperately wanting to know how Hanna was doing.

"You're right, Jamie and I are properly engaged now. I'm outta the game for good, and he's moved into the apartment. We've boxed up all of your stuff, but we'll keep it safe for you. Don't you worry, sweetie." Hanna seemed like she needed her to know they hadn't forgotten about her, and she was glad. Cassie was pleased they were getting on with their lives, the lives she'd kept safe by leaving. Another tear fell down her cheek as she thought back to that terrible day at Leo's home.

"I'm so happy for you both. So, when's the wedding?" Cassie wiped her cheek in an attempt to hide her tears, but Victor had already seen and was watching her again.

"Not for a while. We'll have to wait until the baby's born first," Hanna replied, her smile so very clear in her tone, and Cassie broke down in irrepressible tears at her best friend's wonderful news. "Don't be so soppy. You'll set me off, and trust me, you don't wanna hear a pregnant woman have an emotional breakdown!"

"Hanna, you are just the most wonderful person. You and Jamie are going to make amazing parents. I love you." Cassie watched as Victor stretched out his hand toward her in blatant expectation of having the phone back. "I have to go, sweetie. I'll speak to you when I can, but in the meantime look after yourself, and that wonderful baby. Say hi to Jamie for me, love you."

"Thanks, Cassie. You look after yourself, too, and stay safe. Love you," Hanna replied, hanging up the phone.

Cassie handed the cell to Victor. She smiled across at him, so grateful for his gesture. It had been lovely talking with Hanna. Her heart was full of pure love and emotion, thanks to her friend's wonderful news, and hearing her voice had been amazing.

The tears still fell, even though the call was over. For some reason she couldn't control them, but Cassie didn't fight the wave of emotion, and Victor didn't seem fazed. He flicked through the paper some more, but then stood.

He walked around to the other side of the table, where he lifted Cassie into his arms and carried her out to the garden. She rested her head on his shoulder, feeling tired after her tears, and wondered where they were going. She braced herself when they reached the pool's edge, realizing at once what he was about to do, but this time Victor didn't jump in to soak them both, he just threw her in.

When she broke the surface of the water, Cassie laughed. It was a genuine, happy laugh, and Victor soon joined in.

"I told you I can't stand to see you cry." He sat on a lounger and watched as she lay back in the cool water to bask in the sunshine, her dress billowing beneath her in the water, but she didn't care.

***

A few weeks later, an invitation arrived in the mail. It was addressed to Mr. and Mrs. Victor Sanchez. Inside was a lavishly decorated and embossed white card, announcing they'd been invited to Leonardo Solomon's birthday celebration. He was holding a masquerade ball at his home to celebrate his thirtieth birthday, and had also included a handwritten note. Leo informed Victor he was now clean and sober, just in case Mrs. Sanchez still had her reservations about the party.

He sneered at the note, crumpling it up and throwing it in the trash. He kept the card, staring at it while wondering whether Cassie could be trusted to accompany him to New York. This would surely be the biggest test of her loyalty to date, and part of him hated the idea of her being anywhere near Leo. The other part wanted to see for himself what her reaction to her ex would be. For now, though, he would wait and see. They still had a while to reply, and he was enjoying the good life far too much to complicate things.

Victor hid the card in his desk, locking the drawer shut. He then wandered off in search of his wife. He found her lying in a shady spot by the pool, her stunning body on display in her tiny bikini. Only his most trusted men would see her, and they all knew never to take a lingering glance, or else risk losing a treacherous eye to his jealousy.

Grayson was sitting beside her, as always. He had a Spanish novel in his hands, and was reading her one line at a time. Together they were telling the story, he paused at the end of each sentence for her to repeat it in Spanish, and then translate into English. She was doing pretty well, only struggling over the odd word here and there, and Grayson was proving to be a good teacher.

Her art supplies were beside her on the table, the stunning array of colored pastel or grey penciled drawings each portraying just a snippet of her talent. Victor lifted each one to admire while he listened to her saying the lines back to her tutor. He came across his own portrait and stared intently at the face she'd chosen to portray. It made him happy to see she'd chosen his seductive smile and bright eyes, rather than his smoldering stare or stern expression he knew he'd often shown her.

"That's who I've seen every day since I came here. I think I might even love him," Cassie said, and at first Victor thought she was still reciting the story. He soon realized she was no longer translating the book with Grayson, but looking up at her husband from her lounger. It was the first time she'd ever made him feel she might genuinely love him. It was the one thing she'd told him she could never do, and Victor grinned down at her adoringly.

"I like when he's around too. Maybe together we can try and keep him here so you can be sure whether you love him," Victor replied thoughtfully. He slid the picture back down on the table and then joined Cassie on the lounger. She didn't resist at all as he pulled her close and began kissing her, savoring her taste and the feel of her half-naked body against his suited frame.

After one last kiss, he stood and headed off to gather his men for another of their meetings. Grayson carried on reading once Victor had finished his passionate moment with his wife, nodding to his boss in respect as he left.

Just before he reached the door, Victor turned back. He considered calling off his meeting, wondering whether to take Cassie out shopping in the city for the afternoon instead. He paused, deciding to listen in on their conversation after hearing her voice drift over from where they were still lounging. His men could wait five more minutes, and then he'd surprise her.

"Do you like working for him, GG. Being my nanny?" Cassie asked her guard. He ignored her at first, re-reading the same line of their story again, but she didn't play along. Grayson eventually lowered the book and scowled at her, but nodded and shrugged.

"I have no life away from Mr. Sanchez. No family of my own, and no friends outside of this complex. He's been good to me. He took me off the street when I was an idiot teenager with a chip on my shoulder, always looking for a fight and a swift buck. He trained me, took me into his employment, and I've never looked back. There's nothing I enjoy better than spending my days with you, and making sure you're safe, Cassie."

She laughed, seeming to assume he must've been joking, but he seemed sincere, and Victor caught her smile as she basked in his kind words. "I was never any good with drugs or whores, not my style. But protection I am good at, and he knows he can trust me never to take advantage of my closeness to you." Grayson stared off into nowhere thoughtfully. His assumptions were right, Grayson was the only person in this entire complex he would've ever trusted with her safety and virtue.

"Because you're gay?" Cassie asked, one eyebrow raised, and he nodded.

"Yep, I'd be crushing on him before I'd be making eyes at you," he replied, grinning widely, and they both started laughing.

"Clever girl," Victor whispered before heading into the house in search of Eduardo.

Chapter 34

More weeks passed in which Cassie seemed to be doing everything she could to keep Victor satisfied, and in return he did the same with her. They were blissfully happy, each of them surprised by it. She utterly captivated him, and Victor never wanted their happy bubble to pop.

The morning before Leo's party, he summoned Grayson to his office, watching the man who'd grown close with his wife during her time here with suspicion. He understood his chosen protector had no desire for his wife's attention sexually; however, their bond had developed into a connection far stronger than just business. At times, Victor wondered if he should replace Grayson, but there really was no one else he trusted not to take advantage of his beautiful captive.

"Hey, *Chicano.*" He greeted Grayson in a relaxed way, even though he felt far from composed. His mind was racing, still unsure of the best approach, but he set the plans in motion anyway.

"Morning, Mr. Sanchez. What can I do for you?"

"I need you to pack my wife a weekend bag. We're going away for a few days." He decided not to tell his trusty henchman where. Victor knew he was taking a risk by going to Leo's party, but he had to know if all of this was real. He would put his wife to one final test of loyalty before he could fully put his trust in her.

Cassie had asked for no explanation for their trip when she joined him at the limo. Victor was glad she'd learned to bite her tongue, and now knew better than to question. He couldn't deal with her accusations today, bristling so visibly that they made their way to the runway in tense silence.

The pair of them, along with Victor's group of top henchmen, boarded his plane and took off. They didn't need to worry about check-in times and passport control, and Victor could tell she enjoyed traveling this way. Her fears of flying seemed long gone now, and he knew they'd been replaced with far more real fears thanks to Victor's domineering nature and consistent threats.

He softened a little once they were on board, but she seemed to know he was wound up, so showered him with kisses and affection once they were settled. He enjoyed the distraction and let her keep him busy in bed as the miles disappeared, her body completely at his command.

When they neared New York, Victor climbed out of bed to make them both a drink. He slipped a strong sedative into her coffee as he stirred in the sugar, watching with a satisfied smirk as she drank it down. As soon as Cassie was out cold, he instructed Grayson to get her ready for the cool weather on the other side.

Victor watched as he slipped her into a warm coat and jeans in readiness for the cold, before carrying Cassie out to the main seating area. He checked to be sure she was okay, and buckled her in as they prepared for landing. After a quick passport check, the group left the private jet behind and traveled into the suburbs. Victor had rented them a large house, making sure to choose one with plenty of room for his men to stay close by during their visit.

***

By the time Cassie roused, she was lying in a strange bed. She tried to figure out her surroundings. She felt rested, but had a vile taste in her mouth, and a dizziness which let her know for sure Victor had drugged her again. She frowned when she spotted him in an armchair across the room, the dim red light of his cigar the only thing giving him away in the darkness.

"Why did you drug me, baby?" She sat up in bed, peering into the darkness. Victor said nothing. He pulled the cord to his side that opened up a huge set of curtains. The scene before Cassie quickly became clear, and she didn't know whether to laugh or cry. "We're in New York?" she asked, but still Victor said nothing in response to her questions.

"Get some rest. We have a long day tomorrow." Victor stood and turned to leave, his entire demeanor sending her into a spiral of fear. She jumped off the bed and wrapped her arms around her husband's back. Victor stopped, his hand on the doorknob. He turned to face her in the still heavy darkness of the bedroom.

"Why are we here, baby?" She leaned closer, kissing his lips in an attempt to read his mood. Victor pushed her away. Cassie's breath caught in her throat, and she began to cry. "Why are we here, Victor?" she asked again, louder and more insistent. He stepped forward, grabbing her face in his hands and yanking her toward him for an almost violent kiss.

"Because I fucking said so." He let Cassie go, and she retreated. She slid back under the covers, where she cried herself to sleep after Victor headed back downstairs.

***

The next morning Cassie awoke to Grayson's warm smile as he stood over her, and she tried her best to smile back. She'd had the worst night's sleep since before Victor had come into her life, and knew she must look terrible. Grayson said nothing, offering her coffee and a bowl of chopped fruit with yogurt, which she wolfed down in record speed. She hadn't realized how hungry she was until the spoon hit her lips.

She showered and dressed, waiting for Victor to come get her, and it felt like hours. All the while Cassie looked across the water at the vast metropolis she had once called home. She yearned to go into the city and see her friends, to catch up with Mrs. Brown, Hanna, and Jamie. Especially Leo. Part of her even wanted to check on how Jonah was doing, but for now she knew she'd have to sit and wait for Victor to tell her why they were here, or what he wanted from her. Either way, Cassie could not be sure if it was going to be a good visit or not.

Victor came storming into the bedroom later that afternoon, with a dress bag over one arm and a box in the other.

"We're going to a party, and I want you to wear this. I cannot stress enough how important it is that you stay by my side at all times during this event, Cassie. Is that understood?"

She climbed off the bed and took the items from him, forcing herself to smile, even though she could tell he was still in a bad mood.

"Of course, I won't leave your side. I promise," she replied, kissing his cheek softly. "What's wrong, baby?"

Victor ignored her question and left her to get ready.

Inside the bag was a stunning black lace gown with a high front that covered her cleavage, but it had an open back, and was so long it dragged along the floor behind her. In the box were shoes and a jacket to match, and a mask. It was the sort of filigree design she'd seen many times before in the theater. It tied behind her head securely, rather than being on a pole for her to hide behind only when necessary. Cassie knew Victor must want her face hidden. This mask covered more than half her features. She knew she'd need her hair pinned back to accommodate it, which was an easy task for Grayson. He set about perfecting her hair and makeup, and she was glad to have him around to help.

When Cassie was ready to go, she looked in the mirror and saw a young woman, just like any other girl. She was a blank canvas, and knew that was exactly how her husband wanted it. In this outfit, she could play whatever role Victor expected of her, and she was determined not to let him down. When he came back, Victor had on a black suit, black shirt and tie. The whole outfit created a darkly seductive air, and Cassie looked him over with a smile. He looked hot, and he was all hers.

As he eyed his wife's efforts, he smiled as though impressed. He donned his mask and held out his arm with an expectant stare. Cassie took it and followed his lead down to the car. He barely spoke during their ride to the party, but when he did, his voice was harsh and terse. He was seriously on edge.

"You can trust me, baby." Cassie leaned in close and nestled into her husband's neck.

"We'll see," he replied.

Cassie soon realized why he was so tense when their car pulled into the driveway of Leo Solomon's house. She looked at Victor, staring at him with tears in her eyes, and she shook her head. Every bone in her body suddenly felt heavy. Daggers stabbed at her chest and stomach, dread sweeping over her in waves, and they made her feel as though she might be sick.

"I won't go in, I don't want to see him. Please,

Victor. Is this a test?" she asked, desperate to know his plan, and he just smiled.

"Of course it is. This is the biggest test you'll ever take, and if you pass, I'll never question your loyalty again," he replied, making her stomach drop. Fear gripped her in a way that shocked Cassie to her core. She began to realize at last how right Victor had been about breaking her will and owning her. She was scared to see Leo, absolutely terrified of him and what he meant to her. It was as though he was every one of her nightmares personified, and in that terrible moment Cassie hated the person she'd become.

By the time they reached the front steps, she forcibly steadied herself and took her husband's arm, smiling sweetly at their greeters before climbing the steps to Leo's front door. She followed Victor's lead every step of the way, eager to show him she was telling the truth. No matter what, there was no going back. She had chosen him.

Being in the house again was surreal. Cassie had so many memories of this place. So many of her hopes and dreams still lingered here, but they were forever lost. Her hand held onto Victor's sleeve as tightly as she could without making her knuckles turn white, and together they wandered the house. He chatted with many guests along the way, whom he seemed to know through their crooked business dealings.

Cassie stayed quiet, playing the dutiful wife, but when she spotted Jamie and a very round looking Hanna standing a few feet to her right, her tiny yelp gave her away. Victor continued his conversation, while she watched her friends fawning over one another and bickering just like old times, and she longed to go to them. She was desperate to see and hug them both, but Victor maintained his control. He even began leading Cassie in the other direction after finishing his conversation, and she had to beg him to turn around.

"Very well, but you owe me," he whispered, grinning down at her.

Cassie nodded. She was desperate for some time with her friends, so any treat would be worth giving him in return for this moment. As they reached them, Cassie gave Jamie a wink along with a dazzling smile.

"You've gotta be shittin' me!" he cried, grabbing Hanna and turning her in the direction of her long lost friend, and his fiancée squealed in delight. She threw her hands around Cassie, forcing Victor to let her go for a few seconds, much to his obvious distaste. Cassie hugged Hanna tightly, but watched as Jamie eyed her husband with a scared, yet clearly vengeful stare. He greeted him politely, out of courtesy, but didn't bother making small talk. Cassie was glad he seemed to have made a full recovery, and was obviously still working for Leo. She wanted to ask after him, but didn't dare. She just held onto her dear friend and lapped up the affection she felt pouring into her in their embrace.

Standing there, Cassie suddenly felt very afraid that Jamie might be considering something foolish. He looked as though he wanted nothing more than to punch Victor in the face and make off with his wife. There was a purpose in his stare, but she knew he was no fool. They could all see Victor's guards around the room, watching their every move. Most of all was the huge man who watched Cassie like a hawk, her Gentle Giant, Grayson.

Even she had figured out that if things kicked off, he would be the one to watch out for. She knew he'd not only watched over her all this time, but he'd learned her tells, and more than likely knew things about Cassie she didn't know herself. His protective affection had given Victor one hell of an advantage, and she'd been so desperate for a comrade, she'd never even realized how dangerous her friendship was.

Having a loyal henchman who had an incredible insight into his prisoner's psyche was worth its weight in gold to any strategist, and Grayson would no doubt track her with ease if she got away.

"You look so beautiful," Cassie said, pulling back from her hug with Hanna and rubbing her tummy. She felt Victor's hand return to the small of her back, gripping the low-cut edge of her dress between his thumb and forefinger in a possessive way, so Cassie was mindful not to make him jealous of her in any way, just in case.

"I've missed you so much. I can't believe you're here," Hanna said. Her eyes flicked over to Victor, but she didn't say anything to him. Cassie guessed he would expect a thank you from her for bringing his wife along, but Hanna was not about to inflate his ego by doing anything of the sort.

This attitude was what Cassie loved and missed about her. She remained focused on her old friend for as long as Victor would allow. They chatted for a few minutes, until a huge cheer erupted around them, and the crowd divided.

Leo waded through them like a god who had parted the sea. The men and women fawned over him and hung on his every word, cheering him on with sultry smiles and affectionate gazes. He paused when he saw faces he recognized, stopping for a quick greeting, but then carried on.

Cassie's heart stopped when he wandered right past her, not knowing who she was. Only then did he clock Victor. Underneath her careful façade, Cassie's mind and body were going into overdrive. Seeing Leo again after so long, and after so much had happened, sent her spiraling into a whirlwind of fear and anger, passion, and even a throb of love. She hid it all as best she could, barely smiling politely when his gaze briefly swept over her.

"Victor, so wonderful of you to have come all this way. I hope you and your wife enjoy the party," he said, wandering away again without so much as a backward glance.

Cassie felt weak, nauseated, and heartbroken. Leo had barely looked at her, let alone shown her any sign of affection. She had paid the price for his mistakes, and now he treated her like nothing more than a stranger. The hangers-on followed him, as did the rest of the crowd, Hanna and Jamie included. Leo and his guests made their way to the terrace, where his huge cake sat awaiting his attention.

"Victor, baby, I need to use the bathroom," Cassie whispered, fighting back her tears. He was tense, and she knew he'd been watching her every move since Leo had appeared. He seemed coiled tightly, ready to attack, and Cassie was terrified of him. She felt like this whole thing had been a terrible idea, and she wanted to run out the door, screaming and throwing things on her way. "I think we should go. I don't want to be here," she added, stroking his cheek gently.

The crowd of minions and whores began singing to the birthday boy, wishing him well and praising him loudly, but Victor didn't move or say a word.

"We're not going anywhere," he eventually told her, before waving Grayson over to take her arm. "She needs the bathroom. I'll be at the bar. Bring her straight back to me when she's done," he told his henchman, and Grayson nodded.

He led Cassie down the hall, eyeing her warily, but didn't bother to ask what had gotten them so shaken up. She knew he must've seen their interaction with Leo, and couldn't even begin to tell him how lost and angry she felt about it.

"You have one minute," he told her when they reached the bathroom. His voice seemed cold, but Cassie nodded. She slid into the small room and didn't bother to lock the door, knowing all too well her watcher always expected unlocked doors where she was concerned.

Inside, Cassie had a quick pee and sat for a minute, trying to regain her composure. She smiled as she felt a breeze on her face from the window beside the toilet, the slight draft cooling her hot cheeks. Looking at it, she realized the window was so large and wide open that she could easily fit through. They were on the ground floor as well, the grass on the other side just a short climb away, and she could see the gates to the mansion from here.

Cassie was suddenly filled with an overwhelming urge to shoot through the window and make a bid for freedom. She longed to feel free at last, but then a panic attack sent the air rushing from her lungs, and a stabbing pain to her chest. She'd been right earlier when she had come to realize how much power Victor had over her. She was terrified by the sheer idea of running away, and she truly hated who she had become.

"Breathe, Cassie. Just breathe," said a voice, and she looked up into the warm brown eyes of the only friend she had in all of Mexico, Grayson. "Don't do it. Don't even think about it. He would never trust you again."

"I wouldn't. I'm too weak, GG, and I hate myself for it. Would you have stopped me?" she asked, still trembling, and Grayson nodded.

"Of course, but I would dislike doing so, and I would hate having to tell him what you'd done even more. You know I would have to," he said, reminding Cassie that his allegiance was to Victor, not to her, and no matter what, he would always follow his boss's orders. She wanted to sneer at Grayson and call him Victor's lapdog, but thought better of it and bit her tongue.

"It's a good thing I wasn't planning on doing anything so silly then, isn't it?"

"Yes. Don't forget, you chose Victor over Leo a long time ago. It's my job to keep you safe, but also to remind you of the promises you've made, as well as ensuring you keep them."

"I get it, GG. Please just take me back to Victor." Cassie washed her hands at the sink. She took a deep breath, and then held onto Grayson's arm again. She followed his lead back to the main hallway of the mansion, where he deposited her at Victor's side but didn't say a word about what had happened in the bathroom, and she was grateful.

Chapter 35

The party continued around them while Victor held Cassie tightly to his side, watching everyone and everything as though they were all predators stealthily trying to get one over on him. He knew he was being paranoid, but his fraught mind was in overdrive, just like Cassie's seemed to be.

He hated being here with her. Testing Cassie was just as hard on him, and he longed to take her back home and never look back. He'd been surprised by Leo's reaction. He genuinely seemed unperturbed by her presence, and had not looked over at them once since making his entrance. Victor wondered if Leo had been telling him the truth when he'd promised he had no intention to try and take Cassie from him.

After a while he'd had enough of the party, and led Cassie upstairs to one of the guest rooms, needing some space and to let off some much needed steam. He knew she wanted to leave, but he wasn't satisfied, so wanted to see if she would let him have her here in her paramour's home.

Spending some time in one of Leo's open guestrooms was not his idea of a better alternative to the bustling party, but he pulled Cassie upstairs with him anyway. He was glad she was so agreeable. After all, he'd taught her many times she had no choice but to go along with his desires, and she did as she was told, as always.

"You remember how you wanted it hard, and you were dying to fight me off, to tell me no?" he whispered once they found a room to his liking at the end of the hall. Victor pulled Cassie's back into him, and gripped her biceps tightly in his hands. He held her immobile and nuzzled from behind, kissing his wife's neck, and biting her a little as he nibbled at her earlobe.

She tensed, seeming not to want this here under the watchful eyes of Leo's hidden cameras. Her reaction only made him want it more.

"Not like this, baby. Not here." Cassie tried to reason with him, to make him understand. "I don't care if you want that kind of night together, but I don't want to do it here," she whispered, and tried in vain to pull out of his grasp. "Please Victor."

"Tell me no, go on. I fucking dare you." He slid down the zipper at the side of her dress, and he pushed the shoulder panels forward to expose her breasts. The dress slid to the floor. Cassie seemed completely unable to keep it from billowing down to her feet, and she gasped as his hands grabbed at her breasts, cupping them roughly.

"Please," she groaned, but Victor silenced her with a bite to her shoulder.

"Tell me to stop, baby. Go on," he insisted, but

she gave him no response, and he grinned. Victor threw her onto the bed forcefully before removing his jacket and shirt.

Cassie lay on her front, frozen in fear. He watched her tremble and pant in anticipation of his advances, but he didn't care about her trepidation. He wanted to claim his woman, whether she wanted it or not.

He loosened his belt and removed the rest of his clothes, then joined his wife on the bed. His body pressed into hers on the mattress, while his hard-on poked between her thighs, and rubbed against the tiny sliver of her lace panties. Cassie turned her head to look at him just as a shadow moved through the dark hallway. Victor caught her fear and didn't stop the man as he wandered inside the room and took a seat on the sofa opposite the end on the bed.

Cassie groaned her disgust, but a second bite to her shoulder silenced her pleas. They all knew the rules, and as long as he wasn't planning on trying to join in, Victor didn't care if the man watched.

It was only when he spoke that Victor finally reacted to his presence. The dark shadows still hid their watcher's face, but his voice gave him away.

"Go on, Cassie. Tell him no. I want to see him fuck you harder than you've ever been fucked before. I wanna hear you scream for him to stop," Leo said, as he relaxed back in the seat. He laid his arms across the top of the sofa. Victor knew it was so he could see he had no weapons, and wasn't there to fight.

"Not like this, not with him here. Please, Victor, no," Cassie whimpered. She'd uttered the words before she could hold them back, and as soon as the word 'no' left her lips, Victor pounced. He ripped the panties off her hips, his fingers shredding the material in less than a second, and then he was inside of her a moment later. Victor pummeled her hard, slapping her ass cheeks with his stomach as he pressed into her firm and fast. He heard Leo take a loud breath, but he otherwise stayed silent, continuing to observe from the shadows.

***

Cassie felt wet and hot from Victor's relentless thrusts, both hating and loving his forceful advances. Having the added combination of humiliation and anger at Leo being there somehow spurred her onward too. Cassie dug her hands into the bed sheets and pushed back into her husband's powerful thrusts. She cried out as Victor's body crashed into hers, and then fell limply onto the bed when her orgasm burst through her in an eruption of hot pressure. Victor flipped her over and slapped her across the face, sliding back inside her aching cleft during her moment of shock.

"I didn't give you permission to come. Did you do it because he's watching? Did he make you so hot you had to come for him?" His face was contorted with venomous fury as he continued his heavy thrusts, but she was lost in the power he delivered to her body, reveling in the pleasure and the pain.

"No, I hate him. I don't want him to see me come, that's just for you, baby. I want you to show him how much you love me, show him how I gave you all of me, and not him," Cassie replied, letting out all of the spite and anger she felt at Leo for having moved on without her. Victor stared down into her eyes, his body trembling as his release claimed him. He fell onto the bed and kissed her lips so gently it was as though they'd just made love, rather than having fucked so violently right in front of her ex-boyfriend.

"You're so beautiful," Victor whispered, still staring at her, and she shook her head. Tears were streaming down her temples, and she stared up at the ceiling in a daze. Her body curled up and she felt so frail and tiny.

She hated that Victor had treated her this way, but knew he'd needed to show Leo she belonged to him. He could do anything he wanted to her, and Cassie would always go along with it, and she had. He'd never treated her that way before, even when she asked him to, and despite it having felt good, Cassie vowed to herself that she wouldn't let it happen again.

Leo stood and hovered near the bed. He peered down at them, before lifting their clothes up from the floor and placing them on Cassie's other side. Victor stood from the bed, still naked, and she watched as he put his hand out to Leo, who shook it, smiling back warmly. He seemed about to leave, but then appeared to think better of it, and held his ground. He held onto Victor's hand for another second before he spoke.

"You think you've got it made, don't you, Victor?" Leo asked him, his smile turning into a grimace. "You've spent all this time thinking you'd won, when you should've realized we are both losers. There are no winners in this game for Cassie's heart, because neither of us is worthy of possessing it. Thank you for coming to celebrate my birthday. The last thing I ever expected was for you to bring her here, but now I can see for myself how broken she's become, thanks to you. I will look forward to seeing the happiness return to her face when you meet your demise, Victor Sanchez."

"Oh, really?" Victor replied, his dominant pose back in full force, but Leo didn't seem swayed by it at all. "You think you can take me down? You think you can win her back? I own every inch of that girl, and she would fall to pieces without me. I tell her when to eat, speak, think, or fuck. You are nothing, Leonardo Solomon. I would rather slit her throat myself than ever see her go back into your arms," Victor added, the two men at a standoff, and the air around them grew thick with tension.

Cassie watched them in horror. Victor's awful words made her want to vomit. She was suddenly filled with all the hatred she'd pushed aside the entire time she'd been with him, and saw red. She wanted to hurt him, to make him pay for what he'd done to her. Cassie wanted to punish her husband for how broken she'd become under his control, and that was when her finger traced the edge of the sheath on his belt. Cassie's eyes darted to it, realizing Leo had put the knife directly beside her, hopefully on purpose. The sheath's snap was already open, and she silently pulled it into her palm. The weight of it surprised her, but she gripped it tightly and rose up onto her knees.

"Baby?" she whispered, smiling at Victor when he turned to face her. "I wonder if this will feel as good as I hope it will," she murmured, delighting in his surprised expression. Fear then claimed his features when Leo grabbed his arms from behind and pinned them back, rendering him immobile.

"Do you want to be free of him forever?" Leo asked, looking at her over Victor's shoulder, and she nodded. "Then do it." Leo grinned with sinister satisfaction as she flung herself at Victor, making contact with his chest, and the heavy knife pushed down between his ribs and disappeared inside.

The only sound was a wet gurgle as Victor opened and closed his mouth in an attempt to speak, but it was no use. Cassie watched without a hint of guilt as he went limp in Leo's arms and then dropped to the floor, taking his last breath as they watched.

"Am I free?" She looked up at Leo and found the old, real him staring back at her. He was the version she'd known so well once upon a time, and that was when she finally fell apart. He grabbed her before she could fall, hugging her tightly in his bear-like grip, and they both began to cry.

"I'm sorry, I'm so sorry," Leo told her. He kissed her cheeks and lips, and the person Cassie thought was gone forever came back to her with every one of his kisses. She was terrified, but so happy, and couldn't quite believe she'd done it. Victor was dead, and she'd killed him. "You're not free, Cassie, not yet, but I'm doing everything I can to make sure you get there. Don't say a word, only talk to the lawyer I send for you."

"What?" She stared up at him, and Leo looked far too sad for her liking. She knew something was up, there were clearly other games at play here that she'd had no idea about. Cassie couldn't get her head straight, she couldn't figure any of it out. "Leo, please."

He handed her the crumpled dress, helping Cassie into it, before taking a seat on the bed, and telling her to do the same.

"They're coming for you, the police. I ratted him out, and you," Leo told her, looking at his hands. "It was the only way to save you, Cassie," he managed to say.

Before she could ask for any more information, a team of police officers burst into the room, shouting at them both to put their hands where they could see them.

Chapter 36

"Cassandra Sanchez, you are under arrest for the murder of Jonah Smith, and the suspected murder of Victor Sanchez. Anything you say can and will be used against you in a court of law," an officer recited, cuffing Cassie's wrists behind her back while reading the remainder of her rights. Leo was being read his, too. He accepted them, allowed himself to be cuffed, and then silently followed another officer away. His eyes bore into Cassie's, and despite the situation, he had a satisfied half-smile on his lips.

"Leo!" she cried, desperate not to be separated from him again.

"It's okay, love. We've won. I don't care what happens next, the only thing that matters is you're safe." He gave her one last lingering look and left. Cassie felt as though she'd been punched in her gut. She trembled uncontrollably and shook her head. This didn't feel like winning.

The partygoers watched in shock as Leo and Cassie were led outside and into the awaiting patrol cars. Victor's other men, Grayson included, were lined up against a police van, and none of them said so much as a word as she passed. When Victor's dead body was loaded into the coroner's truck, they remained still. It was as though they were indifferent to the situation and the man who lay dead before them.

Cassie stared out the window in stunned silence, trying to make sense of the last few hours. Jonah had died. The arresting officer's words were resonating in her head, and she felt sick. Cassie had used him in a bid to instigate this very scenario. She'd let Victor hurt him in return for the hope of a warrant for her arrest, and her removal from her captor's side long enough to seek help, but it had backfired. Jonah had died because of her foolishness, and regardless of who had delivered the beating, she decided to plead guilty to his murder. She had to pay for what she had done to her ex-husband. He hadn't deserved to die because of her, no matter what had happened between them all that time ago.

She caught sight of Hanna and Jamie as they watched from the crowd. Their faces were pained, but they were the only ones in the group of onlookers who didn't seem shocked by the night's events, and Cassie wondered if they might've known Leo was going to turn himself in.

When they reached the station, Cassie was processed and put in a small room. She was trembling, unsure whether from the cold or the fear that still coursed through her. She wished the old, strange numbness would come back again. She yearned to feel nothing.

Cassie was joined shortly afterward by a tall, skinny man who shook her hand and took a seat opposite her at the grey table. She was still in shock, but otherwise fine. Cassie had refused to be seen by a doctor as she had no injuries, but part of her wished she could see a psychiatrist. She hoped she might be allowed a visit from her old doctor who'd helped her get through the trauma with Jonah, but then again she had no idea if he would even want to see her after her apparent murder. He'd not so long ago signed her off his books as being well adjusted and ready to move on with her life, and would no doubt be angry she'd taken such a huge step backward in her recovery.

The man who'd entered leaned closer, breaking her reverie. He removed a notepad from his briefcase as he looked over at her, and he began talking quietly.

"Ms. Taylor, my name is Justin Hawke. I'm an attorney. Leonardo Solomon is my client, as are you," he told her with a warm smile. He'd called her by her maiden name, and it was nice to hear. Cassie was delighted to know Leo had hired him as her attorney in readiness for this night. "We're safe to talk honestly with each other now, anything you say is strictly between us. Mr. Solomon is already in custody. He'd given the authorities a full statement before tonight, and has confessed his wrongdoings. Leo has made a deal with the FBI, and will be going to prison without trial."

"What? No, he can't have. I need to see him," Cassie said, her voice hoarse, and she shook her head, trying to make sense of it all.

"I'm afraid that's not possible. He's been sentenced to twenty-five years imprisonment, but that sentence has been drastically reduced due to his cooperation. He should be out in eighteen months, with good behavior," Justin told her with a glint in his eye.

This guy was good, Cassie could tell. Everything about him screamed money and dirt. He was clearly a shark, and had gotten Leo off on most of his charges in exchange for his testimony. He had procured him an incredibly light sentence, which Cassie thought was probably all for show as far as the FBI's books went, a slap on the wrist of sorts.

"Okay. So, what do I need to do?" Despite her not wanting to follow Leo behind her own set of bars, she knew this man was her only hope at getting justice for Jonah's death. If that meant her going to prison, so be it. She had faith he would give her a good defense in the process, and Leo wouldn't have sent her someone she couldn't trust.

Justin grinned and began telling her the plan. He explained how Leo had contacted him almost as soon as Cassie had left with Victor, asking how they might instigate a rescue strategy for her retrieval.

"Leo knew he needed to be clever and bide his time rather than act rashly. While he got himself and his assistant some medical care, I started thinking. It wasn't long before Jonah was found, and a witness testimony put you and a man fitting Victor's description at his apartment the night he was beaten. You were wanted for questioning, but the assault was not enough to extradite you, or even put the matter of your disappearance on the FBI's radar. Then Jonah unfortunately died from his injuries a few days later, and the case took a turn in a direction I could use." Justin paused as Cassie began crying into her hands.

He handed her a tissue and perused his documents, allowing her some privacy as she mourned her ex-husband. Cassie was truly sorry for what she'd done to him and promised herself she'd find a way to bring him some peace. She would tell the whole truth about everything with Victor. She hoped it must already be evident that she hadn't inflicted those wounds herself—she would never have been strong enough. Still, she would serve her time if a jury found her guilty of his murder. Cassie would do anything to get rid of the deep well of guilt in her gut, but she also considered that maybe it would never go.

"Carry on, Mr. Hawke," Cassie said after a few minutes. Her face felt swollen, but the tears had stopped, and she listened intently as the man continued with his story.

"Leo spoke with your roommate, and your boss at the restaurant. Each of them corroborated his version of events, and they told me they would be willing to testify, if only we could get you back on American soil. Leo then went to his contact at the FBI, the same man he'd passed information to before about Otis Simmons, and he told him everything. They would only pursue a warrant for Victor's arrest if Leo cooperated with their investigation and took them evidence, which he agreed to do without hesitation. As long as you were free he didn't care, he would sacrifice his own freedom for yours, Cassie," Justin said, smiling at her again. Cassie nodded in grateful understanding.

"Just like I did for him," she mumbled, more to herself than to Justin. He nodded.

"Absolutely. He came to Mexico and visited Victor, but you were kept locked away the entire time. Unfortunately, Leo had begun using drugs to help him deal with your loss, something he deeply regrets now, but he played it up for Victor's benefit. He perfected the role of the depressed junkie in order to gain Victor's trust again, and they rekindled their relationship nicely. Leo then put the entire birthday party together, praying he would bring you with him, and lo and behold, he took the bait."

"Leo came to visit?" Cassie was shocked Victor had somehow kept it from her, but then again she knew she shouldn't be surprised. All those days she'd spent locked up in that room, he could've been doing anything, and she would've never known. One lengthy period of isolation came straight to mind. "Let me guess, was it right after we were married?" she asked, remembering those few days when her promised freedom was withheld, and Victor was absent for most of it.

"You're right. Leo said he had no contact with you, but Victor showed him the photographs of your wedding, among other things," Justin replied, but didn't let on what he meant.

Cassie felt terrible. It must've been so hard on Leo, and she hated the spiteful way she had spoken about him earlier at his home. She wanted to take back every vengeful word she'd said, and every spiteful thought she'd had about her patient savior. Leo had evidently been playing his own role all along.

She should've guessed it, but Cassie also knew her mind was not in the right place. Thanks to her overbearing husband, she probably would've never seen or felt anything he didn't want her to. She truly had been under his control, but vowed to herself she would break away from all of that now.

She and Justin spoke for hours, going over Cassie's version of events from the night of Jonah's beating, and her captivity between then and the night of Leo's party. She told him honestly that she had stabbed Victor, not withholding a single detail.

"Clearly self-defense. He was an abusive man who kidnapped you and forced you into a life of servitude, and an involuntary marriage. His death will not be the issue. It's Jonah's family who are pushing for a trial. They never knew what he did to you, they just thought you were a disgruntled ex who lashed out at their son, and murdered him. They'll soon learn the truth, and I believe that once the facts are heard, you will not be found guilty. It is likely you'll be deported back to England, but otherwise you'll be free." Justin grabbed his things and offered Cassie a supportive pat on the shoulder.

She thanked him, grateful for having been able to tell her story at last, and Justin left. Once she was alone, her thoughts swallowed her up, but all in all, Cassie was glad. She might not be free, but she was free of Victor, and that was all that mattered.

Chapter 37

A few months later, Cassie was tried before a jury for the manslaughter of Jonah Smith, and the murder of Victor Sanchez. She'd spent the time between her arrest and the trial date in a low-security prison, where she'd had sessions with a psychiatrist daily, and was treated well by the guards and other inmates. They'd heard her story and viewed her as nothing more than a victim, many of the inmates respecting her for finally killing Victor. Not all women were lucky enough to get away in one piece. Those few she'd grown relatively close with understood her reasons for having Jonah hurt in an attempt to save herself from becoming a sex slave, despite the awful consequences.

Justin defended her brilliantly. He started at the beginning, opening with a brief history of Cassie's life before falling into a relationship with Leo. He then called Mrs. Brown to the stand, and asked for her account of the night she'd overheard Victor and Cassie talking at the restaurant. The lovely woman spoke slowly and clearly, telling the jury about the ultimatum she'd heard Victor give Cassie, and that she'd told Mrs. Brown she had no other choice but to go with him.

"Cassie is a lovely girl. She just got mixed up with the wrong people, and they took her choices away from her. I didn't know Jonah, but I know for sure she would have never hurt him willingly," she said, gazing warmly at Cassie as she sat behind her defense table.

Mrs. Brown was cross-examined and dismissed, her testimony ironclad, so they didn't go too hard on her.

Then Leo Solomon took the stand. He was handcuffed, but had been allowed to dress in a suit and tie for the occasion. He looked well, and smiled at them all after saying his oath. Cassie couldn't take her eyes off him. Her body yearned for his touch, and as he regarded her with the same intensity, she felt herself blush.

"Mr. Solomon, please tell us what happened on the night of September sixteenth, last year," Justin requested, pacing slowly as he listened to Leo's testimony.

"Absolutely. I was entertaining Victor Sanchez and his men at my home, when he slipped a sedative into my drink, and tied me to a chair in my hallway. When I came to, he interrogated me at length and shot me in both kneecaps. He also tortured my assistant, Tina, for information regarding the whereabouts and personal history of my girlfriend at the time, Cassandra Taylor," he said, receiving gasps from the few onlookers, and grumbles from the jurors. "Victor then left for a while, his men having taken possession of my home, and we were kept there while he went off in search of his prize, Cassie."

"I see, and could you please tell the court what happened the following morning?" Justin continued, drawing out more of the story, while Cassie fought back her tears as she relived the awful day.

"Victor returned in the early hours. He didn't tell me where he'd been, or what had happened. Later that morning Cassie came to the house. It appeared Victor Sanchez had delivered her with an ultimatum. She was to go with him to Mexico and become his whore, or he would kill me, as well as all her friends. I begged her not to go with him, but she couldn't do it, she couldn't let me die, and so she went. He took her with him, where he turned her into his forced subservient. I know this because he insisted on sending me proof, and told me during our few meetings that followed how she was at his full command." Leo took a deep breath, shaking his head as though trying to clear away images his mind had pulled into focus again.

He took a sip of his water, eyed Cassie intently, and carried on. "I didn't see her again until my birthday party on July twenty-third this year, when I helped set up a raid with the FBI to ensure the arrest of both her and Victor Sanchez at my home."

"And what happened that night? How is it that Victor Sanchez ended up dead before the agents could apprehend him?" Justin pressed, wandering the court slowly while resting his chin on his fingertips.

"They both attended the party, and I knew I had to keep them at my property until the authorities arrived. I played it cool so as not to rile Mr. Sanchez in case he got offended and decided to leave. Victor eventually took Cassie upstairs where I found him forcing himself on her sexually. I confronted him, but he wouldn't stop, and that's when Cassie reached for the knife Victor always carried with him, and she stabbed him in the chest. It was completely in self-defense. She'd endured months of forced submission, and finally snapped. I couldn't blame her," Leo told them, peering over at her longingly, and she had to wipe the tears from her cheeks as she listened to him.

Leo was asked a few further questions from the prosecution, but he remained calm and spoke of Cassie with nothing but warmth and even pity, clearly using her fraught past to help plead her case.

He was later dismissed and taken back to his transport to return to his prison cell. The pair of them hadn't had any time alone together during his brief respite from jail, but it was enough just seeing him, and Cassie's heart felt a little better for having heard him speak so lovingly of her in front of the court.

Soon it was Cassie's turn to take the stand. She trembled as she made her way up to it, but she stood tall and spoke eloquently. She told the judge, jury, and onlookers exactly what had happened toward the end of her marriage with Jonah. Cassie held nothing back regarding their dreadful few days spent enduring his meltdown, and the injuries she'd sustained.

In order to prove her story was true, her medical records were brought forward as evidence by Justin. The psychologist's report corroborated her story as well, thankfully forcing the prosecution to leave that part alone.

"I hated Jonah so much, but there was still a huge part of me that loved him, so I never pressed charges. I moved on with my life, and he did the same. I was lost and alone, but I found a new home, and new friends. Maybe they weren't the right people to have around me, but they made me happy, and Leo did everything he could to keep me separate from his business dealings." She gazed into the faces of the jury members, hoping they believed her story. She wondered how many abused and tortured women had sat in this chair before her, telling a similar story. She was a victim, regardless of all the times she'd told herself she wasn't, and she hated both her dead husbands for having made her that way.

"Victor happened upon me, and I knew right from the moment I met him I was done for. He was a predator, and saw me as nothing but Leo's favorite toy, a plaything Victor wanted for himself. He set about making that happen in the only way he knew how, violence and intimidation. I was terrified of going with him, but I had no other choice. He made it quite clear that he would kill my friends if I ran, and he would kill Leo if I didn't choose him," Cassie told them, readying herself to give them the full details of Victor's attack on Jonah, and the room fell silent, hanging on her every word. She took a deep breath and forced herself to carry on.

"After I left the restaurant that night, Victor approached me outside. He asked to give me a ride home. I wasn't tired, I was freaking out, thanks to his ultimatum, and had been trying to think of a way of reaching out to someone for help without him realizing it. Victor was an incredibly clever man, and in the ten months I lived with him I don't think I ever really fooled him, not even once. He always had the upper hand, and even that first night I knew how as soon as I said yes to him, my life would no longer be my own. The only person I could think to help me that night was Jonah." A sob forced itself out of her, and the judge spoke up from his seat for the first time since the trial had begun.

"Would you like to take a minute?" he asked, but Cassie shook her head. He nodded, and motioned for Justin to bring her a fresh glass of water, and she took a sip with trembling hands.

"I knew if I could get Jonah to suspect foul play, rather than me having run off into the sunset with my new lover, I might be in with a chance. He still loved me, despite all of our hardships, and I trusted that he would not just let me go without at least looking into my reasons why. So, I asked Victor to take me to his apartment. I told Jonah I was going away, that I had gotten mixed up with the wrong people, and that was when Victor beat him up. I hated every moment of it, and called him away, but he just wouldn't stop. He took a knuckleduster and pounded into Jonah's groin with it, and then I ran for the car, unable to see any more. I was sick outside in the street, I couldn't bear it, but Victor was calm and drove me home afterward without a flicker of guilt. I saw what a monster he was, and while I sat in his car crumbling under the pressure he was putting on me, Victor simply reminded me that I had twelve hours left to make my choice. He drove me home and left me to say goodbye to my roommate without a care." She clutched at her stomach, the ache deep within making her feel as though her water might make a comeback.

"What happened next, Mrs. Sanchez?" Justin asked, and she cringed at hearing her married name, but knew it was unavoidable.

"After going to Leo's mansion the next morning to make my choice, I left with him, and we took his private jet to Mexico. I was locked in a bedroom for most of the time to be his personal whore. Victor dominated every part of me ruthlessly, and without ever showing any guilt for what he'd done. I played my role. I'm not ashamed to say I went along with it and did everything he asked of me, all out of sheer self-preservation. I married him and forced myself to pretend I was happy. Along the way I think I even believed my own lies, so I played the part of the dutiful wife, and remained in Mexico, until the day before Leo Solomon's birthday party. I wasn't told where we were headed. I was allowed to attend the celebrations with Victor, but had been warned against trying anything foolish. He was testing me, but I was too afraid to go against his orders anyway, and hated every minute we were at Leo's party."

"And can you please tell the court what then happened once the two of you were at Leo's house?" Justin asked her, his expression warm and calm. Cassie stared back at him, finding comfort in his gaze, and she carried on, pushing herself to keep going no matter how hard it all was.

"He didn't care how well behaved I'd been. He was seething. Victor was so angry that nothing I said or did could calm him down. I think he hated being there too, but he wasn't finished testing me. It seemed he wanted to know how I would react to seeing Leo after so long, but I didn't give him what he wanted, neither of us did. I think he was looking forward to punishing me, but I didn't give him the satisfaction. Leo and I were like strangers that night, and although Victor seemed satisfied that our bond had apparently been severed, it was evidently a bittersweet victory."

"Is this when he took you up to a guest room of Leo's mansion?" Justin urged, keeping her going.

She nodded. "Yes. He forced me down on the bed, and ripped off my clothes, forcing himself on me, and I let him. I had to, just like always. Leo found us and tried to pull him off me, but the damage was already done, and I snapped. I think having finally seen Leo again had set me off, and in a desperate bid for freedom, I acted at long last. I saw the knife Victor always carried, it was right next to me, and so as soon as he went to lay his hands on me again I stuck it in his ribs," Cassie told them. She panted as a flurry of panic rose in her chest. She knew she was lying. Both she and Leo had elaborated the story to cover up his involvement, but it was all fundamentally true, and the thought of that night still brought her to the brink of tears again.

"Thank you, Cassie," Justin said. He handed her

a tissue, and she dabbed at her eyes. The prosecution cross-examined her, but they seemed to have little to ask other than for clarification of details here and there. The case seemed cut and shut, and so they went easy on her. No one seemed to want for her to be made an example of. The only thing they needed was the truth so the case could finally be closed. Cassie was glad. She was truly grateful for Justin having spoken with the prosecution lawyer before the trial had begun, and that together they seemed to have already come to an understanding.

Before long the questions were over, and Cassie sat opposite Hanna and Jamie in the holding office of the courthouse. Their baby daughter, Sandi, was in Hanna's arms. She was a happy child, smiling and cooing sweetly, and Cassie was so glad they were all okay.

"He never stopped loving you, Cassie," Hanna told her, clearly talking about Leo, and she nodded.

"I know, I never stopped loving him either, but how can we possibly get back to where we were before? I don't know if I would even want to, Han. I can't be the mob-boss's wife ever again, and I cannot expect him to leave it all behind for me. I think we both just have to draw a line in the sand and say our goodbyes. My track record for lovers is looking pretty bad right now," she replied, shaking her head at herself, and Hanna just laughed.

"Well, you spent the night with us and look where we are now. I think you need to stop attracting gangsters and you'll be fine," she said, making them all laugh. Cassie was glad to have had some time with them before they needed to head back into the courtroom for the final moments in her trial.

Cassie thought of all the truths that had come out during the hearing. Learning about Leo's hidden cameras in the apartment had come as the biggest shock of all. It was an intrusion she wasn't sure she could ever forgive. As much as she wanted to get back to some semblance of a normal life, she didn't know whether Leo could fit into it anymore. Cassie was sure there would need to be some very strict ground rules in place before anything could ever begin again. She couldn't let herself be vulnerable.

"He won't be a mob-boss any more, don't forget, sweetie. You know he'll have to say goodbye to that part of his life after his incarceration. His legit businesses are fine, but the drug trade is now closed for him. Don't forget that," Hanna repeated. She smiled affectionately, seeming proud of Cassie. She was glad knowing Hanna would be happy to go along with whatever she eventually decided, but she would stick by her all the way.

The guard came in and ushered them back to the courtroom. They made their way back inside, and the onlookers took their seats while Cassie and Justin stood eagerly awaiting the ruling. A woman from the jury stood and readied herself to read out the verdict from a sheet of paper, fidgeting nervously.

"Madam foreperson, has the jury reached a verdict?" the judge asked.

"We have, Your Honor."

"What say you?"

"In the charge for the manslaughter of Jonah Smith, we find the defendant not guilty," the spokeswoman said, pausing for a moment while Cassie exhaled loudly, and began to shake. She needed a moment to regain her composure, but wasn't afforded it.

The woman said, continuing to read from the paper in her hands. "And in the charge of the murder of Victor Sanchez, we find the defendant guilty."

Chapter 38

Noise erupted from the court in an instant. Cassie could hear shouts and pleas from her friends behind her, and she hung her head, waiting for the sentence to be given.

"Order in court!" the judge shouted, slamming down the gavel, and silence descended. "You find the defendant guilty?" he asked the jury spokeswoman, and she nodded, but added a little more explanation to their findings.

"Yes, your honor. But, we believe the murder to have been in self-defense, and recommend that Mrs. Sanchez is sentenced to time served," she said, and then took her seat. Cassie lifted her head, watching the judge to see his reaction to the jury's recommendation, and he thankfully seemed to agree with the verdict.

"I concur. Cassandra Sanchez, you are charged with the murder of Victor Sanchez, carried out solely in self-defense. I hereby release you from custody in light of your current time served and good conduct throughout. Your visa to live and work in the United States of America has been revoked, and you are to leave the country immediately. The Mexican authorities have seized your husband's assets, however the IRS has found several offshore accounts in your name. Regardless of his intention, it seems your husband has left you with some compensation for your time as his prisoner. Those funds have been transferred into a holding account, which you will be able to access and transfer over to your British bank account when you get there. The case is now closed, and I wish you well," the judge said. The loud whack of his gavel resonated through the room, and within seconds Hanna's arms were wrapped around her from behind while the room emptied. Justin shook her hand with a smile, and escorted her from the courthouse to an awaiting car that would take her to Hanna and Jamie's apartment.

***

The next afternoon Cassie gave baby Sandi one last hug, along with her friends and even Mrs. Brown, who'd come to see her off at the airport. She checked her luggage and waved goodbye from the security gate, taking one final glimpse of the few people she truly cherished, and would miss with all her heart. Jamie and Hanna had decided to get married in England the following year, though. They told her they'd opted for a long summer visit, and Cassie couldn't wait to see them. Despite hating having to say goodbye, she left safe in the knowledge that this was not forever.

After a long flight and an emotional reunion with her family in London, Cassie finally set off in search of herself again. She found a reputable accountant and set about gaining access to her funds, the rather strange inheritance Victor had somehow left for her. She almost fainted when he told her how much was waiting in the account.

"Eighty million dollars?" Cassie shrieked, almost falling off her seat, and the rotund man nodded, happily setting her up with high interest savings accounts, and a platinum bankcard before she had even left his premises.

Before long she got used to the idea of having the money, and bought herself a stunning apartment in a safe and posh area in the center of London. Cassie also purchased a small, run-down theater in dire need of renovation and updating. This was her baby. It soon became her little piece of new normality, and Cassie loved it. She became herself again inside those walls, and while she found the person she used to be, she also discovered a newer, better version there too. Cassie became the person she'd always wanted to be, thanks to her old and new selves standing tall and strong as one, rather than at war with one another. Her confidence reached new highs, and her love of the theater and passion for the arts combined in a way that made her proud of who she had become. Cassie wasn't a victim anymore. She was determined she would never play a role again. Her scars ran deep, but she would wear them on her sleeve, and never let anyone give her fresh ones.

***

After just over a year of being back home in London, Cassie's theater hosted a lavish party for its opening night. After a full renovation, followed by rehearsals and set design, she was finally ready. They were showing a new play written and choreographed by a talented up and coming composer named Alex Clarke, whom Cassie had discovered at a poetry reading in Covent Garden. She'd decided to give him a chance to wow her, and he had not disappointed.

After seeing what talent was out there, unnoticed and spectacular, she'd had an epiphany. Cassie had to turn her new theater into place where unknown artists had the chance to showcase their talents, helping give them a much-needed foothold in the theatrical world. So far the journey had been wonderful. Cassie had every hope Alex would finish up at her theater and go on to greatness. She loved helping him make a name for himself, and liked how this made her feel. Helping discover hidden talent was what she knew she wanted to do with her life from now on.

The party was heaving that night, their guests enjoying champagne while chatting with the team before the show was due to begin. Cassie wandered the crowd, talking with many of the guests confidently and gracefully. She'd never lost that kind warmth she naturally exuded, and she enjoyed the affectionate gazes and hopeful stares that some of the men gave her, but she just wasn't interested in starting all over again.

Just as the speakers announced the guests should take their seats, the hairs on Cassie's neck suddenly stood up and her core tensed. It was as though she could sense something powerful and intense directed at her from somewhere in the crowd. She watched as the audience filed inside, unable to shake the strange feeling. She was about to head backstage when a voice she knew all too well whispered in her ear.

"Do you have any chardonnay? I'm not really one for champagne."

Acknowledgements

Thank you to my wonderful friends, you crazy bunch of ladies. You're my encouragement, my support, my betas and proofreaders. You were on hand to give me a kick up the arse when I needed it, but also an understanding ear and a shoulder to cry on when the pressure ever got to me. You crazy stew pots have been part of this amazing journey right from the start—thank you!

Thanks to my mum, Sue. You've always supported my creativity. After all, I do get it from you. You ring me up with amazing ideas and have always told me I'd make it. Despite what you and Lisa say, I'll always keep you both close to my heart—as they say, you know too much!

And last, but certainly not least, Brian. You're a wonderful father, husband and friend. You always joke and say I'd be fine without you, and thanks to your travels across the globe, you might be right. But, that doesn't mean I don't miss having you near. I love the way you love me, and I adore the way you love our family. You are my hero, always.

About the Author

Laura Morgan lives wherever the military sends her, well technically her husband, but, as any soldier's wife will tell you, the life involves all the family working together as one unit. She started her writing career putting together short stories and fan fiction, usually involving her favourite movie characters caught up in steamy situations, and wrote her first full length novel, Embracing the Darkness, in 2013. A self-confessed computer geek, Laura enjoys both the writing and editing side of her journey, and regularly seeks out the next big gadget on her wish list.

She spends her days looking after her two young children and their cocker spaniel Milo, as well as making the most of her free time by going to concerts with her friends, or else listening to rock music at home while writing (a trend many readers may have picked up on in her stories.)

Facebook:
www.facebook.com/lauramorganauthor

Twitter:
www.twitter.com/lauram241

Website:
www.lauramorgan.co

Lightning Source UK Ltd.
Milton Keynes UK
UKOW02f0708011116

286544UK00002B/12/P